ImmaKulate

John A. Marble

John A. Marble LLC Publishing
Slidell, Louisiana

Please send any communications with the author to:
jmcrnabook@gmail.com

one – filthy

Three…

Two…

One…

Pause…

[there's several seconds of inaudible mumbling in the background]

And suddenly there's a blinding flash of light that pierces through the twilight of introspective thought. It's both irritating and disconcerting. It's also unsettling insofar as being abruptly awakened from an intense dream, caught somewhere between what's real and what isn't, with rational thoughts initially supporting both worlds as reality.

And as the glare slowly starts to fade a man is left standing there staring at himself in the mirror. Just out of the shower, he's naked with only a towel around his lower body, wiping the fog off the glass surface in front of him using a circular motion from the lower palm of his fist. A pull chain and light bulb dangles and swings, swaying back and forth behind him like a pendulum, the shifting incandescence highlighting the residual steam that's slowly dissipating around him and accentuating the sunken cavities of his eyes…

The bathroom, itself, is small and dingy. A dirty rug has withered away over time and fused itself with what's left of a tattered linoleum floor. There's a spot near the tub where an exposed subfloor is rotting, barely bearing the weight of anyone stepping into or out of it. The toilet appears as if it was an afterthought, having somehow been squeezed-in between the sink and a mildewed shower curtain. A constant, steady drip of water is heard in the background originating from the faucet, even though the nozzle appears to be closed tightly.

The individual leans in and squints for a closer look at himself.

There is no emotion displayed at all, whatsoever.

It's simply where he's at.

There's a bottle of bourbon sitting upon a nearby shelf that he instinctively reaches for before taking a swig, turning, and staggering down a narrow hallway with it by his side.

It's obvious that he lives alone and there's no pride of ownership therein. The carpet lining the corridor is frayed, stained, and coming apart in numerous places as it approaches the base of the surrounding walls.

He somehow makes it through without falling and reaches the living area before stopping, swaying one way and then the other, and passing out awkwardly.

***

It's later in the evening and a distant thunderstorm is drawing near. There are windchimes outside a worn-down trailer that are slightly oscillating as they dangle from a make-shift front porch consisting of a beaten-up canvas awning, a dilapidated pre-cast concrete stairway, and a rotten wooden pallet landing area. The screen door underneath has been torn off the spring that once closed it and a faulty latching mechanism therein is currently causing a growing reverberation of sound all along the exterior as the slowly intensifying breeze begins to rattle it within the frame. An old pick-up truck sits atop a gravel driveway close-by, its bed littered with empty beer cans that also start to wobble and clank in the growing unrest. In all, it's an eeriness that, aside from the approaching inclement weather, might otherwise cause unease to one's spidey-senses.

Meanwhile, inside the mobile home there's disarray everywhere, with empty whiskey bottles and backwashed beer cans strewn about. The sink is so full of dirty dishes that it appears the plates, glasses, and forks on the top of the stack would otherwise crumple and crash upon themselves, if not for the petrified food particles that have somehow kept them glued together. A handful of cockroaches take advantage of the excess and scavenge nearby.

The stench of stale alcohol and cigarettes permeates the air, while the white noise of an old television set is getting progressively overrun by the worsening weather that now appears to be only a few miles away.

Just within the front entryway there's a deteriorated sleeper-sofa. Much of its stained mattress is exposed under a worn-out fitted bedsheet that no longer has a grip on three of its four corners. It is occupied by a Caucasian male who still has a towel wrapped around his waist, somehow barely hanging on. He's emaciated and disheveled in appearance, roughly thirty years of age, and passed-out clumsily – all while the remnants of some type of spilled alcoholic beverage soaks into a cushion nearby.

He appears to be stuck somewhere between apnea and death, with random periodic lower brainstem function sensing the high carbon dioxide levels in his blood, thereby signaling to his cerebral cortex that he needs to either arouse or risk transitioning further into a coma – his response to the stimulation apparently just enough to allow his obstructive breathing pattern to both involuntarily and temporarily transition into air moving in and out, now free of obstruction, if only for a moment, before the cycle ultimately repeats itself over and over again.

The wind soon picks up as the storm gets louder and rain begins falling on the roof. Tap. Tap. Tap... Progressively getting heavier and beginning to leak into parts and corners of the run-down trailer, eluding what would otherwise appear to be strategically placed buckets attempting to catch it.

And all of a sudden a gust of wind falls upon said windchimes, thereby loudly making a distinct sound, immediately followed by a deafening clap of thunder just outside the door – the lights now dimming on and off throughout the mobile home...

The individual in question abruptly jars awake.

Startled, he quickly sits up to find a stranger inhabiting the chair in front of him. It's a middle-aged to elderly black man with a long grey beard who's dressed in slacks and a dress shirt. The intruder, looking him straight in the eye, says nothing at all. The frightened man suddenly lunges for an adjacent table…

"Looking for this?" The outsider puts his hand on a nearby handgun.

He rushes to get out of bed and tries charging towards the trespasser, but somehow can't, as if he's being held back by something unseen and unheard…

"Sit down!"

"Who the hell are you!? Why are you here!?"

"Actually, that's funny that you ask, because YOU are the one who brought me here. So, are you ready?" [very matter of factly]

The man remains confused and angry. "Get the hell out of my…"

[interrupting] "I asked 'Are. You. Ready?'"

"Go away!"

And in an instant the well-dressed man swiftly vanishes into thin air.

Totally freaked out, the mobile home's occupant stays up for the rest of the early morning until, just after sunrise and still in a trance-like state, a familiar knock on the door captures his attention. The visitor then opens it, himself, towards the end of his short, rhythmic hammering, and enters.

"Hi…"

"Spencer, you look awful…"

"Thanks…"

"Did you get any sleep last night?"

"No. Storm kept me up…"

"Spence… I'm worried about you. This is no way to live. You're throwing your life away…"

[interrupting and upset] "It's my life! It's what I've chosen…"

[interrupting] "Nobody chooses this…"

"It's all I deserve."

"Son, you can't justify this lifestyle…"

[interrupting] "Yes, I can."

He then grabs his keys and walks hastily by his father, who's still standing at the door, only to climb into his pick-up truck and peel out along Myrtle Drive, which is the gravel road that leads from his trailer up towards a bigger byway that winds on further into and out of town. Lighting up a cigarette and rolling down the window, he eventually passes by his old high school and notices a faded banner – "Forest Hill High School – 1991 Division 5A Baseball State Champions" – and quickly looks away. It's a habit he's grown accustomed to over the years while cruising these roads, purposefully choosing to recognize the mundane oddities surrounding the area instead of focusing on the realities of his previous life and the inability to live up to the expectations of others.

But before Spence can get too deep into thought, his instincts and cravings start to kick in and he almost involuntarily pulls into a liquor store. Afterall, it's the beginning of the weekend now and he's gotten dangerously low on alcohol back at home. It appears to be a familiar place to him. Everyone, from the bum sitting outside the door to the cashier within, seems to know his name. He quickly strolls the aisles and makes a purchase. And while exiting the building he gives a dollar to the vagrant that's just outside the door. He can hardly get back into his truck before he's opening the bottle and taking what appears to be a much-needed swig of whiskey, his body hurting, nearly lusting after it, and what seems like literally every cell within welcoming and absorbing it. He lets out an "Ahhh…" and almost smiles. It's a high that's difficult to explain and only understandable to a fellow addict.

His longings now temporarily satiated, he pulls out of the liquor store and eventually passes by his old high school on the way back home, where he once again notices the faded championship banner. And before he can pivot his thoughts, his mind helplessly begins to drift back to when he was once a Division-I college prospect as a pitcher with a low to mid 90s fastball. Spence struggled at times with control, but he had a knack for putting runners on base and then pitching out of jams with his live arm. There were very few high schoolers that could catch-up to his heater. And when they started to hone-in, he kept them off-balance with a 12-6 curve ball that often froze them and made them look silly. He was projected by most as a 4th to 6th rounder in the upcoming professional draft. But large conference schools and their coaches assured him that he'd be a for-sure first-rounder in two to three years, if only he attended THEIR specific university.

Arriving home, he snaps out of it and notices that his father is no longer there, before stumbling up the precast stairway and nearly falling down on the make-shift front porch. Unsurprisingly, the loose and wobbly screen door has now been fixed, not to mention the spring that closes it and the latching mechanism within the frame. Once inside, he can't help but recognize that the dirty dishes have all been washed and stacked neatly. There's also a couple of hundred dollars cash sitting on the kitchen counter.

Spence then plops down onto the sofa-bed and takes a deep breath, before continuing to drink the alcohol that he brought home. There's nothing really on the television that interests him and, even so, if he really wanted to watch anything, the choices are very limited because he only gets the local channels. That noted, the bunny ears flared out at the top of it and riddled with tin foil don't exactly get the best reception either. So instead of getting up to channel surf using the dial, he just sits there and drinks, eventually passing out while watching a weather report describing the previous night's torrential downpour, as the screen blurs in and out and turns over upon itself.

two – flawed

It's Monday morning now and Spence is apparently just functional enough to hold down a job, as he instinctively gets up without showering, grooming himself, nor changing his clothes for that matter. His travels and schedule are very simple, if not routine, back and forth from his mobile home, and to and from his place of employment – the "town factory" that's about twenty-five minutes southwest of Jackson, Mississippi – with frequent stops at the liquor store, in order to satisfy the primal needs of an unabashed alcoholic, and periodic visits to the convenience store for more cigarettes.

And once at home again, like every other night before, he simply passes out while drinking and watching whatever local station that he can get using the antenna of his beaten-up television set. One thing that he doesn't seem to care about seeing is any type of sports broadcast, specifically baseball – which, of course, he played at an elite level back in the day.

It's a pretty pitiful and pathetic existence. There are seemingly no friendships. And outside of relatively polite gestures in and around the liquor store, he rarely speaks to anyone. Priority is placed on one thing: drinking alcohol and drowning his thoughts, which he has apparently perfected over the years. He rarely eats anything, save for an occasional grilled cheese sandwich or peanut butter and jelly, and his emaciated and unkempt body shows just how unhealthy he is.

The money that was left on the counter over the weekend by his father is gone by midweek. He does this often and can't help but want to assist his only son at life, even if it means knowing that he's spending it all on booze and cigarettes.

To his credit, Spence is cognizant enough to keep his alarm set at 6am every morning, before eventually stammering out of bed to make it to work relatively on time, give or take an hour or so. And at least two nights a week he frequents the liquor store to restock, usually on his way home from work. There are no bars that he patrons and no social life to speak of.

He is keenly aware that most of the people he encounters outside of his home view him with some degree of pity, as if he's a wasted talent. Many of the old-timers around town will even try to speak with him from time to time about the glory days of Forest Hill High School baseball; however, Spence quickly and rather rudely will often just walk away, giving absolutely not one second of his time for acknowledgment or feedback on the matter.

The more this has happened over the years, the less it occurs now because the locals simply know that he's uninterested in speaking about it. Spence would have it no other way.

***

It's the end of the week and, even by Spence's standards, it's been a tough one. He's still a little paranoid about hallucinating over the previous weekend when a stranger suddenly appeared in front of him, brandished his own gun on him, and then vanished into thin air. And as a result, he likely hit it a little bit harder this week with regard to consuming alcohol – the aftermath being his appearing a bit more jittery and on edge than usual.

Almost understandably, his alarm goes off for fifteen minutes before he even grimaces, eventually waking up and rolling out of bed. It's now been six days since he's showered or brushed his teeth, and today apparently won't be the day, either, as he quickly hops into his beaten-up pick-up truck and heads to work. Like beforehand, he drives by his old high school and sees the faded state championship banner, before quickly looking away. And before long he's pulling into the parking lot of the "town factory." Putting his truck in park, he reaches over into the glove box and downs the last few swigs of the liquor that inhabits the flask inside.

Many of the people from Spence's hometown, both male and female, grow up to work in the factory that's just southwest of Jackson, closer to the Raymond area. There are other businesses scattered about, a mall, restaurants, convenience stores, and a few car dealerships, but some of these establishments are starting to go out of business and the trend over the last ten or so years isn't looking too good for those that are left. And unlike the greater metropolitan area of the city that's been bustling on the northeastern side over the same period of time, with expanding neighborhoods, corporate institutions pouring in money, and the state investing tax dollars into an infrastructure of new roads and bridges to accommodate the growing population, this more rural sector of central Mississippi appears to be stuck in time with a keen ability to keep a lot of the individuals raised nearby from dreaming of something bigger and leaving – especially those without college degrees – and the "town factory" is therefore viewed as a safe and reliable option for employment.

Once inside, he rarely looks up. After clocking in and proceeding to the assembly line as a machine press operator, he doesn't ever tend to acknowledge anyone else working around him and shows very little interest in engaging in small talk with others during breaks. And while working at his post that morning the alcohol begins to slowly wear off as he harkens back to his high school baseball career once again. If there was one player that could catch up to his fastball back then, it was his cross-town rival, Joshua Waters, who grew up in the town of Brandon – just east along Interstate 20 in the adjacent county of Rankin. While Spencer had been a well-recruited Division-I pitching prospect, Joshua was largely touted by scouts as a can't miss legit MLB first rounder. Specifically, a shortstop with an above average glove and power at the plate. That noted, he was staring down a multi-million-dollar contract offer shortly after graduating high school. On most boards he was a top five pick and widely considered the unanimous number one ranked shortstop in the nation. And to be honest he gave Spence fits, who often simply pitched around him. It wasn't worth it. Although he played for a pretty good team, there were much easier outs both in front of and behind him. They weren't friends. But they weren't enemies, either. If anything, they respected one another, but didn't necessarily like each other.

Continuing to daydream, work soon begins backing up around Spence, as his coworkers look on in disbelief that he once again can't keep up. His boss, Ralph, a long-time friend of his father, tells everyone else to take a break and comes over to help out.

"You okay?"

"Yeah…"

"Bullshit. You look like shit."

"Uhh… Thanks?"

"You smell like shit, too. Well… Alcohol, to be more specific. When's the last time you bathed or put on deodorant?"

'Last night, I think… I honestly don't remem…"

[interrupting] "Well, it certainly wasn't this morning because you smell like a cross between whiskey, an ash tray, body odor, and Satan's ass-crack… Actually, I think it's your breath!"

"It's prolly been a few days since I brushed…"

"Look…" – He whistles loudly at someone else to come over and help. "Take the rest of the day off." And then he grabs him by his shoulders and looks him straight in the eyes…

"Listen… Don't clock out. I will clock you out, myself, at the end of your shift. Go home, take a shower, and brush your damn teeth… Use soap and toothpaste…" Ralph then gives him an eye-roll before continuing. "Wash and brush your hair… And get some damn rest. Oh. And here's an idea: Try actually shaving. And for God's sake eat something. Twelve years ago you were 6'3" and built like a brick shithouse and now you look like you take 'NoAssettablets' every damn day, your teeth are all rotting and falling out… I know you like the bottle. But are you on drugs, son?"

[Ashamed] "No."

[in disbelief] "Are you sure? Cuz you're very close to an intervention here. Prolly should've already had one. Your parents are worried sick about you…"

[interrupting] "I'll go home and take a shower…"

"Good. I'll see you on Monday."

Spence walks, if not stumbles, out of work and into the parking lot to his truck. He sits in the driver's seat, takes a deep breath, and glances into the rearview mirror, only to be noticeably aware of what Ralph had just told him. His eyes? They're both sunken in and cavernous. His teeth? They're all rotting out. And his beard? Well, it's woefully unkempt. And with that thought in mind, he backs out and begins driving towards nowhere in particular, just lost in the thought of where it all went wrong insofar as how his life has turned out versus the potential that he once possessed.

He knew he was given a gift that was wasted, and his life had since spiraled out of control…

But why?

When?

Where?

And how?

And before long he's once again passing by his favorite liquor store. His truck is simply drawn to it, as if there's a magnetic force pulling it in. After opting for more of his favorite whiskey, Spence decides to spend the rest of the afternoon drinking and relaxing in the bed of his truck at the "The Rez," where there's a nice lake to look at and usually a cool breeze blowing. But there's also a paved walking trail where the good-looking local females tend to get-in their workouts. That ain't half bad, either.

***

It's Friday night and the sun is setting quite amazingly on the Ross Barnett Reservoir. The water glistening as it reflects the sky above, it's all just very serene and peaceful. The local females "fast-walk" heel-to-toe in pairs while conversing with one another, many of them pushing baby strollers and moving just as swiftly as they might otherwise be, if only they were to decide to transition into a more athletically appeasing-to-the-eye slow-jog. There are a dozen or so visitors who don't seem to be in such a hurry, taking the time to stop for a few minutes at the various exercise stations on the path to do push-ups, sit-ups, and pull-ups – some of them more determined than others to make it worth their while. The walking trail, itself, winds over and through some nearby woods on the right, before opening around and traversing along the shoreline headed south, ultimately making its way eastward and back up a small hill towards the parking lot of a nice overlook, where Spence has found a good space to back into and chill.

Drinking a beer from his cooler and chasing it with the bourbon he bought on the way to "The Rez," he has been sitting on his tailgate now for several hours, enjoying the scenery as the sunlight slowly fades. Glancing over, Spence notices a van pulling up close-by and an elderly couple getting out of the front seats, both beginning the process of preparing to open the side sliding door. They're in the closest spot to the path, a parking space that is a bit wider than the others and bordered with the remnants of blue paint. The older male stops, turns, and peers over towards his truck, making eye contact with Spence, before looking back down again. He then turns to his wife, who nods, and goes about opening the side door. There's a handicap lift lever that he pulls down and a metal platform slowly folds out from within the van. An electric wheelchair rolls out onto the platform, it's headrest a little off-center to accommodate its slightly tilted occupant. Spence looks on intently, without ever blinking.

The wheelchair's inhabitant is contracted and barely able to operate the joystick on the arm, although apparently insistent on doing so. Upon closer inspection, it appears to be more like a fancy cross between a motorized scooter and a wheelchair, extremely high tech when compared to what might be the usual handicap mobility device. Although he's obviously well taken care of, Spence can't help but notice how his neck tends to look one way, as his arms and legs face the other, in what appears to be an unnatural manner. There's also a disfiguring scar along the left temporal area of his head that traces all the way back over and behind the ear. The individual steers the motorized electric vehicle past Spence and onto the walking track, unaware of his presence, while speaking in what sounds like gibberish, but passes as a barely intelligible voice to his handlers to communicate basic needs. The couple looks Spence's way as they walk by, causing him to glance downward and let go of what's left of his beer, which falls hollowly clanking and spilling into the bed of his truck. And then, after a short while, he looks back up and watches as the three of them disappear around the corner.

Sweat soon starts beading up on Spence's forehead, as his temporal artery begins to pulsate very fast. And before long his hands commence into involuntarily trembling, as he reaches them up to his face, slapping himself over and over as hard as he possibly can. There are several onlookers that are frightened and confused by his actions, choosing to detour around the part of the path that crosses nearest to his truck. He then begins to wail impossibly hard, so much so that he nearly passes out, before taking a deep breath and continuing to cry, eventually slipping off the tailgate after a few minutes, climbing back into his pick-up, and speeding off.

He's in no shape to operate a vehicle, drunk driving aside, and is now in a mental state where he's speeding quite recklessly through town and throwing back even more liquor, attempting to numb the pain that he's feeling. His mind continues to wander back to the old couple and the handicapped individual that he just saw at the park. In doing so, he runs slightly off the road and back onto it several times, just trying to stay focused enough to make it back home, still occasionally slapping himself and slamming his head upon the steering wheel – eventually reaching Myrtle Drive and pulling up to his mobile home, where he clutches onto his last bottle of bourbon before exiting the truck.

Upon entering, he grabs his pistol and hurries into the kitchen, sweeping everything off the table and onto the floor in a fit of rage. Hopeless, upset, and dejected, he bangs his head with the butt of his firearm several times, before realizing that he's feeling faint, reluctantly choosing to sit down with a now half-empty bottle of whiskey. Likely concussed, he downs what's left of it while trying to gather his thoughts and staring at his own reflection in the opposing window for a few minutes – the desperation and despair seemingly having temporarily subsided with his disequilibrium.

The self-induced respite from his woes apparently short-lived, he starts to think about how much better off the world would be without him; specifically, his parents. Making a Sign of the Cross with his hand across his chest, he begins reciting the Lord's Prayer very emotionally and purposefully, before standing up, taking the handgun, and putting it into his mouth – holding it firmly with both hands and aiming it slightly upward towards the soft palate. Starting to sweat more, he tenses his arms, squints his eyes, and holds his breath as his entire body flinches and convulses over and over several times. The only thing that is not moving in unison with the rest of his frame is his thumb, which is still resting eagerly on the trigger just a few inches in front of his face.

His adrenaline pumping, he decides to climb on top of the table for no good reason at all, other than in an apparent attempt to psyche himself up enough to carry through with task. Sweating profusely now, and with his knees pressed firmly against the cheap Formica and particle board tabletop, he suddenly erects his back and once again faces himself in the window. Hyperventilating, and still a bit woozy from the self-inflicted blows he endured to his head, he's a bit unsteady with balancing himself on the hard, wobbly surface, but is finally committed to killing himself, having been totally disgusted by what he sees looking back at him. He slowly places the handgun in his mouth, just as he did before. This is it. This time it's for real…

One…

Two…

Three!

And once more there's another full body recoil, not to mention a gag. Maybe even a retch… But nothing else. Confused and angry that his thumb is now cooperating, but he is somehow still alive, he pulls the gun out of his mouth and looks at it more closely…

The "safety" is in the "ON" position.

And while fumbling around desperately to turn it off, a leg on the table suddenly snaps under the weight of his body, sending him crashing down painfully awkward and hard, rendering him unable to immediately get up – the gun lying just out of reach.

He then proceeds to pass out on the floor.

three - immoral

Another storm is brewing, and this one seems to be out of nowhere because the chance of precipitation was essentially negligible. Once again, the rain starts tapping onto the roof and slowly filling up the scattered buckets. The trailer begins swaying to the left and right in the weather. The windchimes on the front porch sound like they're barely hanging on now, as the lights are dimming on and off. Slowly becoming aware of the strobe effect, Spence starts to slightly move about on the floor, when lightning suddenly strikes nearby. He slowly works himself to his feet and turns around...

"You okay?"

[startled] "What the fffuu...!?"

He's there again, in the same chair, no less. Apparently, he just lets himself in.

Spence looks around frantically for his gun.

"You looking for this?"

He then jumps back against the refrigerator and knocks over some dirty dishes, in the process breaking many of them.

"Who the hell are you!? Get out of my house!"

"Actually... It's a mobile home. And by all accounts a pretty run-down..."

"Fuck you!"

"Spence... I'm here to talk. You're the one that brought me here. Tell me what it is that's on your mind."

"I didn't bring shit!"

"What's on your mind, Spence?"

"A stranger in my house! That's what's on my mind!"

"Spence... You brought me here."

[confused] "Why do you keep saying that!?"

"Cuz it's true."

"Bullshit!"

"What if I tell you one of your deepest, darkest secrets? Would you believe me then, Spence?"

"I don't have any secrets..."

[interrupting] "Why didn't you check to see if the safety was on?"

[now enraged and lunging towards the man] "You piece of shit! I'm gonna beat your ass!"

But as Spence charges the intruder, it's as if he's being held back by someone or something. The man's face doesn't change. It shows no fear, nor surprise. There's no humor. He doesn't appear to be enjoying the back and forth between them in some kind of cruel, sick, or heartless way. Spence sits back down, exhausted, and still breathing heavily.

Looking him in the eye... "Are you ready now, Spencer?"

"Ready for what!? Why do you keep saying that!?"

"Let's take a walk outside..."

"But it's storming..."

"Come with me."

The man gets up and opens the screen door. Spence reluctantly follows.

"Grab your keys."

To Spence's surprise, it's not raining and there's no evidence that it ever had been. Come to think of it, there was no evidence the last time he showed up, either. They both hop into the truck, Spence in the driver's seat.

"Where to?"

"Well, where'd it all start?"

"Where'd what start?"

"Whatever had you putting a gun in your mouth and hyperventilating until you passed out cold. I guess that would be a good place."

Spence rolls his eyes as he drives off towards his old high school. There are banners strewn around town hanging in front of many of the local businesses that read phrases such as "Beat Brandon!" and "Slay the Bulldogs!" This is confusing for Spence because his alma mater hasn't been competitive in baseball, or any sport for that matter, for the last five to six years. School districts had since been redrawn and most of the local athletic talent had started being recruited away to a nearby private school. But as they get closer, he notices that the lights are still on at the baseball field. Not only that, but the parking lot is packed. He then sees a couple of Brandon High School buses. That was Joshua's old school. They had played each other last in the quarterfinals of the Mississippi High School State Baseball tournament back in the early summer of 1991.

Spence parks the truck and the two of them walk up to the baseball field. There's an obvious game going on. Nobody speaks to them, but they aren't invisible, either. Nobody simply knows who they are. A younger version of his parents sits nearby in the bleachers, next to his old high school girlfriend. This kinda freaks him out...

"Hey... What the hell is going...?"

"Shhh... This part is good."

The stranger purposefully walks up to the backstop and sits in the only open seats on the front row. It's interesting because the place is packed. It's essentially standing room only, yet there's two open seats... Right in front... Hmmm.

A younger, more developed version of Spence is out there on the mound as a high school senior and his team is up 1-0, having not given up any hits yet. But he's struggled with his control early on and just walked his third batter of the game. Joshua Waters is now at the plate, with a runner on first in the top of the third inning, having walked on four straight pitches in his previous at-bat, back in the opening frame.

It's off the plate... Ball 1.

Spence nods in agreement with the catcher and delivers from the stretch...

Ball two is 93 miles per hour, according to the scout's gun sitting in the chair next to them. He seems pretty impressed.

A quick throw to first base and he almost gets the runner leaning.

Joshua steps out and takes a full practice swing, before stepping back in and assuming his batting stance. Spence once again delivers from the stretch...

Ball three is in the dirt, and it's a good block by the catcher, keeping the runner from advancing.

Spence is visibly perturbed out on the mound. He looks uncomfortable and indecisive, taking his hat off and rubbing the sweat from his brow, before glancing towards the runner at first and re-engaging the rubber...

The stranger leans in and whispers, "Tell me what you're thinking, Spence?"

Spence looks down and softly responds, "I'm thinking that I walked him on four straight pitches earlier and shouldn't throw him anything to hit, but that there's no way he's swinging on a three-oh pitch. So, I should just throw it as hard as I can... Center cut a fastball... Groove one in there to show this scout just how hard I can throw it for a strike..."

And as he's finishing that statement, the next pitch is a fastball, just as he described, a bit low and inside at the knees, but still in the zone, and Joshua turns on it, sending it 400 feet over the left field wall, well into the trees. He maybe watched it for a second or two, but then soon looked down and started jogging the bases. There wasn't any bat flip. But there was no doubt that it was gone, as evidenced by the opposing team's players and fans immediately going wild. It was the first homer that Spence had given up since his sophomore year. That, too, was to Joshua.

"What are you thinking, Spence?"

Spence starts shaking his head, before placing it inside his arms, and leaning forward in his seat, seemingly still upset about what he just witnessed and uncomfortable about what may be to come.

"Oh… I'm for sure pissed-off that I didn't stick to my plan of not giving him anything to hit. And the fact that he swung on a three-oh count…"

"But you know your team goes ahead 4-2 in the bottom half of the inning and you don't give up another run going forward? Y'all actually win the game?"

"Yes."

"And eventually the State Championship?"

"Yes."

"So… What inning does he come back up to bat?"

"Top of the 5th."

Spence watches the game, but he doesn't say a word. Instead, he often glances over at his parents and his girlfriend, who seem to be enjoying themselves while cheering him on, completely unaware that a twelve years older, emaciated, and bearded version of their son and boyfriend is sitting less than thirty feet away. He also notices the demeanor of his younger self as he takes the mound going forward with an outright lead and command of his pitches. He's now pitching a gem of a baseball game, but he's simply not happy at all. Instead, he still seems irked about the home run that he gave up the inning before. He strikes out nearly every batter thereafter and his teammates throw it around the horn, before giving it back and slapping him on the butt with their glove.

And before long Joshua is back at the dish....

"And here he is..."

The time in between the top of the third and the fifth seemed almost as if it were only a few minutes...

"Wait... How'd you...?"

"Never mind... What are you thinking, Spence?"

The younger version of Spence out on the mound is staring right at Joshua, who's smiling at his own parents and girlfriend (also in the stands), and doesn't seem to notice.

The scout seated nearby is now more interested in the game than he was before.

In the stands Spence puts his head down into his arms and takes a deep breath.

"Let's go. I don't want to see this."

"You have to see this..."

"No, I don't!"

Everyone turns to look at the two of them as the umpire calls "Time!" and glares in their general direction.

Joshua steps back into the box. The score is now 7-2. Spence is dominating and getting ahead in the count with every batter.

"What are you thinking, Spence?"

"Do we have to do this?"

"I need to know..."

He whispers to the stranger, such that nobody else might hear him, "I want him to pay for swinging at a three-oh pitch and hitting it over the fence. That scout may be slightly impressed with my fastball, but I'm committed to State. He's only here to watch Joshua. And he just took the hardest that I can throw way over the left field wall on a pitch he had no business swinging at."

"So… I need to know… Are you trying to hit him?"

[reluctantly and ashamedly] "Yes."

"Where are you aiming, Spence?"

"At his ribs…"

And just as he utters those words, the pitch comes in at 95 miles per hour, hitting Joshua in the left side of the head, his helmet flying some twenty feet away from his body, at which point he falls to the ground and begins twitching involuntarily.

There's a collective gasp from the crowd as the coaches from both teams rush towards home plate.

Spence, now essentially on an island in his own mind, can be seen on the mound in obvious disbelief, with his arms folded behind his head.

Joshua continues to have seizure-like activity, lying on the ground just outside the batter's box.

"Tell me what you're thinking, Spence."

Putting his head down… "That I just murdered someone."

Soon the sound of sirens begins filling the air and eventually EMS and fire trucks arrive with all their bright lights. They carefully, but urgently place him into a C-collar and then log-roll him onto a plastic gurney. The situation seems critical by all outward appearances. Spence can see Joshua's parents, who are on the field, too, now walking with the paramedics alongside their son. There is no movement or response from Joshua, whatsoever, as they load him up, close the ambulance doors behind him, and speed off into the dark night.

"What happened next, Spence?"

"They took me out of the game. I didn't even go into the dugout. I walked straight home."

"And exactly when did you find out that he had died?"

"He didn't die. He suffered a traumatic brain injury and is a total care invalid thanks to me. I just saw him at 'The Rez' earlier today. He'd be much better off if he was dead, and so would his parents."

"Did you consider going to the hospital to see him or speak to his parents?"

"I went. But I stayed in the parking lot. I just couldn't find the courage to face them."

"And did you attend the semifinals and finals of the State Tournament the following weekend?"

"I did not." He then looks at his hands and says, "I haven't held a baseball in my hand since that night."

"I think that's enough for today, Spence."

"You believe me, right? That I didn't want to ruin his life."

"It doesn't matter what I believe, Spence. It only matters what you think."

The man disappears again, and Spence is left all by himself at his old high school baseball field in the present tense, lights off, nobody there, the field unmanicured and the stands rotting away, his truck parked off somewhere distantly in the now empty parking lot.

He lays down on the bleachers and gazes upon the night sky.

four – defective

Spence awakens the following morning on the kitchen floor. His lip appears to be busted and his eye is bruised. There's also remnants of blood on his chin. The hand-held firearm is still next to him, but it remains slightly out of his reach. Mustering to his feet, he looks over towards the chair, but finds no visitor. He glances out of the window to see his truck exactly where he'd previously left it, before passing out after the unsuccessful suicide attempt.

It's Saturday morning and way past time for a shower. While in the bathroom, he hears the unmistakable sound of his front door opening. And before long there's lots of clanging about, as if the place is being ransacked. Thinking it's the stranger again, he emerges in a towel to confront him.

It's his parents, Dan and Joy Taylor, who've come over unannounced to visit.

They love their only son, who's now thirty years old, and worry about him immensely. Frequent visitors to his mobile home, they recognize him as a shell of the potential that he once possessed, even without taking baseball into account. He was once good-looking, intelligent, and very personable. They knew that he carried guilt around with him and attempted multiple times in the past to get him the help he needed. But nothing has ever worked. Even so, they didn't love him any less.

"Hi, son. We knocked, but you never answered. What's with the blood on the floor? What happened to your lip!? Your eye!?"

"I'm fine. I fell."

His dad looks at his mom with concern. Joy has brought in several bags of groceries and cleaning supplies. She is currently washing the stack-full of dishes in the sink, while also not buying the story that her son is trying to sell – but purposefully being non-confrontational about it with him.

"Ralph called and said he sent you home early yesterday to take a shower and rest your mind. Are you sure that you're okay?"

"I'm good, dad."

"Good. By the way, you're coming with us to eat breakfast this morning… So get dressed."

"I don't feel up to…"

"I don't care. Get dressed. You haven't had a conversation with your mother for nearly six months now."

His mom, looking downward, continues cleaning until they leave.

He rides along with them in the back seat of their vehicle to a local Cracker Barrel for a late breakfast, and a familiar face seems surprised to greet them and take their order.

"Christa!"

Joy absolutely loved Christa. She had been Spence's girlfriend for several years, leading up to the incident with Joshua. Always wanting a daughter, but unable to have more children, she was basically adopted into the Taylor family early on in their relationship. But everything changed on a Friday evening in May, twelve years back.

"Hi, y'all! I've missed y'all so much!"

Spence looks on, emotionless, until she locks eyes with his…

"Hi, Spence…" – her voice almost cracking from holding back her feelings.

It's obvious there's still an attachment there. She and Spence went their separate ways the summer after high school. He was simply never the same after hitting Joshua in the head and she ended up falling into her own depression, not really having an identity outside of being "Spence Taylor's girlfriend" at the time. Already throwing the "marriage" word around loosely between the two of them at an early age, they were madly in love and her only plan was to follow him to Mississippi State University, where he was to play baseball, while pursuing her own degree as a teacher. Of course, that never materialized, and she ultimately ended up getting into an abusive relationship with someone else, having two children, a boy and a girl, but never marrying.

"Hi, Christa…" – her ex barely making any eye contact.

Joy senses the awkwardness and goes on to make small talk with her about the children, how cute they are, and how big they're both getting. They go on to order their food and, as she leaves to put their order in, reminisce about what a wonderful daughter-in-law she would've made. While hearing everything they're saying, Spence stares forward into nothingness – lost in thought and craving an alcoholic drink.

"Spence. SPENCER?! Your food has been in front of you now for ten minutes. Aren't you going to eat anything!?"

Instead, he eats nothing. He's deep into thought about nothing. But he does suddenly have to pee, so he gets up and walks to the restroom.

Once done with urinating, he moseys up to the sink and glances forward, once again hardly recognizing himself in the mirror. Not only is he disheveled, but he looks like he just got his ass kicked. Walking out of the restroom, he suddenly bumps into Christa, who's now entering the area. At this point they're physically closer than they've ever been since they dated. She even smells like she used to. He tries to leave, but she stops him with her hand on his chest.

She tears up, looks into his eyes, and whispers, "I still love you…"

But there is no reply from Spence.

He starts to, only to stop abruptly and walk away.

***

Windchimes and yet another thunderstorm.

Spence, lying there after passing out drunk again on the sofa-bed, rolls his eyes with anguish that he didn't take those noisy things off the front doorstep.

"Spence..."

"Spencer."

He startles awake and suddenly he's no longer inside his mobile home, but instead he's standing in front of Hinds General Hospital alongside the stranger, who's now come around by his count three times.

He's no longer afraid of him. Rather, he simply thinks he's a figure of his drunken imagination and decides to ask the stranger if he can touch him because he doesn't think he's real.

"Oh, I'm real..."

The stranger then puts forth his arm for Spence to physically touch.

"So, I'm not hallucinating?"

"No, son. Remember our first meeting? You are the one who brought me here."

It's late at night and the town around them is quiet. There's distant movement that's noticeable throughout a handful of backlit windows scattered sporadically across the facade of the hospital. An ambulance and two police cars are parked outside of the Emergency Room entrance nearby. The lights on top of them are turned on and rotating for no apparent reason, aside from perhaps being forgotten, and therefore periodically highlighting the interior walls of the darker rooms with what would otherwise appear to be a revolving nightlight – both the occupants therein and those outside having been thankfully spared from also hearing the piercing sound of their sirens.

He recognizes Joshua's parents walking out of the lobby. It's obvious that this is another flashback because they are much younger and conversing with their son's high school girlfriend, all three of them eventually embracing as if they're saying goodnight to each other. As a matter of fact, Spence sees that he's also the eighteen-year-old version of himself from back in the day through the reflection in the car window beside him.

Like Spence and Christa, Abby and Joshua had been dating for a couple of years. They were the Homecoming King and Queen. Mr. and Ms. Brandon High School.

"Go speak to them."

"Absolutely not. I almost killed their son. Her boyfriend! I permanently disfigured him!"

"They need to hear from you. You also need to visit Joshua…"

[interrupting] "Shut up! I will not!"

"Spence. Do you feel bad about what happened?"

"I do."

"Then go talk to them. This is you, then. Look at yourself. You're eighteen years old again. Your life changed several nights ago. You are not a stranger to them right now. This is a chance to make some type of amends…"

"Make amends? Make amends!? I basically killed their son…"

Spence begins to weep softly.

"The guilt is overwhelming. I don't deserve to live. I don't deserve to be here at all."

He begins to hear the sound of birds chirping and awakens on the sofa-bed inside his mobile home, his right cheek and ear marinating in a puddle of his own drool. His hair is matted. He actually looks as if he's lost even more weight, which might seem impossible at first glance.

IMMAKULATE

But it's back to present day and it's Monday, so it's time to go back to work. He gets into his truck and heads off, distracted by thoughts of his nightly visitor. Who was he? And if he was hallucinating, how could he physically touch him? All these feelings are racing through his head, so much so that he gently nudges softly into the car ahead of him at a 4-way stop-sign.

He suddenly stuns back into reality. He's just bumped into Abby, Joshua's ex-girlfriend. There's no noticeable damage to her car that he can see, but she's out of it and walking up to his drivers-side window.

Abby is now a local elementary school teacher in the town of Raymond and is on her way to work. She never married or had children after the incident between Spence and Joshua. She recognizes who the driver is, a shadow of the teenager she once saw competing on the baseball diamond, and takes a deep breath as she bends over towards the driver's side window...

"Are you ok?"

"I'm very sorry. I'm on my way to work and not sleeping well. How's your car?"

"My car is fine. But you don't look all that well..."

"I'm not..."

She looks again at her car and the surrounding traffic backing up behind them, which is slowly starting to detour around their mishap.

"Spence... Can I be totally honest with you?"

"Yes... please." He grips his steering wheel and braces for the worst...

"What happened on that night years ago was tragic. I've still never really gotten over it. That's one thing. But you? You are killing yourself slowly because of it and the whole town knows it."

Spence begins to get emotional, as tears start falling down his face. But he keeps staring forward with both hands tightly on the wheel.

"Spence... Look at me."

29

His nose running and his lips now quivering, he reluctantly looks her way, and they make eye contact.

"I forgive you. I really do. And I think it might be time for you to consider forgiving yourself."

She leans in and gives him a gentle kiss on the cheek, before walking back to her car and proceeding on to work.

Spence doesn't move at all. Instead, he stays there weeping inside the truck where it came to rest for a full five minutes, with both hands still at ten and two, until a slight siren and a quick flash of the lights by a local sheriff's deputy startles and encourages him to move on.

five – tainted

The deep south is a funny place. People's reactions to events are as difficult to predict as the weather. Spence drives along the backroads of his hometown after getting off work later that evening, while pondering the last twelve years of his life. It was bad enough that Joshua was injured. But multiple lives had been affected in the aftermath, including the two girlfriends and both sets of parents.

Joshua was the life of the party and loved by all. He was very sarcastic and goofy, while including everyone in his circle of friends. He played no favorites and was a well-known practical joker. This came off to people who didn't know him well as being "cocky." But the truth was he was the nicest kid in the whole school, despite being a superstar.

Spence was a bit different. He was more serious – but also down for a practical joke or two.

One thing was for sure though: Both were elite athletes.

Cruising these backroads on that particular night felt a little less heavy than it had before. Spence couldn't believe that Abby was so forgiving towards him. But there's still an obvious burden that he's carrying around.

Arriving home, he pops open a beer, sits down, and turns on the television set. The local news is on…

"Once promising 1st round MLB draft pick Joshua Waters died today in his home after a recent battle with pneumonia. Waters was hit in the head with a pitch in the playoffs during his senior season of high school and suffered a traumatic brain injury. Before that, he was projected to be the first shortstop taken in the 1991 Major League Baseball draft, and possibly the first selection overall. Waters was only 30 years old."

Spence quickly throws his full beer can at the television set in disgust, in the process cracking the screen, and then reaches for the hard liquor.

He wants to drive somewhere, anywhere, so he darts out the front door, pushing it open so forcefully that the screen door his dad had fixed beforehand now comes off the hinge once again, thereby angling the door's frame upwards and slamming it into the hanging windchimes, rattling them loudly. He hardly seems to notice and quickly gets into his truck, liquor bottle in one hand, throwing it back, and keys in the other...

"Spence."

He startles so hard that his truck stalls...

"What the fffff!!!???"

"Throw the bottle out and drive, Spence."

"Where to?"

"Just drive..."

Spence tosses the bottle and the two of them drive around town in circles in that old beat-up truck, saying nothing at all, for well-over an hour.

The stranger then looks over at him... "Are you ready now, son?"

Spence looks back, confused.

The stranger then reaches over, grabs him by the shoulder compassionately, looks him in the eyes, and asks again...

"Spencer: I asked you a question. Are. You. Ready?"

Knowing that he's heard these words and this question before, Spence exhaustively, if not sarcastically, replies "Yes."

"Ok. Stop!!!"

"What!?"

"Stop the truck right now!!!"

Spence slams on the brakes in confusion.

They've come to rest in front of a modest ranch style house that has a big 'W' hanging on the front door, a handicapped equipped van in the driveway, and what appears to be the remnants of some type of batting cage in the side-yard next to the carport. Spence knows exactly where he is and is questioning the intent of the stranger within his own mind.

"Go knock on it."

"I can't. I just can't."

"Go."

"What do I even say?"

"Whatever comes to mind."

He reluctantly makes his way toward the front door. It's a slow walk, with so many things going through his head. He didn't know beforehand where the Waters had lived. Also, he had never even had a conversation with their son before. And yet, strangely, he seems like he's just lost his best friend. He knocks on the door and waits…

The porch light soon comes on and a series of locks begins to unlatch. And before long Mr. Waters is standing right there at the front door looking at him. Spence, once he sees him, immediately begins sobbing, and then buries his head into the chest of Joshua's dad, essentially pushing himself inside the home.

"I'm so sorry! I'm so sorry that I did this…" – His voice now muffled by Joshua's father's chest, while still embraced in his arms.

"I don't want to live anymore. He didn't deserve this at all! You don't deserve it! I'm the one that deserves to die!"

Mr. Waters says nothing at all and just holds on to him as he continues to wail.

By now, Mrs. Waters has emerged at all the commotion from the bedroom in her nightgown, and begins to get emotional, too. Spence leaves the arms of Mr. Waters and falls into her arms, almost knocking her down, and continuing to weep at an even higher level.

"I'm so sorry for what I did!" Spence is now emotional to the point that he may pass out.

The two of them quickly grab ahold of him tightly, attempting to stabilize his body before he falls, listening to his cries, and consoling him by rubbing his back and offering tissues – both of them now crying, too – before eventually easing him down on the couch in front of them…

"We know you're sorry, son. You don't have to say it. You have shown it by how you've lived your life since that night. You never played ball again, drank yourself into oblivion, and ruined all your relationships. You still had so much potential, and we saw your guilt get the best of you. We've often thought about approaching you first, but figured that you had to do it on your own."

"I don't deserve to have a good life."

"Yes, you do."

Mr. and Mrs. Waters then tenderly put their hands on his shoulders and ask him to look up…

"Listen, son… We forgive you. You know, Joshua used to talk all the time about wishing that he was your teammate, instead of having to always play against you? He certainly did. He said there was something special in you and that nobody had a fastball that moved like yours. And that your curve ball was the best strikeout pitch he'd ever seen. He said he hated having a two-strike count when you were pitching, because he had to sit on a fastball and couldn't ever adjust to your curve ball. He even said that maybe you'd be on the same MLB team one day. He knew that you had it in you."

Spence begins to sob once again, this time even heavier than before.

Mr. Waters reaches out, gently touches the bottom of his chin, pulls it up, and looks him in the eye…

34

"Son... I want you to know this and hear it straight from us: You're released. We forgive you. And now we think it's time for you to go get your life back..."

Spence feels a heaviness in his heart subside as he's sitting there on the Waters living room couch, and in that moment it quickly becomes much easier for him to breathe.

Three...

Two...

One...

Pause...

[there's several seconds of inaudible mumbling in the background]

And suddenly there's a blinding flash of light that pierces through the twilight of introspective thought. It's both irritating and disconcerting. It's also unsettling insofar as being abruptly awakened from an intense dream, caught somewhere between what's real and what isn't, with rational thoughts initially supporting both worlds as reality.

"Spence... Can you hear me?"

"Spencer?"

The sound of those windchimes start to... But wait... He's not even at home, and he's somehow still hearing them... It's all so confusing right now.

"Spence."

He then turns towards the voice and the stranger is sitting down in a chair inside the Waters' house, while holding the windchimes from Spence's front porch. The occupants are nowhere to be seen. He was just embracing them, and suddenly they're gone.

"Spence... I'm going to redirect you here. You can see and hear me right now, and think that you're totally awake, but you're actually in a very deep trance-like state of being. A hypnotic state, if you will. The windchimes you've been hearing have been to redirect you, as you've strayed off in your thoughts, and I had to appear before you to help you refocus. When I count to three and you hear these chimes again, you will be totally awake. You may or may not remember much about what we've talked about. But hopefully your subconscious mind is forever changed. Are you ready?"

Spence is still confused…

"One…"

"Two…"

(windchimes) "Three…"

Once again there's a blinding light, as if someone flipped on a switch too quickly and then began dimming everything into focus.

"Welcome back, Spence. You've been in a deep hypnotic state for the past four hours."

The person speaking to him is the same well-dressed stranger, black, long beard, and everything, that's been "terrorizing" him by appearing out of nowhere. He's dressed in the same outfit and sitting in a chair directly in front of him.

"How do you feel?"

Spence thinks about it for a second, much like when a dream feels so authentic that you wake up and for a split second think it was real, and he slowly begins to understand that his reality is much different. He reaches up to his face and feels that it's completely shaven. He then looks down to see that he's wearing a dress-shirt and khakis. Not only that, but he's no longer emaciated. In fact, his arms, legs, and body, in general, are completely filled-out.

His wife… Oh my. He has a wife!

His wife, Christa, is sitting in the same room, over in the corner, observing everything with a very concerned look, just beyond the shoulder of the would-be stranger. The stranger…

He then remembers that the "stranger's" name is Dr. Olgivy.

Christa walks over to him with tears in her eyes and kisses her husband on the lips.

"Welcome back, baby."

She looks over to Dr. Olgivy. "Can he come in now? I'm sure he's dying."

Dr. Olgivy nods affirmatively.

Christa walks over, opens a side door, and says, "He's ready to see you now."

And in through the door walks Joshua Waters, a 6'4" thirty-year-old freak of nature athlete that plays shortstop for the Boston Red Sox and is a 4-time league MVP.

"MEAT!!!" He says while smiling, as he walks over and hugs Spence.

The psychiatrist warns Joshua sternly to be careful because Spence is still in a state where reality is revealing itself, saying that he's just relived the last twelve years of his life in a totally alternate universe.

"Meat! You remember me, right?! We're best friends! Ever since the night you beaned…"

[interrupting] "JOSHUA!"

"Oh… I'm sorry Doc. Hey… Can Abby come in now?" Yelling loudly to the other room… "ABBY! Get in here. He's fixed!"

[interrupting again] "JOSHUA!"

And just then Abby walks through the door and straight over to Christa, hugging her neck. She then looks over at Spence, who's still a bit confused.

"Spence…" Pointing towards her husband… "This goofball has been worried sick. I think he may love you more than he loves me and the kids."

Kids?!

Joshua and Abby have two kids! A boy and a girl. The boy's name is Spencer! OMG! He then remembers that he and Christa have kids, too! A boy and a girl, also. The boy's name is Joshua!

"Spence," Dr. Olgivy explains, "You've had a very long day and been through a lot. Go home, get some rest, and something to eat. And I'll see you back here in several days."

Looking at Joshua, he strictly warns him, "You... You are not to talk to him for the rest of the day."

Joshua looks confused at first, but after grinning mischievously, he then makes a buttoning the lip gesture towards Dr. Olgivy, before quickly turning around and smiling at Spence...

"Meat, I love you, man! We're gonna win the World Series again!"

six – unblemished

TWO WEEKS EARLIER

"It's been a remarkable season so far for the Red Sox. Led by their MVP shortstop, a talented pitching rotation, and a dominant closer who not only has the career record for saves (479), but also just two nights previously set the single season record (58), tonight they're going for the single season record for wins here on the last night of play before the postseason begins."

"Tom, they want it badly and nobody on the roster is resting, as they aren't simply content with coasting unassumingly into the playoffs as the number one seed. You'd think they'd have sat on their ace, 22-win veteran Adam Ledbetter, to have a better pitching rotation set for the playoffs… But here they are! All of them are either playing or available tonight! Everyone, and I do mean 'everyone,'" adding finger-quotes for emphasis as per Manager Skip Jenkins, 'is available!'"

"That's right, Ted, it's all hands-on deck, so to speak, for Boston going for win number 117. Not that they need any more motivation, but a record-breaking win tonight would also put a dagger in their rival's sub-par season. Yes, the Yankees are in town to finish off what has been an ugly 2003 campaign."

"In all honesty, I don't think they could've picked a better team to play and try to beat in order to keep them from making history here tonight."

"Yep… The Yankees would like nothing more than to spoil their plans here in Boston. Make no mistake, as long-time divisional rivals, there's absolutely no love lost between these two rosters and BOTH teams want to win this game!"

"It's been a close one for sure. Both starters have pitched gems and each only allowed two hits, the difference being a solo home run over the monster by Joshua Waters, his 48th of the season. But Ledbetter isn't coming out for the 9th after reaching his pitch count limit, and instead will be handing it off to fellow future Hall of Famer Spencer Taylor."

"Taylor has been dominant and has come close to pitching an immaculate inning on three separate occasions this year, alone, only to fall short by one pitch. In fact, he holds the distinction of having pitched the most ten pitch innings ever, while recording three strikeouts and allowing no base runners, in MLB history. Of course, with his track record and distinguished career, I think anyone would be content with that little nugget of notoriety. But sources do confirm that it eats at him, though. And many that know him have corroborated that with every single outing, despite who's batting, it's always his goal to overpower every batter with a three-pitch strikeout."

"Well, Ted, we'd be remiss in not mentioning that he also holds another MLB record for the most innings pitched without hitting a batter. In fact, for nine full seasons as the Red Sox closer, he has never beaned one single batter, save for one player who leaned into the strike zone with his chicken-wing elbow pad, but was quickly and assuredly called out for it by the umpire, ringing him up for strike three as he began casually taking off the guard and trotting over to first base."

"Yep, that's the closest I think he's ever come, which is rather astounding, in and of itself, when you really stop to think about it."

"For sure. Taylor has made a good living working the outer half of the plate. It's been all heat for his entire career, rarely venturing inside, aside from an occasional two strike two-seamer that often runs up and in on righties for either a swinging strikeout or a bat-breaking jam session. It's no secret at all. You know what you're going to get with him. And if he has an umpire that's been giving some off the plate for an entire game, then you'd better believe that not only does he know it, but that he's also going to exploit it to the point where he's essentially unhittable."

"You're exactly right, Tom. And here he is tonight trying to get the last three outs, attempting to propel the Red Sox to an MLB record 117th win."

"As Taylor does his patented slow, methodical entrance into the game on this cold night, you might remember that he attended Mississippi State University on a baseball scholarship, developing a reputation as a dominant closer who not only threw very hard, but also had pinpoint accuracy. After giving up his only home run allowed in college on a curve ball, he basically abandoned the pitch and now almost exclusively prefers to throw fastballs with movement. He was drafted #6 overall in a bold move by the Red Sox, who traded up in the draft to get him after his sophomore year, ultimately making it through the minors in less than a year, being called up on his birthday in late September when the roster expanded. And since that time, Ted, he's been regarded by pretty-much everyone in baseball as a true southern gentleman…"

"Well, he's certainly a fan-favorite here in Boston and enters tonight's game sporting a career ERA of 1.97, with only 48 blown saves in 527 opportunities."

"And don't forget two World Series rings, Ted."

"That's right, Tom… And as he toes the rubber to deliver his last warm-up pitch, I would like to stress that Taylor has never known a full season in Boston without a post-season appearance, with many of those saves over the years having come in late October – when it just means more. Thusly, the Red Sox rewarded him with a 5-year guaranteed deal before his rookie contract expired, thereby making him the highest paid closer of all time, and likely ensuring that he one day retires wearing a Boston uniform."

PRESENT DAY

Joshua leaves the psychiatrist's office and Spence is still a bit confused about everything. Dr. Olgivy assists him out of his chair and looks him in the eye.

"Some dream, huh?"

Spence can't yet recall or fully understand the depths that his mind was taken to – but starts to remember that Dr. Olgivy is a world-renowned sports psychiatrist who specializes in rehabilitating athletes.

He and Christa hold hands and then start walking slowly towards the door, when the doctor stops them just before reaching it…

"Spence… Aren't you forgetting something?"

Dr. Olgivy is holding Spence's handgun. He's a licensed concealed carry and has always been "packing" since he and his wife were robbed at gunpoint while exploring Downtown Chicago during a mid-season All-Star game road-trip several years ago.

Slightly embarrassed, Spence grabs his gun and holster and walks out the door with his wife. Christa insists on driving home. She decides to avoid telling him that he's forbidden to drive for twenty-four hours. His mind is still bogged down, anyway, so he doesn't argue. Along the way he notices everyone around town wearing Red Sox paraphernalia and the surrounding business all decked out with team spirit. Tired, his mind begins to drift…

"Taylor will face the top of the Yankees order, which is no small feat in and of itself, while attempting to garner his record-expanding 59th save of the season and the record 117th season win for the franchise. It's only two days into the month of October, so we don't really expect it to be warm here in Boston. But a passing cold front earlier in the day has plunged the temperature down into the high 30s. I mean the football and hockey players are happy, but baseball!?"

"You're exactly right, Ted. Spence, a southern boy at heart, is visibly uncomfortable with how cold it is and incessantly blowing into his pitching hand before taking the rubber. Worth noting, he still has that patented slow, full wind-up and high leg kick as he's about to deliver…"

"Strike one with a 100 miles per hour fastball," high in the zone that the batter couldn't catch up to.

"Taylor, now ahead in the count as he delivers… Strike two! One-oh-one, that caught the outside corner."

"I don't know. I think this umpire might be a 'Spencer Taylor fan,' because that one looked a little bit off the plate…"

"Well, I mean how are you not? How do you not like one of the nicest and most respectful players in all of baseball? I'm sure it's given him the benefit of the doubt more often than not over the years."

"Taylor delivers… And it's strike three swinging on a patented 'Taylor special' – a two-seamer that ran up and in at the top of the zone," as he circles around the back of the mound, still blowing into his right hand, before receiving the ball from his third baseman.

"You know, Ted, that pitch seems to defy the forces of gravity. And it's a tough pitch to track when you not only have to look away, but you also must account for a ball or two off the plate…"

Spence then jars awake when he feels the wheels of the large SUV that Christa is driving touching the curb, before pulling into his driveway. It's a far cry from the run-down trailer that he's seemingly lived in over the past twelve years… But then he remembers that this is his house. Actually, it's his mansion.

He and Christa open the door, enter their house, and immediately hear barking and the shuffling of little feet while turning the corner…

"Daddy!!!" – as they jump into his arms, the dog spinning around on the floor below the three of them and waiting for its own turn, whimpering with joy. At first glance it's not overly apparent who loves him more, the kids or the golden retriever.

And not far behind them stands his parents, smiling from ear to ear, watching their grandchildren embracing their son with happiness.

"Hi mom and dad."

"Spencer."

"We've been worried sick about you, son. How do you feel?"

Christa soon steps in with "He's a bit off, but that's apparently normal. Dr. Olgivy explained that he's relived the past twelve years over the last four hours in an alternate universe, so there will be an adjustment period. He says he can't drive for twenty-four hours."

"Alternate universe?" – his mother says with both question and concern.

"Yes."

"What do you remember, son...?"

[Christa interrupting] "He said he must process it subconsciously, before verbalizing it. But that he may never truly remember all or any of it. He said it's normal to only recall bits and pieces, but others can remember everything. Time will tell..."

Spence, now on one knee and loving on the dog since his children quickly went back to whatever they were doing, listens to them speaking about him and understands that he had some sort of psychiatric intervention, but he still isn't exactly sure why or what it was. He moves forward towards the kitchen and overhears a newscaster on the television speaking about tonight's World Series game one in Boston, before his wife abruptly turns off the TV.

"I play for Boston..."

"Yes, you do, honey."

"Then why am I not there getting ready?"

Christa stops what she's doing and hugs him tightly.

seven – modest

It's later that evening and the game isn't on the television inside the Taylor home. Instead, Christa has insisted that the family get out of the house and decides to take everyone to the Disney animated movie that the children have been wanting to see. The concession line at the theatre understandably isn't very long. After all, there's a World Series game being played just ten miles away. The kids are visibly excited about seeing the film with their parents and grandparents, when a sudden flash of lights and the sounds of nearby camera shutters startle them...

"Spence! Spence Taylor! Why aren't you at the game tonight!? Are you planning on playing in the World Series at all!? Do you feel like you've let your teammates down!?"

Spence appears confused, as Christa and his dad usher the would-be paparazzi away, while scolding them for having no life.

Once inside the theatre, the family settles down to watch the movie. His son insists on sitting on his daddy's lap. Spence's attention towards it fades shortly after the opening credits, as his son giggles and shovels popcorn...

"Taylor steps off again and blows into his hand. You know, Tom, he grew up in Mississippi. His hands just aren't used to this cold weather. He settles back in and delivers... Strike one, foul. He just reached back and challenged him on that one."

Spence takes his time in between pitches, blowing into his hand multiple times, trying to get more feeling back into his numb fingertips.

"Strike two, outside corner. Give Taylor credit there. If the umpire is gonna give him an inch or more off the plate, he's gonna take it..."

"You're absolutely correct, Ted. He's too good of a pitcher and too accurate with his control to not take what he's being given."

"Taylor steps off again. And here comes the pitching coach out to the mound. Tom, you've pitched in cold weather before. What's it do to your control…?"

[interrupting] "Well, if you're not used to it, it's bothersome… But for someone like Taylor, who has both velocity and impeccable control, it can definitely cause issues at release."

"It appears as if the meeting on the mound is over, as Waters has a few words of encouragement for Taylor and the rest of the infield…"

"And it's a swing and a miss…"

"I think that ball was tipped, Tom, but Palmer held on to it for the second out. High in the zone and once again on the inner half, that pitch was a bit less than his normal at 95MPH. A very formidable Yuli Rodriguez is up next."

And suddenly his child's laughter towards the movie awakens him out of the trance that he's in. Christa is watching him closely with concern from the seat next to him.

***

Arriving home from the movie, the Taylors begin getting the kids into the bathtub and then ready for bed. Spence, less than ten hours since undergoing deep hypnosis, is still instinctively the best daddy ever in the eyes of his wife, as he spends five to ten minutes in the bedroom of each child, tucking them in and praying out loud with them, before handing out ample amounts of goodnight kisses.

Dan and Joy spend a few moments downstairs tidying up, loading and starting the dishwasher, and then moving the laundry through, before ultimately retiring for the night to the guesthouse out back.

And later on that evening… Actually, it might be considered early the next morning, if you're being truthful, they both finally settle into bed – at which point the landline phone on Christa's nightstand begins ringing…

"Hello… Is everything okay!? Well, it's past midnight here, so I was concerned that you were calling so late. No. No. We didn't watch it. We took the kids to a movie with Spence's… Mr. and Mrs. Taylor. What!? Oh dear… Yeah… It's gonna be all over the TV tomorrow, but for tonight I'm just gonna let him sleep. Ok. Thanks for calling. Love ya! Bye."

Rolling over and looking at Spence, "My parents say 'Hi' and that they love you."

"What happened?"

"Baby… You've had a really long day. Can we just talk about it tomorrow?"

"Why did I not go to the game tonight?"

"Because Dr. Olgivy said…"

"Why did I have to go see Dr. Olgivy!?"

"I know you're upset, baby," starting to caress him. "Tomorrow we'll talk more about what happened… In the meantime, we're here, we have a wonderful life, the kids are healthy, and we're both tired. Let's get some sleep and tomorrow will take care of itself."

eight - imperfect

The sun has barely risen the next morning when the phone rings, startling Christa awake. Spence opens his eyes slowly, still a little bit groggy, but more alert than last night. Christa reaches for her nightstand.

"Hello…"

Spence can hear a muffled male voice speaking on the other end.

"Let me tell you something! You have some kind of nerve calling my house, especially this early! Get a life!"

She then slams down the phone.

This is very unlike his wife. He looks on with concern and wants to know what's going on. She turns to look at her husband… "Spence. You pitch for Red Sox, correct?"

"Yes."

"Do you remember what happened the last game that you pitched…?"

And suddenly they are interrupted by a child at the door, proclaiming to be hungry. Spence appears to be trying to formulate an answer, before Christa puts one finger on his lips in the form of a "Shhhh…" and decides to quickly get out of bed and cook breakfast for everyone. The TVs throughout the house are purposefully powered off. Abby comes through the side door without knocking and hugs Christa, the kids, Spence's parents, and ultimately Spence – who's just joined the others after leaving the bedroom.

"You wouldn't believe what I had to do to keep that clown from coming over with me!"

"Joshua?" – inquires Spence.

"Yes!"

"Why not?"

Abby realizes that Spence has questions that probably don't have really good answers, at least coming from her.

Spence waits for a second and then walks away to another part of the house, announcing that he's going to take a shower.

Abby looks over at Christa…

"He's just now putting it all together."

Spence, moving slowly on purpose, actually hears her saying that just before opening the door to his bedroom and closing it behind him. Once there, he turns on the television out of habit, before walking into the bathroom, turning on the shower, and beginning to undress. It immediately opens to a sportscast…

"The Red Sox blew game one in the top of the ninth last night at Fenway Park when, with a two-run lead, would-be closer Mike Spratlin came in and surrendered two consecutive walks, a sac bunt, and a go-ahead bomb to San Francisco's Mateo Encarnacion."

"Yeah, Stuart, let's be honest. The Red Sox bats still had a chance to tie or win it in the bottom half when Waters doubled with two outs. But again, just being honest, they haven't been put in that kind of 'do or die' situation after surrendering a late lead since before Taylor arrived and established his dominance as a closer."

"And speaking of Taylor, who usually lives a quiet life with his family out in the Boston suburbs, he's now being thrust into the spotlight and tabloids. Last night, during game one of the World Series, mind you, Taylor was photographed at a local movie theatre with his wife and kids. During game one!? A game in which he could've closed it out!?"

"That's right, Stuart. But I think there's a little more going on here than just a case of 'the yips.'"

"Yeah, Keith. I believe you are correct."

Spence, naked and having worked his way back into the bedroom as the bathroom is steaming up from the shower being on, is visibly concerned while watching the broadcast, when suddenly the television cuts off inexplicably. He then turns around to find his wife standing there holding the remote control.

"Go take a hot shower and I'll drive you up to the stadium later this afternoon. You are not to speak to the press at all, whatsoever. And do not even think about answering the phone."

Spence steps into the shower and begins thinking things over. Having been on for nearly ten minutes now, he can hardly see his hands in front of him as he bathes due to the denseness of the steam. He then looks up directly into the nozzle and starts rinsing his face and hair…

"There are now 2 outs in the bottom of the 9th and the Red Sox are on the brink of making history. You know, I've been to so many games here at Fenway, but I've never seen the crowd so electric."

"Yeah, Ted. They've been kinda spoiled over the last decade with the team they've put together here, including this closer."

"Strike one, swinging!"

"Yuli might've chased one there, wanting to tie it up with just one swing, but that one was likely over the chalk line in the left-handed batter's box."

"Taylor continues to blow into his right hand. He's obviously not comfortable. But the results he's having so far don't demonstrate that."

"You're right. And as a matter of fact, and I don't want to jinx him here, but if he gets a strike on his next offering, he'll only be one pitch away from throwing that elusive immaculate inning that he's known to have been chasing. We've seen lots of innings from Taylor over the years where he had three strikeouts, and several of them with only ten total pitches thrown. But he's never actually thrown a perfect nine pitches and recorded three strikeouts in any one inning at any level of baseball."

"And here's the oh-one…"

"Strike two! Still using that generous outside zone, and Yuli is not happy at all with the home plate umpire. In fact, here comes the Yankee's manager Jim Anderson, and he's apparently not thrilled with him, either."

"You're absolutely correct. And as Jim argues, Skip has all the Red Sox infielders convening at the mound talking to Taylor, giving him words of encouragement and patting him on the backside. And his best friend, Joshua Waters, is the last one to disperse after giving him a smile, a wink, and a pat on the behind for good measure."

"This argument took a little while, and the whole time Taylor was blowing into his hand. At one point he even stuck it inside of his back pocket."

"Yeah. He just wants this one pitch as the crowd stands to its feet cheering in anticipation."

"Yuli looks like he's a little closer to the plate now, obviously in an effort to reach the outside pitch."

"And Taylor agrees with the catcher and begins his wind-up in a bid for an immaculate inning to end a near perfect, historical season for the Sox…"

"OOOOOOOOOH!!!!!"

"Oh my God, Ted. That was 98 miles per hour that ran up and in, and Yuli is on the ground."

"I'll tell you what, Tom… You can hear a pin drop here in Fenway Park as the trainers are out assessing the situation. I'm not sure if it hit him in the face just yet or not."

"Well… Here's a look at the replay. Nope. It glanced off the top of his shoulder and went on to hit him near the ear guard of the helmet. Thank

Goodness… It appears as if he's going to be okay. And, as they stand him up and escort him to the first base bag, the Boston fans give him a polite applause. That certainly could've been much worse, Ted."

"Tom. What shouldn't be lost here is the fact that this is the first batter that Taylor has ever hit in his entire MLB career."

"You're absolutely correct, Ted, and he looks visibly shaken as Waters and the rest of his teammates talk to him at the mound."

"Well, he's still in the driver's seat here, so let's see how he responds."

"Taylor from the stretch. Comes set. And he steps off."

"You know, there's never anybody in the bull pen when Taylor pitches. But now there are two arms out there frantically warming up."

"Taylor again…"

"Wow."

"At first glance it appeared they had a pitch-out called right there, but then again Palmer never even came out of his stance. Instead, he had to stab at it to keep it from going to the backstop."

"Ball two. Again, well off the plate."

"Taylor… And once again he steps off… And here comes Waters in from the short-stop position to try to settle him down."

"Would you look at that? He won't even look at Waters, Ted."

"You're right. He won't. And now Waters is gesturing for the manager to come out."

"Wow."

"Something's up."

"So now you've got two firsts. Taylor has never hit a batter in his MLB career, nor has he ever been given the hook."

"You're right. He's never 'not' finished the inning, either way…"

"Taylor… Now with his head down as he walks off to a standing ovation from the Fenway faithful…"

"He never looked up while walking off the field, Ted. Not even once."

"I don't think anyone would've ever accused him of throwing at Yuli, especially considering the cold hands and the situation he was in. But there's something that's obviously bothering him."

And at that point Spence's daydream is interrupted by Christa walking into the bathroom, asking if he needs a towel for when he gets out of the shower. He's fully aware of what all has transpired now for the first time since his session with Dr. Olgivy.

"Christa. Dr. Olgivy. What kind of doctor is he?"

[handing him a towel] "He's a world-renowned sports psychiatrist. He came highly recommended. In fact, you're going back to see him on Monday…"

[interrupting] "The hell I am!"

Christa is taken aback because it is very unlike Spence to raise his voice…

"Christa… He did stuff in my head that I never want to experience again!" [now beginning to cry] "I had a whole life outside of you and the kids that I thought was real. Like the worst nightmare possible that lasted for what seemed like months – and with memories that didn't include you or them."

"I know you did, baby. He told you all of that. You even consented to it. He explained that due to time constraints, he needed to do a deep dive without all the usual pre-treatment therapy that goes into it. He doesn't like to do it that way – but, in your case, he said you needed it. He gave both of us all the warnings and we said 'yes.'"

[now crying harder and falling into her arms] "I didn't know you or the kids. It was my own hell that I couldn't get out of. It was so real…" – His voice now muffled by her shoulder as they are embraced…

Christa, now crying too, "So you remember?"

"I remember everything so vividly. It was no different than standing right here with you. It's just that you weren't there, and my life was completely eff'd up."

"He said he had to get to your primal instincts and fears in order to fix…"

"He hasn't fixed shit!"

"I'm so sorry, baby. He said it might take several days to process…"

"I'm not going back!"

"If you don't want to go back, that's fine. You have nothing to prove to anybody."

"What do you mean 'I have nothing to prove to anybody?'"

"The Red Sox team of physicians all recommended that you see Dr. Olgivy and you agreed. He is the only one that can release you to play again. They flew him in from South Africa. He's had amazing results with golfers."

"I don't play golf, Christa!"

Trying to calm him down. "I know, baby. And I'm sorry. We'll go up to the stadium later so that you can be with the team tonight."

nine – decent

The radio is conspicuously off during the mid-afternoon commute to Fenway Park. Spence is dressed in a nice pair of jeans, cowboy boots, an oxford, and a blazer that Christa picked out. Barely twenty-four hours out from his session, he still hasn't been cleared to drive by Dr. Olgivy. That should come sometime after the next meeting on Monday, if he even goes – which currently doesn't look good.

Christa pulls the plus-sized luxury SUV into the player's parking garage and they go through all of the checkpoints, before she walks with him to the entrance of the locker-room. He's a little bit late showing up, but everyone understands that he isn't expected to play tonight. The attendant at the door lets him in, as Christa proceeds to the family entrance and suite.

Spence works his way down a long hallway and into the locker-room...

"MEAT!"

It's Joshua, who's happy to see him.

"I'm so glad you're here," as he gives him a big bear hug.

Spence manages to smile back at him.

"Meat... Uh... Look..." Joshua gets up close to his ear and speaks as softly as he can, which isn't very soft at all... "I thought we were past all of that. I had no idea that it affected you so much. You need to know that..." [Joshua looks around] "... I love ya and we're here now as adults living out our dreams. We're best friends and practically neighbors – ok, across the street and down a few. We planned that though. Our wives are best friends, too. Hell, even our kids..."

"I know…"

"No, you don't know, Meat! Because if you did you wouldn't be all messed up in the head right now. This whole team loves you and needs you…"

"Taylor." His name is spoken in a very matter of fact tone from across the room.

"Yeah, boss."

"Come to my office."

Spence looks at Joshua affirmingly, before walking into the manager's office, closing the door, and sitting down.

"Taylor. We lost a World Series game that we should've won last night. It's been almost two weeks since we played the Yankees to end the regular season and we made it through the American League Conference Series against the Mariners by the skin of our teeth. We need our closer ASAP. When do you think you'll be ready?"

"I'm ready tonight, Skip."

"Bullshit! No, you're not. I can see it in your eyes. You're scared shitless. You pitched a bullpen session with a live batter before the start of the ALCS and you were so far off the plate that we had to halt it after less than 10 pitches. And even if I thought you were ready, Major League Baseball and The Player's Association both say that I can't put you out there until I get written permission from some wacky-doo head doctor. I'll tell you what, times have certainly changed since I played…"

"What do you mean 'Head Doctor?'"

"Some bullshit neurologist or something has diagnosed you with Post Traumatic Stress Disorder and they've called in some Voodoo Doctor from Africa or something, who's holding you hostage. Hell, for all I know he has a plate lip and wears face-paint. He wouldn't even let us talk to you the past couple of weeks. Not even Joshua. He's now allowed you to come back to the ballpark."

"Well, I'm not going back to that basta…"

"The hell you aren't! Don't come in here telling me that you're 'ready to play,' but you're not going back. The Red Sox are paying you $10 million a year to pitch, which is way more than I make coaching and twice as much as I made while playing for twelve years. You're going to go in there on Monday and tell that wacky-doo Voodoo piece of shit that you're a baseball player and the team needs you."

"I can't go back to him, Skip. He messed me up."

"Son… You have to go back if you want to play. And quite frankly if we're going to have a chance at winning the championship. You do what you need to do. But I can't have you sitting around, dressed out in the dugout or bullpen tonight, if you're unavailable. You can't travel with us. Nothing…"

Spence looks surprised.

"Really!? It's too much of a distraction, Taylor, with the circus media and stuff. The movies!? During game one of the world series!? Whose brilliant idea was that!? They are eating this shit up! The crowd is going to be chanting for me to put you in, not knowing that I'm handcuffed. And we can't have that. We need to stay focused because we must win game two before we go to San Francisco. You're gonna have to sit in the box with the ownership tonight if you want to see the game. Your wife can sit with you, too. Try to stay away from the windows, please. And you really need to rethink not going back to the Voodoo doctor. I can't help you, son, unless you help me."

Spence walks out of the manager's office. By this time most of the players have taken the field for pre-game warm-ups. There is one local reporter that's just finishing up an interview with the game one starting pitcher who sees Spence and walks up to him…

"Spence. Are you dressing out and will you be available for the pivotal game two match-up tonight?"

Spence has a deer in headlights look as he responds "No comment…" and walks away.

***

The ownership suite at Fenway Park is state of the art, especially in relation to how old the ballpark is. There's an open bar, buffet, and private restroom with a butler, all littered with live game broadcasts on a half dozen televisions scattered about the enclosure, all so that one might never miss any of the action if he/she was to choose to partake in any of the available amenities.

Just outside the suite, but still enclosed behind tempered glass, are three rows of stadium style seats about eight across, roomier than the standard issued ones below, and with more than adequate leg room. About 50 feet behind and above the backstop, it gives a panoramic view of the entirety of the field and stadium, completely within the comforts of both air conditioning and heat.

After finding Christa chatting with the wives of the other players, he escorts her along with a chaperone up to the ownership suite, at which point a hostess, who's been told to expect them, explains all the conveniences and luxuries therein. The two of them are then approached and greeted by the team's general manager, Michael Thompson, who is the longest tenured GM in all of Major League Baseball, and who was instrumental in drafting both Spence and Joshua. In fact, Joshua Waters was the first pick that he insisted on taking. And a couple of years later he urged the Red Sox to select his best friend, trading up in the draft to take him. Throw in a few key free-agent signings, and combine them with a well-organized farm system pipeline, and you, too, can perhaps one day build what Michael has since built in Boston.

"Spence," shaking his hand.

"Michael."

"Christa," embracing in a casual hug.

"Come join us. There's plenty of food and drinks."

"Thank you."

"Spence. We're pretty shielded from the view of all the cameras in here, but just so you know, the minute that you step out there…" [pointing to the stadium seats] "… you're fair game. They have several camera angles dedicated to just this one box, so any facial expressions that you make, they will zoom in and see it. They even read our lips from time to time in here."

"Good to know. Thanks."

"So, tell me, Spence, how are you doing?"

Christa is very defensive of Spence. She looks on and listens cautiously, waiting to intervene, if necessary. But Michael isn't acting like a dick. He genuinely seems concerned about his well-being.

"I'm pretty good."

"You know, we knew that Joshua got hit in the head by a pitch in his last high school game. We had lots of our doctors fly down to Jackson to check on him because he was our guy that we were set on acquiring in the upcoming draft. However, we never put 2 + 2 together that you were the pitcher that actually hit him."

"It was a close call."

"And did you ever go to any therapy afterwa…"

[interrupting] "He didn't need therapy, Michael. He was the most dominant high school pitcher in the state of Mississippi and a Golden Spikes award winner as a sophomore in college."

He then looks at Christa… "Oh, I'm well-aware of that. That's why I wanted him to come pitch for us. I'm just trying to understand…"

Christa interrupts again… "There's nothing to understand. He's a two-time World Series champion and a first ballot Hall of Famer. If he doesn't touch a baseball again for the rest of his life, there's still nothing for you to 'understand' about it. Please leave that to the medical professionals because, comparatively speaking, he's more than returned your investment in him over the years, and then some."

He then glances over at her husband with a smirk. "She's right, Spence. And you're a very lucky man to have her."

Christa grabs her husband by the hand and hastily steers him away towards the stadium seats, all while giving the GM a go-to-hell look.

"Christa!? That man gave us a $2 million signing bonus before I ever threw a pitch for him, several million dollars more in salary arbitration, and then a $50 million contract four years ago, which was unheard of for a closer. You have to be nice to him because he's still paying me not to pitch right now."

"I know. I'm sorry, baby. I'm just mad. They should allow you to sit with the team."

"Skip said I can't play until I'm cleared and that it's too much of a distraction for the team with all of the media involvement."

"Baby, you are the reason they are here! I just can't…"

Christa suggests that he sits down while she gets them something to eat. She then runs into other people that she knows and begins conversing with them. The teams are taking batting practice below when Spence's mind begins to drift…

The opening music of the X-files television series plays in the background as Christa, Spence, and his parents are at the Taylor's house listening to an AM radio broadcast of the Major League Baseball draft from Radio City Music Hall in New York City.

Baseball is a tricky sport. Historically there's always been an old school approach to making batting line-ups and deciding which pitcher to put into a game, depending on the opposing team's tendencies, the situation at hand, and the coach's gut-feeling on the matter. However, SABRmetrics, short for the Society for American Baseball Research and a term used to describe a new form of decision making based upon the empirical analysis of baseball statistics, was starting to gain favor in the early 90s. Mississippi State University's long-time head coach, Art Miller, was an early adopter of the approach. He recruited a professor from the school's Department of Mathematics and Statistics, who also happened to be a big baseball fan, and tabbed him with pioneering a system to both collect and summarize relevant data from in-game activity, analyze it, and then implement the findings into the everyday decision making of the coaches.

For instance, originally a Friday night shut-down starter for the Bulldogs with several complete games under his belt, empirical analyses of Spence's outings determined that his dominance, control, and velocity drastically decreased after 60 to 70 pitches. But based on how effective and commanding he was on pitches 1 through 40, it was suggested to the coaching staff that as a sophomore he should be moved to both a position that the team needed and one that afforded him a better shot at long term success in the major leagues… Closer.

Spence never looked back, and as a sophomore he overpowered the best hitters in college baseball one inning, and sometimes two (when needed) at a time, winning the Golden Spikes Award as the best amateur baseball player in America.

He was clearly the best pitcher in all of college baseball and thusly had been projected as an early first round pick. The only problem was most of the teams with picks in the early first round already had an established closer, so the suspense of the unknown and the prospect of sitting there at Radio City Music Hall with the glare of the lights and cameras as team after team skipped over him was enough of a deterrent to keep the Taylors from attending the event, choosing instead to monitor the festivities from the confines and comforts of their own living room.

One thing was for certain though: Spence was going to be a millionaire before the night was over. What was uncertain, however, is exactly how many millions he would be signing for, based upon how early or late he was taken. He also didn't know how good or bad the organization would be that selected him. Most of the early picks were from teams that finished way back in the standings the year prior.

And so the Taylors decided to just grill some food while they listened on. Christa's favorite show and actor were still playing in the background as the draft began.

Of no surprise, Spence wasn't among the first three picks, who all went with high school position players. The team with the 4th pick was on the clock and had shown some interest in him, although he wasn't too keen on their franchise, history, and how they managed their players.

Make no mistake, though… Any team that invested in him, he'd pitch his heart out for.

The team then chooses and goes with a pitcher, the top prospect high school arm out of the state of California.

Spence is kinda bummed, but doesn't show it. Christa is still engrossed in the television episode in front of her and his parents continue to casually speak as if there isn't going to be a big change in their son's life at some point tonight.

And just then the cordless phone, strategically placed close to Spence, rings loudly.

Everyone jumps.

Spence lets it ring a couple of times, looks around at everyone else, and then answers in his calmest voice…

"Hello."

"Meat!"

Spence can hear Christa, who's turned down the TV, telling his parents "It's just Joshua."

"Wassup, buddy?"

"Uh… I don't know. I'm just hanging out here at Fenway in the war room with my old buddy Michael Thompson!"

Spence immediately spits his drink out all over the coffee table in front of him.

"Joshua. This isn't even funny. There are at least twenty more draft picks until the Red Sox can select someone."

"I know…"

"So why would you call and tease me on tonight, of all nights!?"

"Because the GM that I'm sitting next to asked me to…"

"Joshua!?"

"Meat!?"

And then at that moment on the radio…

"This just in. We don't know all the details yet, but we just got word that the Boston Red Sox have traded WAY-UP in the draft to the 6th position on the board!"

"Joshua?" As Spence starts to get emotional…

"Meat… How'd you like to come to Boston soon to play baseball with your best friend?"

Spence drops the phone in shock as Christa and his parents rejoice around him. Joshua is so loud and boisterous, they could hear nearly every word he said.

She then picks up the phone off the floor…

"Joshua!?"

"I've got some pull up here in Beantown, Christa. Abby and I can't wait until y'all can join us!"

Again, from the radio…

"Well, it's usually a ten-minute time allotment between picks, and generally speaking most teams tend to use the entire time, but it's only been two minutes since the fifth one and here's the commissioner already coming up to the podium with the 6th…"

"With the 6th pick in the 1993 Major League Baseball draft, the Boston Red Sox select Spencer Taylor, Pitcher, Mississippi State University."

The four of them go wild while Joshua listens-in and smiles from the other end of the phone line.

"Meat! Meat!? Are you there!?"

Spence can barely hear his friend's voice coming through the handset now.

"Yes, I'm here."

"Congrats, buddy. I'll give you a year to get up here. Oh… And by the way, Abby already has your house picked out."

And with that Joshua hangs up.

Christa, who's crying, embraces Spence as he picks her up and they both spin around in a circle. He then sets her back down, reaches deep into his pocket, pulls out a single solitaire diamond ring, grabs her left hand, and gets on one knee. Spence's dad, already anticipating the moment, now has his VHS video camera out.

"Christa," He then takes a deep breath… "You've always been my forever…"

Spence quickly shakes his head back and forth and tries to concentrate on saying something else as he slides it onto her left ring finger. He then tries again… "Christa…"

She suddenly interrupts him… "Stop it. Stop it! That's so perfect! Don't ruin it!"

"Spence. Spence. Spencer!?" Christa is nudging him on the shoulder…

Spence shudders back to present day reality. His wife has been trying to get his attention for several minutes now. The player introductions are now over and the Star-Spangled Banner is starting down on the field. She's telling him that he needs to stand up.

***

Spence and Christa arrive home later that evening after what was essentially a blow-out win. San Francisco's starting pitcher struggled with his control and the Red Sox put up large, crooked numbers in each of the first three innings, cruising to a 10 to 3 victory, with all the Giants' runs coming in the top of the 9th inning.

He is relieved that the lack of late-inning relief pitching didn't contribute to the ultimate outcome of the game, even though it still showed that there was a glaring problem in the arsenal for Boston.

His parents greet them at the door, having been up for a couple of hours since putting the children to sleep and watching the end of the game. Spence and Christa both silently enter the kids' rooms and gently kiss them goodnight, before retiring for the night, themselves.

Lying in their bed together, she suddenly turns to him and says, "I love you no matter what. I'd love you if you weren't a baseball player, and I'd be just as in love with you if we still lived in our hometown, you worked at the factory, and we lived in a mobile home. My love for you is not contingent upon your success. It is unconditional. It always has been."

Spence looks on and wonders what precipitated that remark, especially considering the alternate universe he experienced under hypnosis.

She then kisses him softly on the lips and says, "All of these ball players get famous and make lots of money, and then either divorce their wives for greener pastures, or don't get married until later in life. But you and Joshua are the exceptions to that rule. You both married your high school sweethearts, you're both excellent fathers, and you're both superstars that could live totally different lives, like some of your teammates. Abby and I were just talking about how fortunate we are to have found you both and each other."

Spence, trying to think of something to follow that up with, "Well, Christa, I think you're totally hot…"

Christa interrupts with "Oh my God!"

Spence, confused: "What? I'm trying to pay you a compliment…"

"A compliment!?"

"Yes."

"Spence, I just poured out my entire heart to you about how fortunate the kids and I are to have you and how none of this [as she points around at the oversized master bedroom and high ceilings] really matters, as long as it's you…"

"I'm trying…" – Now amused and smiling.

"Oh... 'I'm trying...'" – Christa says sarcastically, while purposefully and outwardly rolling her eyes and giggling out loud...

"There."

"What?"

"Right there. The way your eyes dance when you're laughing at me..."

"You mean the way they roll?" – As she playfully hits him on the shoulder and laughs out loud.

This soon turns into intimacy as Spence, now lying on his back and quickly straddled by his wife, begins recalling how it all seems both new and strange for some reason when they start kissing, but in a good way. Christa, not anticipating the spontaneous moment when she came to bed wearing a silk pajama set with short bottoms, takes off her top and buries his head in her breasts. What initially began as heavy petting in high school slowly evolved over the years and eventually culminated into the full exploration of each other's bodies in consummation after they were married. That noted, there had always been some degree of progressive mutual familiarity between them that had developed over the years. But with his mind having been bogged down lately, not to mention drifting in and out of reality, a very satisfying moment of mental clarity ensues, allowing him to appreciate being widely alert and keenly more aware of her presently, while also noticing that she's a bit more active than usual – the two of them ultimately reaching climax together and voluntarily falling asleep in each other's arms...

"Spence... Spence..."

There's someone knocking at the front door. He can hear his dad opening it and greeting the person. Spence opens his eyes to find himself inside his childhood bedroom, lying down, and staring at the ceiling. There are about a dozen posters of past MLB pitchers adorning the walls of his room, Tom Seaver, Nolan Ryan, and Steve Carlton, just to name a few. There's also a framed picture of him and Christa on his bedside table.

"Spence... It's Coach Gray."

It's his mom's gentle voice and she's tapping on his arm, concerned that he is not exactly sleeping, but instead appears as if he is in a trance-like state, just lying there staring at the ceiling fan.

"Coach Gray is here and he wants to talk to you."

Coach is a big man. Not very tall, but wide. And many of the kids find it funny that he still dons the uniform just like everyone else, belt cinched very tightly above the belly button, with large rolls of fat folded both over it from above and under it from below. But right now he's in the Taylor's living room in his 2nd choice of outfight, undersized "coaches shorts," no belt, a way too tight polo shirt adorned with the school's emblem, a comb-over, and some very unflattering matching striped socks.

Spence walks into the living room and greets the coach.

"Spence. We won the game. We couldn't find you afterward. I called your dad and he said you were pretty torn up. We had practice this morning and all of the kids are worried about you..."

Spence interrupts him. "I'm not coming back."

Coach Gray is surprised... "Why not?"

"I just can't... Not after what I did..."

"Spence. These things happen in baseball..."

Interrupting, once again... "They happen? They happen!?"

"Yes, son... Unfortunately, they do."

Spence rolls his eyes.

The coach looks at his parents. His mom appears to be the most concerned.

"We just want him to take the time he needs..." – Joy replies.

[interrupting] "Well, I'd otherwise be inclined to agree with you, but we don't have the time available. We have the State Semifinals and hopefully the Finals in five days; and Spence is our ace. I'm not sure we can do it without him."

Spence looks on.

"Look. I've been on the phone with Brandon High School's coach. We're actually really good friends. Your dad and I played baseball with him growing up. He's been in touch with Joshua's parents and is closely monitoring the situation. He suggested that Spence visit him and his parents at the hospital…"

"No way."

"Spence… This will help give you some closure and hopefully the ability to…"

[interrupting] "The ability to what!? Kill someone else!?"

And just then the youngest child, who's now up, climbs up into the bed, jarring both he and Christa awake, and imploring him to get up and throw the ball. But instead, he just holds on to him and kisses him all over, before sending him out of the bedroom to find one that they can toss.

ten – snafued

Dan Taylor is simply a dad that is proud of his son. He still has his house in Mississippi, but he and Joy spend most of the year in their son's Boston suburban home – specifically the guesthouse, which has all the amenities they could ever ask for – and it keeps them separated enough from Spence and the family, such that both sides can keep their privacy and easily help one another out when the need arises. That's a one-way street of exactly who helps whom, but the proud grandparents wouldn't have it any other way.

The truth is he wanted to buy a more modest home several miles away, but Spence and Christa insisted that was unnecessary and, in fact, put them both on the official payroll as "personal assistants," even though they likely don't do much more than any other grandparents would.

One thing Dan does do is grocery shop for the entire family compound. And on this morning's trip he has a cart full of items at the cash register, when he glances over towards the tabloids. There, on the front page of the National Enquirer, is Spence and the family at the movies, from two night's prior, with the headline: "TAYLOR ABANDONS HIS TEAM!"

Dan walks into the house and places the tabloid magazine on the kitchen island.

Christa: "Oh my God!"

"Well, son, it's looks like you're now an official celebrity."

Spence looks on with concern.

"ABANDONS HIS TEAM!?" – asks Christa. "ABANDONS HIS TEAM!? He's given that team over 10 years of his life and even turned down more money to play elsewhere!"

And suddenly the phone rings…

"Hello. Oh, hi Abby. No. No. I'm just sitting here looking at a picture of my family ON THE FRONT PAGE OF THE NATIONAL ENQUIRER! And it's not even a good one!"

Everyone can hear Abby's voice muffled through the handset…

"What do you mean?"

More mumbling…

"People Magazine!?"

Joshua is a bigger "celebrity" than Spence, based upon his larger-than-life personality and the fact that he's been a superstar baseball player since his rookie season, making his Major League Baseball debut while still only nineteen years old. But both are more local athlete/celebrities than national and have generally shunned the spotlight over the years, unlike many of their colleagues, in favor of a more normal family life for their families.

Even so, they could always count on Abby to fill them in on pop culture and recent events because she subscribes to all the gossip magazines, People Magazine and Entertainment Weekly – just to name two of them.

And inside People Magazine there's a "Star Traks" section where the publication purchases pictures of celebrities in everyday life from the paparazzi and captions them with the date, where they are, and what they're doing.

"Star Traks!? Who are we, Tom Cruise and Nicolle Kidman!?" – Says a frustrated Christa. "What's the caption say?"

Again, they can hear the muffled sound of Abby's voice in Christa's ear through the phone line.

"What!? Of all the things they could've possibly written, they want to now be on par with the National Enquirer insofar as gossip and not reaching out to us personally for comment!?"

"Christa… It's fine," proclaims Spence. "They can write whatever they want – and technically they didn't say anything that's untrue."

"You did not abandon your team!"

"I know. But I said 'technically.'"

And just then Joy walks in from the guesthouse… "It's all over ESPN and talk radio this morning that you're not making the trip to San Francisco with the team?"

"Yeah… About that… Skip says that his hands are tied, and that Major League Baseball and The Player's Association said that I couldn't play or travel with the team until I get written clearance from Dr. Olgivy."

"Well, are you going to go see him so that you can pitch?"

Christa chimes in, "Only when he's ready…"

Christa, still on the line with Abby, hears a "beep" and takes the handset off her ear to look at it…

"Abby. I'm sorry but I've gotta take this call…"

"Christa. I've been your best friend for the last twelve years… How is it that I'm losing a 'call-waiting faceoff…'"

Christa smiles as she clicks the answer button and simultaneously ends the call with her best friend…

"Hello… Oh, Hi…" – As she lip-synchs "It's Dr. Olgivy" and points several times in a hammering motion at the handset.

Spence listens on intently, as he can faintly hear his voice.

"Well, Dr. Olgivy, we're still trying to decide on whether or not Spence is coming back. Apparently there's some post-traumatic stress from his session and he remembers nearly everything from the hypnosis now. He says it was very real and what was only three to four hours to you and me, he swears went on for many years in his own mind."

Dr. Olgivy goes on to explain to Christa that everyone is different, and depending on the individual in question and how deep the suspected issue lies in the subconscious, that it could most definitely be a scary voyage into finding it.

"Christa. I let you sit-in on the entire session. When or how often have you ever heard your husband speak using the language he used to communicate with me? For four hours he was a completely different person. You might even say that he was 'possessed.' But we made progress in finding the core of what's happening. However, he's still vulnerable."

"So… You can't just release him to play?"

"Christa… You've seen him. Is he acting like himself at all?"

"No."

"Right. If I release him right now, he's gonna get thrown to the wolves and the media is going to tear him up; not to mention what it might do to him permanently. Right now, his best option is to never play professional baseball again. But if he meets with me…"

Christa [interrupting]: "Well, he has been discussing retiring soon…"

"Christa… You know Spence. I didn't see him until after the traumatic event happened. But I could tell that he was a broken man – just a shell of the person he once was. Unfortunately, my job isn't just placing a band-aid inside someone's brain who's injured. It goes way deeper than that. If he never plays baseball again, he's gonna be just fine. He's still a Hall of Famer. But the Spence that you know, the one you've known since high school, wouldn't want to accept going out like this without a good fight. He simply needs some encouragement – and perhaps you can help with that. I'm not asking you to force him. I've already been paid. I'm being held here on retainer until the series is over by Major League Baseball, The Player's Association, and the Boston Red Sox because they don't like what's played out on television screens all over the world. They want Spence 'fixed' for selfish reasons. But I don't want him to be 'fixed,' Christa. None of us need to be 'fixed.' I want to see him fully restored. A fully restored Spence is no longer distant, unattached, distracted, confused, or preoccupied. It just so happens that I personally believe that a fully restored Spence is also a dominant closer."

Spence notices Christa starting to tear up after glancing over at him.

"I just feel like a complete restoration in both baseball and in life can only be accomplished if we finish what we started. What we both witnessed under hypnosis, whether with my trained eye or your untrained eye, was a broken person harboring a fear deep down in his core that has been unleashed in the present day and is wreaking havoc in his life, both professionally and personally. I think we can find him and restore him."

"I'm not sure I can get him to come back."

"Well, you have my number. When he decides he's ready, I'll be here…"

Christa hangs up the phone, just as Abby opens the door, wanting to know who she lost a "call-waiting faceoff" to…

eleven – foul

The Boston Red Sox travel in style in their own team logo-adorned Boeing 767 that's decked out with spacious leather seats and about thirty personal "cubicles" that recline to lay down flat, all with personal televisions, radios, etc. – which is more than enough room to handle the number of players on the roster and the coaches, including the prima donnas.

The executives and coaches have already boarded the plane and are meeting towards the back, as the players start to check-in and begin claiming their cubicles. The pilots are going through all their pre-flight checks and the ground crew is loading the team's equipment.

Joshua is dressed in a blazer, and oxford, jeans, and cowboy boots. Major League Baseball, not to mention the Red Sox organization, requires players to "dress appropriately" when they travel on "official business" and most, like Joshua, end up in some form of dressy casual that's based upon their personal preferences and where they are from.

And as Joshua passes one of the outfielders, Cameron Moon, a young, arrogant 1st year player out of the Dominican Republic who bats leadoff and has primarily played shortstop his whole life until being called-up from the minors, he notices him abruptly stopping his conversation with another young player and both of them looking over at him and laughing.

"What's so funny?"

"Ahhh… Nothing." [as they both look at each other and grin]

"Listen, Rook. I've been at this way too long for y'all to talk shit about me behind my back."

"Oh, we weren't talking 'shit' about you. We were talking about your pussy friend that's…"

And just then Joshua lunges at him before he can even complete the sentence, "You barely speak English you cocky mutha…"

And as he does this, he gets sucker-punched by the other teammate in the right eye, opening up a small cut around the outside corner of his brow, at which point the rest of his teammates and coaches intervene and separate them.

They call for a trainer to come look at Joshua and determine that he needs several stitches. The plane is delayed from leaving for nearly two hours while that gets taken care of.

***

Word travels fast, especially when it's juicy and there's evidence to back up something that's more than just hearsay. Perhaps it was the pilots? Or maybe even the crew? The players had strict instructions to keep it all inside the clubhouse after the incident, but it could've been one of them, too. Or maybe it was the airplane's expected arrival time in San Francisco being delayed for what the Red Sox officially stated was for "no reason" at all, thereby piquing the curiosity of the awaiting media.

But the firestorm that awaited the team shortly after their arrival in San Francisco became evident while they were still taxiing to the gate, as the players were starting to get phone calls and texts, prompting Skip to call a meeting before disembarking the aircraft, and instructing everyone, players, coaches, and all personnel, to avoid speaking to the media until after the series was over – the only exception being post-game interviews where it might appear rude to ignore a reporter in front of a national audience.

The manager then asks for a press conference to be set up upon the team's arrival at the hotel, one in which he will address the media about what had transpired. Maybe that wasn't the best idea because, while the team made its way from the airplane to the bus, it was obvious that its superstar shortstop had an injury to his right eye. Upon closer inspection, when the players arrived at the Boston airport before departing earlier in the day, video had clearly shown that Joshua did not in fact have the injury. That meant that it happened somewhere and sometime on the team plane.

Skip walks into the press conference later on that afternoon, sits down, sighs, and reads a prepared statement.

"Before departing Boston, while boarding the aircraft, there was a disagreement and scuffle between three Red Sox players that left Joshua Waters with a laceration to his right upper eyelid that had to be addressed and stitched before we could take off. The team is looking into exactly what happened and will handle it internally. Thank you."

But as Skip gets up and walks off, he's bombarded with questions from reporters yelling over one another. He ignores all of them and walks off the stage.

***

"It's like we're prisoners now in our own house."

Abby has walked over this morning to visit with Christa and check on how things are going. She also brought along her children to play with the Taylor crew. Dan is occupying himself by getting leaves out of the pool, while Joy sits nearby reading a book, having already gotten out for an early hair appointment this morning and successfully navigated the media circus coming back into the neighborhood.

"Well, luckily you live in a gated community with a guard."

There are about a dozen or so trucks camped outside the entrance of their "neighborhood," which is basically just one upscale street in the Boston suburb of Newton that has about twenty homes. Only three houses past the gate on the right side of the street, Christa can walk just down to the end of the hallway, which she is doing more frequently today than ever before, and peer through the plantation shutters of their mud and laundry room to witness the chaos that's building and building.

"Yep… I guess the days of 'living in anonymity' as a 'Hall of Fame' pitcher for the Boston Red Sox are over now," Abby quips as she gives a playful sarcastic eye roll.

Christa musters a giggle.

She and Abby became very close friends essentially by default after their respective husbands became besties. Although they grew up in different towns and attended separate high schools, it was a match made in "Best Friend Heaven" when they finally met, having so much in common besides their boyfriends at the time. In fact, they might argue that they are closer to one another than their husbands.

Spence is still sleeping though. He's never been one to sleep in, but since his hypnosis therapy session with Dr. Olgivy, he hasn't spontaneously awakened in the early daylight hours like he always did before. Christa, concerned, but also assuming that he needs the extra sleep in order to recover and wanting to shield him as much as possible from the turmoil brewing outside of their home, doesn't bother with waking him up.

They turn on the news just to get a glimpse of what's happening and a local television reporter on location begins to broadcast from just outside the gate:

[nodding while holding a microphone in one hand and using the other to cover an earpiece as the traffic passes nearby] "Yeah, thanks, Ron. I'm here [while looking around] as you can see along with many others outside of this swanky New England neighborhood that houses the likes of prominent NFL, NBA, NHL, and MLB players. And we're all just waiting to get a glimpse of Spence Taylor. This hasn't been confirmed, but sources have told us that the beloved Red Sox closer has been under the care of Dr. Olgivy, a world-renowned sports psychiatrist, since the regular season ended. Of course there's details that are still coming in, but word is Dr. Olgivy must clear him medically for Taylor to be allowed to play. And there's obviously some turmoil to speak of in the Boston locker room, as Taylor's best friend showed up yesterday in San Francisco with a visible cut over his right eye. It has since been confirmed that this happened as the team was boarding the plane here in Boston and Waters had a confrontation with a couple of younger teammates, who allegedly made disparaging remarks about Taylor. This, of course, as the Red Sox just finished a historic season on a high note while firing on all cylinders, only to be exposed in the playoffs since that time when their closer became suddenly, and quite frankly without good reasoning, unavailable. Let me tell you, we know that the fans want answers, and we're here to get them, Ron. For the record, there has been no official word from the Spence Taylor camp and all calls are essentially going unanswered. We'll have another update here at 6pm tonight. Until then, this is Gayle Patterson reporting live for WBOS, your Red Sox insider!"

Spence enters the kitchen area from the master bedroom and Abby lunges for the remote control, attempting to quickly turn off the broadcast.

"It's fine. I was watching it in the bedroom."

Abby seems relieved as he hugs Christa tightly, before walking over to Joy and kissing her softly on the cheek. She leans in and pats him gently on the forearm.

Looking across the kitchen island at Abby, "So how bad is it?"

Abby looks at Christa for an acknowledgement to answer and she gives her a thumbs up.

"There are at least 20 local and national news trucks outside of the neighborhood, all of them focused on the comings and goings from our neighborhood. There're also several police units monitoring the traffic as it moves by."

"So... It sounds like you're saying, 'It's a complete circus?'"

"So to speak."

"Have you spoken to Joshua?"

"Yes. Last night before I went to bed..."

"And..."

Abby again looks toward Christa before answering... "He's fine."

"Did he really get into a fight trying to defend me?"

"Yes."

"Against who?"

Abby knows the answer and that it was actually against two teammates, but says she doesn't know.

Spence walks down the hallway towards the mudroom and glances through the plantation shutters – all he can see is the tops of a dozen or more news trucks, complete with satellite dishes, and those with unobstructed views have cameras mounted and pointed at the Taylor house.

And as he sits there monitoring the chaos, Christa walks up and embraces him from behind, before gently asking, "Have you thought about a follow-up session with Dr. Olgivy?"

Spence lowers his head and looks at the ground before softly replying, "I'm not sure if I can. Something he did really messed me up."

"I know, baby. He explained all of that to you before you agreed to the treatment."

Surprised, "Wait. I agreed to that!?"

Christa tears up and nods affirmatively. "He is not the 'bad guy' here that you're making him out to be."

"Christa. It felt like so much more than three to four hours. I feel like I've lived a whole'nother life outside of you and the kids. And I had actual memories of my alternate reality and how I got there. I knew that I had a job and what time I had to be at work. I craved the alcohol and cigarettes so badly and felt the discomfort of the withdrawals. And even worse I had to relive and personally witness what I did to Joshua – not to mention the toll it took on all of us."

"Yes, baby. Dr. Olgivy told you all of that. And I was there for the entire session. In a way I lived it too. I saw it all. You were a very different person. But in my opinion, as hard as it was to watch, I think he found something."

"Like what!? That I was a total loon!?"

"Spence. Look at me. You went from being the most dominant pitcher in recent history with impeccable control to, after just one errant pitch on a very cold night, someone that not only couldn't find the plate, but was nowhere near it. You couldn't even pitch to the next batter. You had a very unsuccessful bullpen session a couple of days later. Whatever happened, it really messed you up mentally and triggered something that was, until that time, lying dormant inside your beautiful, but complicated head."

Spence looks down before Christa lifts him up by the chin.

"Spence. Look around us. If you never pitch in another game for the rest of your life, I'm totally fine with it. You've given us an amazing life and all we could ever ask for. We're set. We have enough money saved to move anywhere we want. We have our house here in Boston that's across the street from our best friends that we can always keep and still come to visit any time we want. But we also have the option to build and live full-time in a gorgeous house back home on 'The Rez' and drink cocktails together while watching sunsets every evening from our dock. Or we can simply pack everyone up and opt to travel the world and 'road-school' the kids."

She then places both hands on his shoulders and makes him look her way…

"But you, Spence. You're a competitor. You don't really even enjoy winning, as much as you simply hate to lose. That's why you're a closer, baby. And a damn good one, at that. Deep down you couldn't accept ending your career like that and, with the agreement of the coaches, Major League Baseball, the Red Sox organization, and The Player's Association, you are the one that actively sought out the help that you needed. You chose Dr. Olgivy based upon his reputation."

"My teammates all hate me now."

"No they don't! They love you! And they are not where they are without you. Your best friend probably over-reacted, but he just misses you. Y'all have been virtually inseparable for the last ten years. He just wants you back. He's hardly played a game that he can even remember that you weren't right there with him."

The phone rings in the background as they can hear Abby picking it up.

"Wait… How'd you get this number!? You have some freak'n kind of ner…"

Christa walks over and quickly grabs the phone from her, before politely speaking into the handset, "We have no comment at this time. Thank you."

twelve – dull

It's later that evening and it has been dark outside for quite a while in New England. But, over 3,000 miles away in San Francisco, there's still almost two hours of daylight left, as the teams are warming up and getting ready for game three of the World Series.

Tied one game to one, they are set to play three games on the West Coast, before heading back to Boston for games six and seven, if needed. The Red Sox winning one game is all that it would take to bring the series back home to Fenway Park for a game six matchup, at the very least.

The Taylors sit down to watch the broadcast and all anyone can talk about on air is the unavailability of Spence and how it relates to the drama brewing in the Boston clubhouse.

Christa tries to turn the volume down on the television, but Spence stops her, wanting to listen to what they have to say.

"Well, it's hard to believe that it's been less than two weeks since we were at Fenway watching another masterful closing performance from Spence Taylor."

"That's right, Ted. He was finishing the night for Ledbetter, trying to cap-off a historic season for the Red Sox, needing just one more strike. And while he was visibly uncomfortable with how cold it was that night, nobody could've envisioned just how the next pitch would've impacted the upcoming postseason for Boston."

"I've gotta be honest: That they've made it this far, with what seems like no bullpen and no closer, is quite surprising."

"Yes. And as such, not only has nobody else stepped up to fill that void, but those that have tried have failed miserably. In the postseason, alone, so far, Boston pitching has blown four saves, three of them by two or more runs."

"It's obviously their Achilles heel."

"And even in the games that they've gone up big while scoring a lot of runs, they've made it interesting at the end, to say the least."

"Correct. It's obvious that this team misses Taylor."

"Waters, however, is still doing all that he can to carry this team. He's batting nearly .500, with two home runs in as many games so far this series."

"But what about the drama?"

"Well, if you listen to Skip, it was 'nothing.' But if you look at Joshua's right eye, it tells another story…"

And just then the camera focuses on Waters in the visiting dugout. Not only is his eye black, but he also has several stitches around the outside of his brow.

Christa lets out an audible gasp, while Spence looks on, obviously concerned.

"Oh my God. He did that defending you. I love him."

Spence smirks, eventually mustering a smile.

And just then Abby walks through the door with the kids…

"Did you see it!?"

"We did!"

"I'm so turned-on right now, I could yank him off that field and…"

And then she remembers that the kids are right next to her, quickly instructing them to go upstairs and find the Taylor kids.

"I know. I told Spence that him defending his honor against two younger teammates…" Christa's voice then starts to crack, "Everyone should have someone like Joshua in their corner."

Spence nods affirmatively, as they all move to the kitchen and begin fixing their plates to eat while watching the game. Christa has catered the evening using a local barbecue restaurant, one of the few "outsiders" they've allowed through the neighborhood gate.

Most everyone is finished eating by the time National Anthem has started. Another close-up of Waters standing at attention alongside his teammates in the baseline shows just how bad his eye looks. But, as he comes up to bat in the top of the first with a runner on, it becomes obvious that it's not bothering him when he jacks a towering home run ten seats deep into the left-center field stands.

The Taylor house erupts in pandemonium as he circles the bases, the kids even coming down to check out what's going on.

"That's my baby!" – shouts Abby.

"And my best friend!"

"And my husband's best friend, who's the baby's daddy to my best friend!"

The two girls chuckle while Spence is still trying to figure out what was just said.

Dan and Joy are cleaning up in the kitchen and laughing at all the goings on in the living room.

"Let's go!" Spence is fired up now as the teams settle in and it becomes a pitching duel, both teams having given up only four hits each by the top of the ninth inning. The Red Sox go down 1-2-3 in the top of the inning.

"Ledbetter has certainly pitched a gem here in San Francisco, but at 34 years of age and 125 pitches into this outing, I'm not sure how much more he has left in the tank."

"Well, you've got to wonder as he walks out to the mound for the bottom of the 9th…"

"There are two arms warming up in the bullpen. Page, a righty, and Burns, a lefty."

"That's right. But it's obvious that Skip doesn't trust the arms he's got."

"And for good reason. They've blown four out of four save chances."

"Well, he's certainly rolling the dice here with Ledbetter."

Taylor watches from home with interest.

"He'll be facing the #3 hitter in line-up, Mateo Encarnacion, who won the regular season batting title, just beating out Waters at .331 by 1/2 a percentage point."

"Ledbetter always locates well, Ted. But his velocity and movement are known to decrease in the later innings."

"Yeah. If you can get seven good innings out of 'the old man,' that's all Skip is looking for. Taylor was good for two innings sometimes when Ledbetter pitched, depending on his pitch count."

"Boy, could they use him now…"

And just then Ledbetter's first pitch is absolutely crushed, a no doubter opposite field shot out of Pacific Bell Park and into McCovey Cove, as the kayaks swarm the ball and the stadium crowd goes wild.

"Wow. Encarnacion has so much raw power. That is the very first ball ever hit into the water by a right-handed batter."

"This should be interesting, as the Red Sox still lead 2-1. Ledbetter is out of gas and the bullpen has yet to prove themselves so far this postseason."

Skip walks out to the mound and decides to bring in the young righty, Scotty Page, who goes on to walk the first batter on four straight pitches. Not one of them was even close to the plate.

Spence looks on with concern, as you can now hear a pin drop in the Taylor house.

"Well, you've got the five-hole hitter here that could end it with just one swing, Ted. Do you try to bunt him over, playing for the tie and extra innings, or do you go for the win here, considering there aren't any outs?"

"That's why John Tonglet is paid the big bucks to live with these decisions as San Francisco's manager."

"I'd make him throw a strike first."

And just then a strike is called – a no doubter, center cutting the plate.

"The oh-one offering… And he bunts it down the first base line. It's a perfect bunt…"

"You couldn't roll it out there any better between the pitcher and first baseman."

"Yep. All Boston could let it do was hope that it rolled foul as the batter raced by them. They're in real trouble now, with runners on first and second and nobody out, Ted."

"Skip is sticking with the young righty here…"

"And it's a wild pitch, as the runners advance!"

"Oh my."

"And here comes Skip out to the mound…"

"I think they're gonna put him on."

"I think you're right."

"I don't think that's a bad idea, Ted. It puts a force out at every base and the baserunner, himself, means nothing, with the winning run now at second. Boy, how nice would it be to have Taylor in this situation!?"

The bases are now loaded. Spence doesn't move a muscle as he continues to watch the television in his living room.

"It looks like the Red Sox are conceding the tying run at 3rd base, instead opting to play double-play depth."

And just then the first pitch is hit. It's a hard grounder up the middle to Joshua's left…

"And it's a diving play by Waters, who spins on his back and quickly tosses it to 2nd base for the out!"

"Simply amazing."

"That ties the game at 2-2, but for sure that was a 'game-winner' if anyone besides Waters is playing shortstop."

"That's absolutely correct. And now a ground ball double-play still extends this game into extra innings for the Red Sox."

"Right now, either that or a couple of strikeouts is what Boston wants."

Skip slowly walks out to the mound and makes another pitching change.

"That ball was hit really hard, so I guess you're looking for a little less contact here."

"Yeah. Skip knows that was a game-winner with anyone else playing in the middle infield, and as a result he's going with his last arm out in the bullpen."

"And as Jason Burns warms up, we're gonna take a quick break. Hold on to your seats, America. You don't want to miss it when we come back."

The television goes to commercial, as Spence looks around the room at everyone else.

"If we lose this game, it's gonna get way worse around here."

Christa chimes in, "It's not your fault, baby."

"It is my fault. I'm the closer. It's my job to save games just like this one."

Christa says nothing in return and instead just leaves it alone.

"We're back here in San Francisco, where the outfield is playing in, and its double-play depth in the middle infield, hoping for a miracle."

"Well, they'd surely rather pitch to Walker here in the 8th spot of the line-up rather than Mitchell, who's now stepping into the on-deck circle to pinch-hit for Kevin Powell, who's been brilliant out on the mound here tonight for San Francisco."

"Yep. Mitchell can certainly beat out anything other than a routine double play. And the Giants have Moorhead ready in the bullpen to come in for Powell and finish the game, should they not walk it off right here."

The young lefty on the mound is visibly nervous, having stepped off the rubber twice now. Waters leaves his position in the infield to go check on Burns and try to calm his nerves. He then says something to make him smile, pats him on the butt, and goes back to shortstop.

"Ball one."

"I'm not sure I'm liking his demeanor out there. He looks overwhelmed."

The second pitch is a foot short of the plate and almost goes to the backstop.

"Game saving block by Palmer right there."

Ball three is high, as the crowd somehow gets louder…

"And he walks him on four straight pitches."

"There's nowhere to put Mitchell now, Ted."

"No there isn't. And I think I'd make him throw a strike here, if I were the batter."

"Me too."

"And there it is. Strike one. That's how you do it, kid."

"The oh-one…"

And it's a hard ground ball straight back to the pitcher. Burns fields it cleanly and turns toward second base. Joshua is moving to cover the bag on time and the throw to him is errant, both high and to his right. He makes a freakishly athletic adjustment to catch the ball, while somehow still finding the bag for the 2nd out, and then quickly fires a rocket over to first…

"He's safe! Mitchell beats it out, barely!"

The Giants fans go wild as the team surrounds Mitchell in right field, jumping up and down, and dousing him with water, while ripping off his shirt."

"I don't know… That one was pretty close, Ted…"

"Here it is…"

[the replay shows on the television]

"He was out, Ted. Pretty clearly. By a few inches."

"This is why baseball needs some form of replay."

"Yeah. It's awful to have the game end on that play."

"Well, the umpires are human, just like the rest of us."

"Terrible. Nevertheless, San Francisco takes a two games to one lead in the World Series. Let's go down to the field and hear from Mitchell, who beat out a double-play on a ground ball back to the pit…"

[Christa abruptly turns off the television]

Spence places his face in his hands and shakes his head, as Christa and Abby join the elder Taylors on the back porch.

"It's best to just let him process it," advises Dan. "Nothing that you say will help right now."

***

There's a familiar "Da da dant! Da da dant!" coming from the kitchen television. Christa is up before everyone else. Or at least she thinks she is.

Unbeknownst to her, Spence is awake, too. The skyline through the trees in the backyard is showing hints of orange, with sunrise imminent.

"Welcome to Sports Center. I'm Keith O'Byrne, alongside my partner Stuart Skenes. Well, Stu, we have a little controversy here."

"A little!? You think!?"

"A great World Series game three was marred in controversy last night after a called 'safe' at first base allowed the winning run to score from 3rd in the bottom of the ninth."

"This is a call that you've simply gotta get right, Keith. Major League Baseball needs some type of replay system, and they need it fast. Look. Obviously, the Red Sox were on the ropes here. I'm not saying they would've won the game. But when you have a superstar like Waters who makes those types of plays and can come in and go yard at any given moment... I'm just saying that he's a game changer if you give him a chance... And, quite frankly, he, alone, earned that chance in the bottom of that last inning."

"That's right, Stu. And can we talk about Spence Taylor?! We all know how great he is. But I'm thinking we may have underestimated just how important he was to this year's team. He shut down so many would-be comebacks this year and everyone had the confidence that the game was in the bag once he toe'd the rubber."

"For sure. It's just baffling. I hope he gets the help he needs, soon, because the Red Sox aren't winning this World Series without him."

"That's a strong assertion."

"Is it though? Outside of their starting pitchers, they can't hardly throw a strike – and when they do, it's hit a mile..."

Christa changes the channel to MTV and turns around, startled by a minute sound that Spence made behind her.

"Sorry."

She walks up to him and smiles really big, before embracing him.

"Please make love to me."

"Here!? Now!? I haven't even brushed my…"

She grabs his hand and pulls him into the laundry room, before shutting the door behind them and locking it.

Christa has always had a knack for being spontaneous in the past and Spence has never been able to deny her requests. And for next several minutes they forget everything around them, bumping awkwardly into the countertops and drawers, giggling in between and taking heavy breaths, both lost in the moment. Spence then looks around at the dark room and the absurdity of their children's dirty and clean folded up clothes all around them, and he bursts out laughing.

"Shhh…"

"I needed that."

"Me, too. Remember…." She looks him in the eye. "I choose you, always, over everything else in this life. I always have and always will. I love you Spence Taylor."

thirteen – modest

The Taylor home is an older one. In fact, it's been around for nearly a century. The houses that surround it populating Newton's exclusive Notwen Avenue were all built around the same time, give or take ten years. Like the Taylor house, all have since been remodeled multiple times over the years, usually while attempting to match the underlying decor of the period or decade in which its occupants chose to renovate.

It could be argued that the Taylor residence is the "most modern" of all the homes on the street, having been purchased, refurbished, and sold by an investor to the Taylors nearly nine years ago.

And it's not just on the inside. The previous remodels have ranged from as small as tiny facelifts to the decor to, most recently, demolition down to the studs, removing walls, shoring up shortcomings, and changing the entire look of the outside of the house, insofar as curb appeal goes. Even the backyard and pool were upgraded to a standard that the Taylors could've only dreamed of while growing up middle-class in Mississippi.

Abby, two doors down and across the street, essentially claimed the house for the Taylors in the middle of the overhaul, and even somehow convinced the contractor and investor handling it to go ahead and consult Christa on some of the decorating decisions.

Spence and Christa were apartment hoppers while he quickly made his way through the minors and, within a year after his call-up to Boston, they had used some of his signing bonus to secure and move into the home – one that Christa was essentially already emotionally attached to.

The gate and guardhouse protecting the entrance to the residential street was added in the 1970s when prominent basketball and baseball players, not to mention celebrities hailing from Boston, started gobbling up the properties and reconstructing them. It, too, has been restored and upgraded over the years, after initially fulfilling its usefulness at quelling would-be gawkers, and later what would ultimately come to be described as "the paparazzi."

Ironically, they, too, were in no shortage on that morning just outside of said gate. Christa had moved quickly back into mom and daughter-in-law mode, freshened up, and was now back in the kitchen, anticipating that the children would want breakfast soon. Spence lingered around and curiosity eventually got the best of him, as he discreetly approached the laundry/mud room window. And instead of just seeing the satellite dishes on the tops of the mobile news trucks, he could now see multiple portable platforms lifted well above the fence-line, along with nearly a dozen or so individuals with cameras at the ready, just waiting for a "money shot" to sell to the highest bidding tabloid.

This had become big news now. In fact, the story was starting to transcend cultures. Those who knew nothing about baseball, or any sport for that matter, had come to learn about the future Hall of Famer that had "the yips." Talk shows, sportscasts, online chat rooms, and the newer social media websites ate it all up. Gossip ruled the day, and the Taylors were front and center.

Spence had never wanted anything like this. In fact, he and Joshua purposefully stayed out of the "celebrity" spotlight, even though you could make an argument for both to be in the mainstream pop-culture press that included the likes of People magazine, Entertainment Weekly, the E News Channel, and MTV. But instead, they used their off-seasons to hunt and go on family vacations together. Essentially their lives were "boring" – and the two couples with their young kids preferred it that way.

Taylor even balked at the idea of a "walk-out" song. Most MLB closers who were anything special had their own "walk-out" song that signaled it was time for the bullpen savior to come in and save the game. Other players with similar roles on different respective teams "walked-out" to the likes of "Wild Thing," "Welcome to the Jungle," and "Hell's Bells." But here was the most dominant closer in recent memory, and the all-time Major League Baseball leader in saves, choosing to opt out of the trend of ringing bells, whistles, and/or music, and instead insisting on a slow, methodical, and calculated march toward the mound – which, after nearly ten years, had ironically ended up with the same intended effect of intimidation that the other pitchers had only hoped for. The slow walk, the stoic lack of emotion, and the "business-as-usual" approach of Spence's entering the game had become a thing at Fenway Park and further endeared him to the fanbase, who in turn always respected his seeming desire for privacy when off the field.

After scoping out the neighborhood gate saga from the confines of his laundry room, Spence eventually makes his way into the master bedroom. Once there, he decides to lie down and rest. And, as he does just that, he begins staring at the ceiling and blaming himself for throwing all of them into the spotlight that they'd tried to avoid in the past.

His eyes slowly begin to fade…

"The boy can't hit, Joy. But his arm… There's something that's there."

Dan played baseball in high school. He was a starting center fielder for the same school that his son would later attend, Forest Hill. While technically within Jackson's city limits on the southwestern side, it had a different identity than the other schools that populated the rest of the city. The area was more rural and had been annexed in the early 1950's, just after the war, right around the time that Dan was born. Out further to the south and west of the area were the towns of Raymond and Clinton, both of which were also in Hinds County. Forest Hill students and parents during the 1980s knew pretty much everyone within the "tri-city" area, both socially and through activities involving sports.

But there was also a larger "tri-county" area made up of Hinds, Rankin, and Madison counties, where the kids all grew up competing against one another during activities like All-Star baseball, based out of the local parks, and "Select" soccer – where a small amount of travel to enter out of state "tournaments" every other weekend would essentially ensure finding adequate competition for the development of the kids' skills.

All the children within the "tri-county" area would ultimately grow up and then attend their respective high schools after a very competitive regional youth sports experience, having already experienced playing against each other to varying extents. So, in addition to Forest Hill and Clinton High School in the most southern and western county, there were also the perennial powerhouses of Brandon High School, Jackson Preparatory School, and Madison-Ridgeland Academy to consider in the northern and eastern bordering counties, all of which also fell within the greater Jackson area – thereby making it a haven for the many prospects found within that would ultimately go on to play their respective sports at major universities, both in state and out, including Alabama and LSU – not to mention professionally.

Dan was a good player back in the day. But he wasn't a Division-I level talent like his son. He went on to play at the local junior college in Raymond, Hinds (named after the county that houses the "tri-city" area) Community College. He did this for two years, before finally hanging up his cleats and attending Mississippi State University, choosing to major in mechanical engineering. It was there that he met Spence's mom, who was from Kosciusko, just up the Natchez Trace, between Jackson and Tupelo.

"Dan, don't be ridiculous. He's only twelve."

"I know. But he didn't make the All-Star team because of his bat. It was only thanks to his…"

And just as he's about to finish that sentence, a yet to be developed pre-pubescent Spence rounds the corner…

"Dad. Wanna throw with me?"

"You bet."

"Just ten minutes, please! I'm not going to eat this dinner alone, once it's ready!"

The two of them walk outside into the backyard. The house reeks of upper middle class. Dan has made a decent living designing hydraulic pumps for airplanes, but he'd have much rather possessed half the baseball talent that he now recognized in his young son.

Spence steps up onto a wooden platform-like mound that his dad made for him. It's topped with Astro Turf and has a gradual one inch per foot descent towards the home plate that's staked into the ground fifty feet away. It's all been measured out to the correct dimensions, down to the millimeter, likely closer to the correct age-standard than most of the fields that the kids are used to playing on. He goes on to gather his momentum, striding towards the plate while using minimal effort, and with the intention of just a warm-up toss, he zings one into his father's glove.

Dan catches the ball, takes a deep breath, and pulls out a handkerchief from his back pocket. He goes on to tap his forehead with it, folds it slightly, and then strategically stuffs it into the palm of his left hand, between it and the glove.

"What's the matter old man!?"

Spence's voice is still pretty high pitched. It's not even cracking yet. In fact, he still has some baby teeth that the dentist is considering pulling, if they don't come out soon. Afterall, they're in the way and he can't get braces until the permanent ones behind them come in. But he's already long and lean, quite high in most of the physical developmental percentiles, and soon projects to begin growing into what's considered to be well-above average in height.

Even so, his arm is already becoming elite. But don't take his dad's word for it. Coach Gray, Dan's former high school teammate and now the baseball coach at Forest Hill High School, has had his finger on the pulse of the local younger talent for several years, and just last week came to watch the championship game of Spence's most recent All-Star tournament.

"He's gonna be a good one," Coach Gray had told Dan with a sly grin, while watching him dominate the other kids from the mound.

Spence had only given up one hit in that particular game, a double to a kid from the Brandon area All-Star team named Joshua Waters. He pitched five innings and had twelve strikeouts, with only one walk.

The sun is now moving behind the tree line as he throws the ball back to his son.

"Try to take it easy on me, son."

And, as he strides and throws, his father attempts to find fault with his form, with his delivery, and with the natural movement that he puts on the ball. He's never had any type of professional lesson, and there's nothing that Dan can really criticize. Not only that, but he swears he can hear the seams of the baseball cutting into the wind, as every pitch pops the mitt that he's holding.

And just then Joy calls out from the house, "Dinner's ready!"

The two make eye contact and smile, inherently racing toward the back door, for no apparent reason other than just silliness...

Spence then peacefully emerges from his twenty-minute catnap, while still in his own bedroom. It was a good one, remembering everything just like he was there again. Nobody even knew that he was asleep.

***

"Well, it looks like the Red Sox faithful can rest a little bit easier tonight here in game four, as we head into the bottom of the ninth and they have a 12-4 lead here in San Francisco, looking to even the series at 2-2."

"I don't know. There's a lot that they can take away from this game. On the positive side of things, Joshua Waters is oh-for-five and the other bats in the line-up have come alive to carry this team to 12 runs. So, there's definitely that. However, the score was 12-0 before the bottom of the eighth started, and once again the Boston bullpen is showing that it can't hold a decent lead."

"You're right about that, Ted. And to think that the last inning ended with two men on base? The Giants almost batted around."

"And there's a leadoff homer to start the inning. It's now 12-5."

"You were saying?" [as all three announcers begin to chuckle]

"The odds are still very much in favor of Boston winning this ballgame. But just how big does the lead have to be for it to be a comfortable one without Taylor here to close it out?"

"Well right now a six-run lead would've sufficed."

"It's baffling."

"I've honestly never seen anything quite like it."

"To be fair, the bullpen wasn't this bad during the season. Who knows? Maybe they, too, were confident in knowing that Taylor was always there to clean things up."

"And there's another hit, Tom…"

"I'll tell you, Ted, Encarnacion had barely rounded first base, before Skip was out of the dugout and on his way to the mound."

"They need Taylor and they need him quickly."

"Yes, they do."

fourteen – meek

It's the following morning and Spence is working out in his home gym that overlooks the pool. He hasn't done anything physical now for a couple of weeks, and it's starting to show. He's much more tired than he would've been previously, before everything began falling apart. Working out feels good to him, despite his struggles.

He watched the whole game last night, one that the Red Sox ultimately ended up winning 12-7. He, too, is concerned about the shape of the Boston bullpen. But the series is now tied at two games to two, essentially guaranteeing that it will come back to Boston for a game six on Friday night. Spence knows that he must do something.

And just then his dad walks in. Spence pauses the elliptical machine and takes off his headphones…

"You ok, son?"

"Yep."

"You sure?"

"I've got to figure something out, dad. I'm a head case."

"Well, let's talk through your options."

"Options? I only have one choice, dad."

"And…"

"I'm petrified."

"Spence. You have nothing to prove. It's all been done already. You're a first ballot Hall of Famer. And the whole world now understands just how valuable you were to the team."

"I've let everyone down. Joshua, Skip, the fans, and even myself..."

"Wait... Are you saying that you can't live with yourself if you don't make it back to baseball?"

"Not just back to baseball, dad. I have to be ready and available when the team comes back to Boston."

"So, what exactly needs to be done, then?"

"I have to revisit hell on earth."

"Back to the psychiatrist?"

"Yes."

"Son, after you hit Joshua, I had no idea that the first several days you spent beating yourself up would have lasting consequences. Had I known then, what I've since come to find out and witness with my own eyes, I would've helped you work through it all, or at least gotten you the professional help that you needed back then. I foolishly told your mom that it was something you had to work through yourself. I'm sorry that I failed you."

"It's not your fault, dad. I never knew that I had lasting issues, either."

"It's crazy. You two became best friends in the weeks that followed and so did your girlfriends. You stood in each other's weddings and even named your children after one another."

"Dad, I was an absolute mess for several days after the incident. Something stuck with me. It's no accident that I pitched for so long after that without hitting a batter. And when I hit Yuli so high and tight like I did Joshua years ago, it unlocked a demon of doubt within me that I'd long suppressed. And the only way to subdue that terror that is still inside of me is to visit hell on earth once again. I don't want to go out this way."

Spence's father puts his hand on his son's shoulder and looks him in the eyes...

"Son... I'm a firm believer that things happen for a reason and that the Lord puts stuff on our plate that we aren't quite sure of exactly why or how, but we eventually figure it out, and in hindsight come to accept and understand. Your incident with Joshua years ago happened for a reason. I have no doubt about that, whatsoever. And what occurred in the last game of the season against the Yankees happened just as it was supposed to, too. It's now a part of your story. I believe that it might be time to reflect and pray about it. I know that sometimes in the hustle and bustle of life, and how crazy it gets, that we often forget to just stop everything and talk to God. It shows maturity and growth to accept what's happened, but it's also appropriate at times to bow your head and respectfully ask Jesus why this is now a part of your walk. He doesn't mind you asking 'Why?' or for assistance in finding a resolution. In fact, He wants you to lean on Him for answers and to ask for help in all things. And knowing 'JC,' not only will He likely send you a revelation, but looking back years from now, you might also find that He actually carried you though it."

Spence begins to tear up...

"Spence... You're very special to me. For one, you're my only child. My pride and joy. But this talent that you have is no accident. And although you've always been quiet and reserved for a professional athlete, like it or not, you now have a platform... And when you're on the other side of this nightmare, you can simply smile, thank your teammates and coaches, and then give all the glory to God. Nothing more and nothing less. And with your legacy that you're worried about not just intact, but with an added exclamation point!"

Dan smiles and walks off, as Spence places his headphones back on and restarts the elliptical machine. He then powers off the television and begins exercising without any distractions, all while focusing somewhere beyond the wall in front of him...

"Spence."

Dr. Olgivy shakes his hand and then turns and looks Christa's way...

"Christa?"

She acknowledges him with a head nod and extends her own hand for a polite handshake greeting...

"Please... have a seat."

They all sit down, the two of them in front of him. There is no desk. It's just an eerily quiet room with no windows, wall hangings, or excessive furniture – and only one door.

"I'm Dr. Olgivy and my time and services have been retained by the Boston Red Sox organization, Major League Baseball, and The Player's Association for the duration of the playoffs and the World Series. I will be readily available to you during that time, and have been tasked with both treating and, if deemed appropriate, clearing and releasing you to play baseball."

Nobody could blame anyone for mistaking his accent as Australian. His words are short and concise, and his voice sits somewhere stuck between tenor and baritone, like he could go either way, should he decide to burst out in song.

"I am based out of South Africa, specialize in the field of sports psychiatry, and have dozens of elite professional athletes worldwide in various sports as patients. I would name names for you, but for confidentiality's sake, I simply cannot."

Spence nods affirmatively.

"There's only one way to explain what we're about to do, should you consent to the treatment."

He then looks at Spence for an awkward 8-10 seconds, almost as if he's trying to gauge his reaction...

"You know, Spence, this session, in and of itself, is much more difficult than the game you play for a living. You've put in hours and hours of preparation time and can therefore go out on the field at a moment's notice and dominate against the best competition that the world has to offer. However, the treatment plan that you require, with regard to the timeline available to us, necessitates that we skip over all of the routine initial therapy that I offer to my clients – which is equivalent to the hours of preparation that you put in, with me getting to know you very well – and instead jump straight into a regimen that involves a less traditional and slightly more controversial technique – which is kinda like jumping into the World Series straight outta spring training and just trusting your instincts, while pitching blindfolded."

He and Christa look on with concern…

Dr. Olgivy then giggles slightly before composing himself and continuing…

"Some people call it 'hypnosis.' A lot of people have a misconception of the hypnotic state as being totally asleep. Nothing could be further from the truth. In fact, under hypnosis you are very much awake. I like to explain it as inducing an intently focused state of being where your mind can wander with both guidance and direction, all while still being receptive to suggestion."

The two of them continue to look on as Christa begins to appear a bit unsettled…

"And what it involves, assuming we can get you there, is digging deep inside your mind, peeling back layers, and taking a good hard look at yourself – specifically in places where everything isn't always very pretty. In fact, Spence, and I'm just going to be frank with you… It can be downright ugly. And once again, it's a whole lot of work just to get you there, not to mention being taxing on one's conscience, just trying to fix whatever the issue might be."

There's no additional reaction from the two of them…

"Let me try to explain it another way… Your brain's primary function is to protect the body at all costs, recognize immediate or potential danger, and send information out into the periphery while attempting to avoid it. And when it's traumatized, it often goes into a self-preservation mode, storing said trauma within the areas inside your mind that can often be very hard to access, lest you were proceed to the next step of it lingering around, which usually manifests in a state of mental shock that can stay perpetual. Then, in the process of your brain trying to find that remote hiding place, the whole ordeal can leave traces of mental residue or scattered psychic disturbance behind, ultimately making it very possible to become triggered – all with little to no accessible information available therein for both processing and/or understanding just why or how it all happened."

Spence starts to lean in...

"Now..."

Dr. Olgivy then looks down towards the end of his nose and through his small lenses at Spence...

"There's obviously something inside of you that was provoked. And I understand that it's frightening. But do you really think all this time, putting up Hall of Fame numbers over the years, that you were operating on talent, alone?"

Spence doesn't answer, but instead continues looking at Dr. Olgivy...

"Son, your brain has been protecting you the entire time and lying to you that you were invincible insofar as mastering the mental side of pitching. That's how you zoned in and hit your spots so well. But it's also no coincidence at all that there were little to no hit batters throughout your career after hitting Joshua. It was indeed protecting you..."

Spence nods agreeingly...

Dr. Olgivy then smiles a wry smile...

"Now go ahead and insert an unseasonably bitter cold night in early October at Fenway Park and the perfect storm of an umpire giving several inches off the plate, you exploiting that advantage like any good veteran pitcher would, and a batter therefore crowding the dish..."

Spence takes a deep breath...

"I have to say, Spence, that although we're crunched for time, both of your parents and Christa were extremely informative regarding the root cause of everything in my initial interviews... 'Hey... Remember that time in high school when...?' So I looked into it more closely, and I have to tell you that I think we've found the source... It wasn't difficult to determine. Your brain did what brains do. What I just described to you. The good news is that you're totally normal in that regard. Many people live with various forms of underlying PTSD, but it lies dormant and isn't as apparent when it's triggered. Yours unfortunately played out on a national stage. And I'm sure you would agree that it was hard to watch. Well, we just need to probe a bit more, attempting to find it and suppress it..."

Spence leans back in his chair...

"And in order to do so, we need both your consent and cooperation..."

"I'll do whatever I have to do," declares Spence.

"Now, Spence... Here's where the 'informed' part of an 'informed consent' takes precedent. Wherever we go in your mind and however we get there, you may indeed remember some or all of it, both immediately or soon thereafter. Or you might not remember anything at all. I can't guarantee you anything regarding the recollection of our sessions. Also, there is a minimum of two sessions required before I will even consider releasing you to play. Do you understand that?"

"Yessir. I do..."

"And do you remember when I said where we go '... ain't always pretty?'"

"Yessir..."

"So, what you may end up remembering is like a bad dream, or maybe even worse, that might seem like you spent considerably more time in an 'alternate reality' than the time period in which you were actually hypnotized – which I don't like to go for more than four hours at a time..."

"Yessir..."

"Good. I just wanted you to know..."

He then turns to Christa...

"And do you understand this too? That he may be processing this for several days afterward?"

She nods affirmatively with reservation in her eyes and looks towards Spence...

"This is what you want, baby?"

He nods affirmatively...

"Yes. I want to be there for my team. I don't want to go out this way..."

The elliptical machine then cuts off at one hour and goes into cool down mode, both snapping Spence back into present day reality and reinvigorating his desire to fight.

***

"Yeah... Doc? Uhh... It's me, Spence. Umm... I've been watching the World Series and I've talked it over with Christa... And..." [he clears his throat and his voice breaks slightly] "... I don't want to go out like this.... To be remembered for not taking the mound when my team needed me the most."

Christa knows Dr. Olgivy is on the other line because she could hear his voice when he answered the phone. But now it appears as if he is strategically letting his client talk through how he feels and what he wants.

"I want to be out on that field..."

And just then she hears his unmistakable voice again...

"Okay, Spence. And you are aware that I'm bound morally as a person, medically by oath, and professionally by my experiences to make sure that your mind and body are ready to take that field..."

"Yes, I do..." – Spence interrupts.

"And that this has always been at least a two-part session..."

"Yessir."

"And that just by coming to see me and 'participating' – in no way am I inclined or obliged to grant you permission to play if I feel that you haven't progressed beyond what's medically acceptable..."

"Yessir."

"And that by putting you back out there before you're ready to be out there, it lends credence to the possibility of exacerbating your PTSD and extending it further into your personal life..."

"Yessir."

"Not to mention that it may also put the health of your teammates and the opposing players in jeopardy, considering that your fastball can top 100 miles per hour..."

"Yessir."

"Because, Spence, I've been doing this long enough to know that, although you've made significant progress, I am not going to rush what was always meant to be a longer treatment process..."

"I understand..."

"And we've already lost a significant amount of time both before and after our initial session..."

"Yessir."

"And I would guess that at least a fair percentage of your motivation is to be ready to play when the World Series comes back to Boston?"

"You'd be correct..."

[interrupting] "Which is Friday night for game six?"

"Yessir."

"And it's already late on Wednesday morning right now?"

[bracing for the worst] "Yessir…"

"Great. Well, we have no time to waste. Are you okay with meeting me at the same place?"

The Red Sox had paid to rent out a counseling room at the Tau Center, a local psychiatric treatment facility in Boston that has a private side door entrance, for the duration of the playoffs and World Series, so that Spence could meet as often as needed with Dr. Olgivy, who had graciously agreed to travel and take him on as a patient, even though his practice was based in South Africa.

"Yes. Same place."

"Can you be there by 1pm today, Spence?"

"Yessir. I think I can. Thank you. I'll be there…"

"Okay. We will discuss it further once you're there…"

"Yessir."

"And again, I won't feel rushed, but I also understand that there's a timeline…"

"Yessir."

"So the session could possibly last well into the evening hours…"

Spence says nothing at all, but is obviously thinking about his last four-hour session that seemed like twelve years of his life.

"Spence. I'll take you where you need to go. But you're absolutely doing the correct thing here, considering the rough part of your treatment plan has already been completed…"

"Yessir."

"Now I'm not saying that it's going to be a cakewalk moving forward by any means…"

"Uh huh…"

"But if we can tap into the part of your brain that's harboring this anxiety and manifesting in your physical abilities, or lack thereof…"

[interrupting] "Yes. I'm ready…"

"Alright, son. Just you and Christa. Nobody else…"

"Yessir."

"And can you possibly slip past the paparazzi outside of your neighborhood right now? I'm not interested in a circus."

"I think so. I have a plan…"

"Perfect. To my knowledge they haven't given up our treatment location yet. I'll see you at 1:00 this afternoon. Eat a light meal beforehand."

"Thank you. Goodbye."

Spence hangs up the phone and looks over at Christa.

Smiling… "This is what you want?"

"Yes."

"And this is for you, and you alone, and you're not trying to please me or anyone else?"

Spence nods affirmatively and adds, "And Joshua. I owe it to him for taking up for me on the team plane, not to mention all that he's done for both of us. Oh… And in another life, he died a slow, agonizing death because of me."

"What!?"

Realizing that she likely has no idea of what he's referring to, Spence replies, "Never mind."

"Spencer…"

He grabs both of her hands, squeezes them gently, and gazes into her eyes with a blank stare, wondering how to explain what he just said.

She begins to cry and asks, "So you remember 'everything,' everything? As in all the details?"

"I think so."

"Oh, Spencer, baby. I'm so sorry…"

Christa had sat in the corner of the room observing the entire previous session with Dr. Olgivy. And even though he explained the hypnosis process, how it was pertinent that she remained quiet and emotionless, and where the discussion and his high-profile client's mind may go, she wasn't quite ready for what she witnessed. She was able to see him as a different person. Physically the husband that she knew in the present tense, but emotionally a Spencer that she's never known, so much so that his appearance actually changed with his frame of mind the further he went. His face had a despair that she'd never known and his temper often flared up with words that he never used on this side of reality. There were times where she was convinced that he was going to stand up and assault Dr. Olgivy right in front of her and was impressed that the psychiatrist was so unmoved by his actions. It was as if he was wearing a seatbelt with shoulder restraints, even though he was comfortably sitting in a chair with nothing at all to hold him back. He mentioned his gun and using it several times. And even though she understood the "details" of the session by the actual words that Spence spoke to Dr. Olgivy, she came to eventually comprehend that what he was experiencing inside of his mind was much more vivid and detailed.

She hugs him tightly and asks, "So it really was another life that you experienced?"

He nods affirmatively and begins to tear up.

"The worst part about the whole thing was being completely outside of you and the kids – feeling like I didn't deserve you and not knowing our children."

"And you still want to do this, baby?"

"Yes. I want complete control of my own mind and physical ability. Oh, and I want to win."

"I love you, Spence Taylor."

fifteen – humble

Abby is on the ground and rolling around in laughter…

"Spencer Taylor… I think you just made me pee on myself."

She can hardly contain herself as she makes it back to her feet.

The Taylors' neighbor, Sergei, comes outside, having heard all the commotion. Spence and his wife are on his side of the fence now. Abby is with them. She sees his face and further bursts out into hysterics, as he assesses the situation.

"Spence. You're a professional athlete!?"

At this point Abby is bent over and says, "That's it. I've gotta go across the street now and change my underwear…"

Christa has a smile on her face, mostly from watching Abby's reaction. But she is also a little bit worried about her husband.

"Spence. We both have gates, you know?"

Spence looks up from the ground, with grass stains on one knee and a wet muddy area on his behind…

"I know…"

His gun is still holstered around his waist.

Christa chimes in, "You're lucky that you didn't kill yourself with that thing."

She then looks at her neighbor and tries to explain…

"I told him to use the two gates, but he said the paparazzi might see us if we just walked out of our yard and immediately back into yours, so he had us walk further down and…"

Spence had helped both Abby and Christa over the fence, but then climbed and jumped off the top of it, himself, into his neighbor's yard, slipping on a random low wet spot, where he landed and fell backwards onto the ground. He was wearing dress pants, a nice belt, and an oxford because he wanted to look good, just in case the paparazzi filmed him on his way to meet with the psychiatrist.

The master plan was to use his neighbor's vehicle, a professional hockey player for the Boston Bruins, and to have Abby drive the two of them out of the neighborhood – and hopefully past the unsuspecting media circus on the way to Spence's treatment.

"I'm not sure if Abby's fit to drive now," he says to Christa with a smirk.

"You know she loves you…"

"Oh, I know."

And just then Abby, who's now apparently composed herself, comes back outside, sees his muddy pants, and loses it all over again…

"That was one of the best things I've ever seen. We told you to use the damn gate. We didn't have to scale the wall, Spence…"

"Abby, you're welcome for me helping you to get over the awkwardly high fence, before I climbed it, myself, unassisted," Spence responds, playfully rolling his eyes.

"I just know there were two perfectly good gates that we could've used, both yours and Sergei's, only twenty feet that way," she says pointing towards the front of the houses. "I can't wait to tell Joshua about this. We could've won America's Funniest Home Videos…"

This was probably the best thing that could've happened to Spence, considering it helped to keep his mind off where he was headed. The three of them eventually walk inside and through the neighbor's house, before then proceeding to the garage and climbing into his large black SUV.

"I feel like we're escaping from prison or something!" – exclaimed Abby, as she backs out of the neighbor's garage towards the street.

"Well, we did scale a big wall…" – quipped Spence from the back seat with a smile.

Abby laughs and involuntarily spits water all over the dashboard of Sergei's car.

"Abby!?" – Christa, also in the back seat with her husband, responds with disbelief.

She suddenly stops the SUV at the end of the neighbor's driveway and spends five to ten seconds trying to regain her composure.

"It's his fault!" – pointing at Spence. "I can't get the picture of him jumping down off that wall, slipping, and busting his ass out of my head."

"But he could've hurt himself, or worse…"

"I know… I know… I'm not saying that it's right. It was just funny…"

Spence interrupts, "Oh, I can't wait for Joshua to hear about this."

"I know, right? I wonder if Sergei has cameras outside of his home?"

"We do…" – Christa responds, as Spence reaches over with his hand to quickly cover her mouth…

"Shut up!?"

"We do. Spence has been so freaked out ever since we were robbed at gunpoint." She then points to his gun. "You think he carries this thing around for no reason!? Our house is protected like a fortress."

And just then the neighborhood gate opens, prompting Abby to look back and advise, "Now… While these windows are 'tinted,' I'd advise you both to lie down in the backseat, just in case."

She turns out of the neighborhood, and when they get on further down the road, she looks back and gives them the "all clear" using a thumbs-up gesture. They both then sit up and look through the back windshield. It appears as if they indeed made it through and are heading to the psychiatrist without being followed by the paparazzi.

"We escaped from Alcatraz, baby!" – as Abby reaches back and high fives Christa.

***

"Damn, that was a whole'lotta fun!"

Spence shakes his head from the back seat as he reaches over to open the door. He then turns and smiles at Christa, who laughs back at Abby, who's still all alone up front in the driver's seat of Sergei's Sport Utility Vehicle.

"You're crazy, girl. But that's why I love you," says Christa as she blows a kiss and gives her a wink.

Spence steps out of the vehicle and looks at the side entrance to the building. His wife comes over, stands next to him, and interlocks her arm with his.

The Tau Center is a facility that is three stories high, with its four facades made-up almost entirely of glass. It operates by offering short-term psychiatric care and providing the much-needed space for treatment. It's also capable of accommodating a dozen or so inpatients up on the third floor for a variety of reasons, ranging from adults with mental illness and addictions to adolescents with behavioral problems and/or suicidal tendencies. But most of its use stems from the medical offices scattered on the floors below, where several psychiatrists are based, large meeting rooms that house weekly groups such as Alcoholics Anonymous, and several therapy rooms that are outfitted with comfortable furniture and surrounded by sound-proof walls and doors – in order to prevent contamination from outside noise.

Major League Baseball, in cooperation with the Boston Red Sox and The Player's Association, has paid for and reserved one of these isolated rooms for the duration of the World Series, in anticipation of Spence's required treatment regimen being completed before it ends – which is the only way for him to be cleared to return to play.

The league is handling this issue very transparently, with the outward appearance of concern, and with an open pocketbook, attempting to perhaps avoid any issues even remotely similar to what the National Football League is currently experiencing regarding long term concussions and Chronic Traumatic Encephalopathy (CTE). They've even held press conferences stating just how important the mental health of their players is to them and announcing the implementation of brand-new protocols to deal with likely concussions.

There are many current players who make jokes about needing the psychiatric help now offered by MLB to get them out of their slumps. Others feel that it's just a "cover your ass" move in this ever-changing world of increased litigation and political pressure from fringe groups.

But the post-traumatic stress disorder issue that's now front and center and national news during the current postseason is something the league never saw coming, and it has the higher tier executives doing all they can to keep the focus back on baseball and away from Spence's, or any player for that matter, perceived mental health.

There are side entrances that can be accessed for privacy at The Tau Center for those in the spotlight that require added privacy, and this is where they are standing while awaiting entrance into the building.

Christa takes a deep breath, as they both hear giggling behind them coming from the SUV. Abby is once again tickled at the muddy stain on the back of Spence's dress pants, while she backs out the neighbor's vehicle and begins rolling up the window partially... Sensing that she may have interrupted the beginning of a serious moment between her two married friends, she offers an apology, as Christa looks back and smiles.

Once again taking a deep breath, she looks at him and asks, "You ready for this?"

Spence takes one too...

"I am."

"Are you scared?"

"I'm absolutely petrified."

"Do you remember where we need to go?"

"I do not."

And as he responds, Dr. Olgivy walks out of the building and towards the couple.

"Did you have a tail?"

Spence looks behind himself, as best as he can, at his own backside in response to question, which he thought was odd.

"No, not that we know of," says Christa, while rolling her eyes at her husband and further explaining to him, "He wants to know if we were followed by the paparazzi."

Spence can hear Abby once again giggling at his expense from Sergei's vehicle, as they turn around and see that she's stopped and watching them. They then thank her and wave her off to proceed back home – or at least back to the neighbor's house, lest they were to be figured out by those currently camped out at the Notwen Avenue gate. Game five of the World Series is scheduled for later in the evening in San Francisco and most experts think that tonight's winner will go on to take the Commissioner's Trophy. If there is more controversy regarding Boston not having a closer to finish games, then they all expect the number of media personnel at the entrance of the neighborhood to grow into a fever-pitch overnight.

Dr. Olgivy reaches out to shake Spence's hand and then he and Christa share an awkward side hug. He touches Spence on the shoulder slightly as they slowly enter the building, before proceeding towards the treatment room and explaining what he can expect during this go-around.

"Spence. As mentioned, this isn't going to necessarily be a cake walk for you. Also, because you recall so much from our first hypnosis session, there's a good chance that you'll remember some of this one, too. Just so you know, I'm not looking to 'patch' things up here. That's not how I work. I'm looking for a complete restoration for you. That's why we dig so deep. It says a lot about you that you're willing to continue with this. But I honestly believe we've found the root cause of the issue that you're experiencing and that we can indeed rectify it. I just need you to trust me…"

"Of course, Doc…"

The three of them walk down a long hallway and into a room that has several chairs, reminiscent of a waiting room, with magazines on a coffee table and such. There's another doorway that opens into an area with three leather office chairs and a chaise lounge over in one corner. There are no windows or doors, other than the last one they just walked through. There's also no decorations or art hanging on any of the walls. There's simply a wooden floor and some painted baseboards. The walls are pale and gray.

Dr. Olgivy closes the door behind him. There's absolutely no outside noise getting through now and all is quiet. He asks Christa to take a seat towards the back corner of the room as he makes himself comfortable sitting down in the middle. He then turns and asks Spence to sit down in the only chair that's left, which is about five to six feet away and facing him.

"Spence, we've gotten the necessary consents from before we started this process, and you understand what we're trying to accomplish?"

"I do."

"And do you have any more questions for me?"

"I do not…"

He then asks Spence to unholster his gun, at which point he almost looks embarrassed that he forgot it was still on his waist, before handing it over.

Dr. Olgivy looks at his watch and notes the time in a hand-held voice recorder that he's holding up to his face… "It's one-fifteen pm and we are about to start the second hypnosis session with Spencer Taylor…"

He turns around and looks at Christa, before nodding his head in a manner that he knows that she already understands not to intervene, and to alert him before any sudden movements, such as sneezing or coughing.

"Spence. I want to ask that you look at my forehead, just above my eyes, and then focus on just one area…"

Spence obliges…

"Okay. Now Spence, I want you to take five deep breaths, near to what you would consider capacity volumes…"

And once again Spence follows his instructions…

"I now want you to close your eyes and imagine that you're outside of your body and looking at the same area of your own face, just above your eyes, and focus in on that one area."

Christa has witnessed this once before, but she's already amazed at how fast her husband seems to be progressing through the two dimensions. She isn't sure if it's the soothing tone of Dr. Olgivy's voice that helps him to feel so at ease or not. But it's something, for sure, that allows her husband to extend what seems like absolute trust to the psychiatrist in the early moments of his mesmeric slide into hypnosis. And although it's most definitely still Spence sitting in that chair, she can see the relaxation of his muscles and the changes in his facial features that suggest he's becoming a different person with each breath he takes.

Spence's eyes are still closed and his breathing remains deep. His hands, once clasped together on top of his legs, now begin to separate and eventually come to rest palms down upon his thighs.

"Spence… I want you to imagine a candle's flame burning in that area of your face. Every once in a while, it flickers, like it's encountering a slight breeze. But it's a strong flame that is right there. It isn't hot, but you can almost hear it, as it is full of luminous brightness…"

Spence appears to go deeper into wherever he's going, as Christa starts to notice that his eyeballs are moving in many different directions behind his closed eyelids…

"And one more thing, Spence… As we take this journey, there are things that we're going to focus on. But sometimes that fixation can wane, at which point I will suddenly appear to you. When you open your eyes in a few seconds, you won't be able to see me or anyone else in this room. You will talk to me and answer my questions, but you won't be cognizant of it. But occasionally I will have to make myself fully known to you. That's why I have these…"

Dr. Olgivy then reaches into his own front pocket and pulls out some small windchimes, ringing them ever so slightly so that Spence can hear them.

"Spence… When you hear these windchimes ringing, I will appear in front of you, wherever you may be, and be able to interact with you… Please understand that my intent is not to startle you."

Spence doesn't respond…

Dr. Olgivy says nothing for the next five minutes as Spence appears to progressively relax into the comfortable leather chair.

"Spence. That candle is getting brighter now as your eyes become closer to it. I want you to imagine where we left off in our last session and take yourself back to where you were…"

Once again there isn't any reaction from Spence…

"Okay, Spence. I want you to take a few more deep breaths. You can see that candle in front of you and your eyes are still behind it. You're getting closer to it though and you can now begin to feel some of the heat coming off the flame…"

Dr. Olgivy can sense that Spence is nearly there and gives him about thirty more seconds…

"Three…"

"Two…"

"One…"

Pause…

[there's several seconds of inaudible mumbling in the background]

sixteen – sinful

And suddenly there's a blinding flash of light that pierces through the twilight of introspective thought. It's both irritating and disconcerting. It's also unsettling insofar as being abruptly awakened from an intense dream, caught somewhere between what's real and what isn't, with rational thoughts initially supporting both worlds as reality.

And as the glare slowly subsides, a likeness of Jesus Christ being crucified on a cross and centered on the most prominent wall of a church comes into focus. Spence is standing towards the back entrance and looking forward. With varying sizes of organ pipes to both His right and left, He's hanging directly above a uniformed choir and seemingly watching over a procession of mourners that are pouring into The United Methodist Church of Brandon.

There are several dozen wreaths of flowers that are perched upon easels and scattered about the stage, while even more stand by beautifully adorning the steps that come down from either side of the pulpit.

And in the center of it all sits a closed hardwood casket that's stained in dark cherrywood and embellished with even more flowers that are draped over the top of it. A high school senior portrait of Joshua Waters stands directly in front, with framed collages of him at different ages flanking it on either side. Some of them are candid and goofy, while others are action shots of him playing both T-Ball and baseball during various stages of his life.

The pews are full of people, ranging from the extremely young to the very old. Several babies are being tended to by their mothers, attempting to nurse and console them in hopes that they might peacefully sleep through the upcoming ceremony. All have come to pay their respects. The choir is almost complete, save for a few that are still standing nearby and talking to others, but will soon be ready to perform. There's a sign upon entering the church that reads "Joshua Waters: A Celebration of Life."

The church organist starts playing and those that haven't yet taken their seats begin to quickly do so. But for some it's standing room only down along the sides of the pews and looping all the way around to the back. There's former teammates, coaches, and classmates in attendance, not to mention extended family and friends.

The mother and father of Joshua Waters grab Spence by the hand and slowly start to walk in. He's cleanly shaven, recently barbered, and wearing a new suit. The three of them proceed to the front row and sit down. Immediately behind them are both Dan and Joy Taylor.

It's an about-face for Spence in comparison to how the town of Brandon, the tri-city areas of Southwest Jackson, Raymond, and Clinton, and the general tri-county communities, as a whole, have become accustomed to seeing him over the last decade or so. For one, he's completely sober. And while he's still malnourished in appearance, now that he's cleaned up there are faint resemblances of what had once been his commanding presence.

As the music fades, the Reverend Buddy Day gets out of his chair that's facing the congregation and slowly walks up with a well-used bible in his right hand, gently laying it down on the pulpit and opening it to what might otherwise appear to be a random page. He then pulls out his readers and, in a classic preacher's voice of hope, begins to read softly…

"1 Thessalonians chapter four, verse thirteen tells us 'Brothers and sisters, we do not want you to be uninformed about those who sleep in death, so that you do not grieve like the rest of mankind, who have no hope at all.'"

He then pauses and glances up for several seconds, scanning the congregation using his bare eyes, with his readers still pulled down upon the bridge of his nose…

"The world tries to tell us 'You know what? This is a sad day for everyone! Joshua is gone! And you must mourn his death because you will never see him again!'"

He then stops and looks over at the three of them seated in the front row, before walking to their side of the stage and staring somewhere towards the back, but at nobody in particular…

"Joshua has not walked in over ten years on this earth," he whispers very softly, almost embarrassingly. "But right now," building up the volume and tone of his voice as he speaks, "at this very moment, I believe with every fiber of my being that he's dancing in the golden streets of heaven!"

There are some scattered "Amens" and "Praise Gods!"

"And I'll tell you something else…" Shaking his head back and forth. "This is not a sad day for him. But our inherent selfishness makes us want to keep him here with us because it's simply tough to let go of someone that you love."

He turns around towards the choir and two or three of them give an obligatory "Amen," before he walks back to the podium and once again faces the congregation…

"2nd Corinthians chapter five, verse eight proclaims that 'We are confident, I say, and we would prefer to be away from our bodies and at HOME with the Lord,' praise Jesus!"

He then pauses for a few seconds, before continuing…

"There's pain and suffering here, where we are. Wouldn't you agree?" He looks around as if he's expecting an answer, only to receive a few head-nods…

"We're all here today trying to mourn a loss of life that we feel we lost too soon. Joshua, as independent and feisty as he could be in that handicap scooter of his," he says with a sly smile, "still needed caregivers to care for all of his basic needs here on earth." Then his voice once again starts to build… "But at this very moment in heaven, there's no more physical therapy, there's no more need for speech therapy, and there's no more choking on his food, no more hospital admissions, and no more feeding or breathing tubes attempting to buy us more time with him!"

He takes a deep breath and then whispers softly…

"That's because he has now been made whole and has all the time in the world, while being completely restored in the presence of Jesus Christ for eternity…"

Again, looking up, with his readers hanging low, and his voice starting to build with each sentence that he speaks…

"You know God knew him! Yep. Before he was born! Jeremiah chapter one and Psalm 139 tells us that He knows us all before we're even born, that He personally weaves our cells together in our mother's womb, and that He fully knows the entirety of our individual lives by the power of His omniscience."

Spence looks forward and ponders on that thought for just a moment…

"Like you and I, Joshua was fearfully and wonderfully made! In fact, He made him for a purpose! We think about all the hardships that he faced here on earth. A once promising athlete who spent the last ten-plus years of his life in total care… Well, the Bible tells us that God, Himself, wasn't surprised by this at all!"

He stops to survey the crowd after getting a few more scattered "Amens." Spence listens on intently, as Mrs. Waters grabs and squeezes his hand gently.

"Genesis chapter two, verse seven tells us that God made us all out of the dirt from the ground and that He, Himself, blew the breath of life into Joshua's nostrils, making him become alive – a living soul! And Ecclesiastes chapter twelve, verse seven goes on to say that the same dust that we're made of eventually returns to the ground from which it came, while our spirit still lives on and returns back to God, who gave it!"

The Reverend then turns to the choir and smiles, before turning back…

"No, no, no… Joshua doesn't want us to cry for him unless they're tears of joy. This, here, is a 'Celebration of the Life of Joshua Waters' and we invite you to sing along with praise to Jesus!"

And just then the organ and piano players begin to duel, as the choir stands up and sings, followed by the rest of the congregation. Mr. and Mrs. Waters both rise to their feet and encourage Spence to do so, also.

A person playing a guitar comes out, adjusts the microphone at the podium, and begins to lead worship, as the choir and congregation support him with backup vocals. Joshua's parents both hold their hands high and sing to the top of their lungs as Spence, slightly uncomfortable at the thought of singing along as loudly, mouths the words softly, as if speaking them, and gently sways back and forth in unison with the two of them.

The worship leader goes on to lead the congregation in several upbeat songs, before slowing down the music and softening the volume, but continuing to play. The Reverend Buddy Day again walks up to the podium and speaks, as the music plays ever so softly in the background and the choir and congregation continue to stand…

"We're going to open this podium and microphone up for anyone who feels led to come up and say a few words about Joshua…"

The Reverend goes back to his seat as the soft music plays on. Some still have their eyes closed and their hands in the air, while others are just swaying back and forth, connected in the moment.

He's not sure why, but Spence walks over to the outside of the pew and slowly continues up the steps towards the podium. He then takes a deep breath, before adjusting the microphone to his height and speaking…

"Good afternoon…"

He then moves it once again so that everyone can hear him and, as the music dims even quieter, he clears his throat…

"Good afternoon. My name is Spencer Taylor…"

He gets a few smiles from those who are now looking at him, including Mr. and Mrs. Waters. Most everyone else has their eyes closed, some with one or both hands still in the air, appreciating the moment…

"I've known Joshua since we played Little League All-Stars against one another…"

Both the Taylors and the Waters smile an encouraging smile as he continues…

"Our paths crossed many times as we grew up and he was by far the toughest person I've ever tried to get out…"

He stops to compose himself as he begins to get a little emotional…

"We were never on the same team. Always opponents of one another. But I felt like I knew him. That he was my friend. What was the most impressive trait of Joshua's was his attitude. I've played with some really good ballplayers over the years, but none of them were as good as he was. Nowhere close. But really good ballplayers start to realize over time 'Hey… I'm a pretty big deal,' and many of them begin to act in ways unbecoming of an ideal teammate… or competitor, for that matter…"

He then points to Joshua's photo that's front and center with the casket behind it…

"You know Joshua had every single reason in the world to be a diva, a prima donna, to get frustrated with his teammates and coaches, to 'pimp' every home run that he hit, and to rub it in the faces of his rivals… But all I ever saw from the guy was a smile, a lot of goofiness, and the utmost respect for the game that he loved. He was the epitome of what it takes to one day be a Major League Baseball Hall of Famer…"

Spence then gathers himself and clears his throat once again…

"And I took it all away from him."

He gets choked up for a second, as his parents look on with concern and those with their eyes closed begin to open them and look up.

"I sat there thirty minutes ago with Mr. and Mrs. Waters and, up until that point, I never once thought that I was simply a part of 'God's plan' for Joshua. I can't begin to tell you how many times I've asked in despair 'Why me Lord?' I've beaten myself up over the last twelve years for what I did to him back then. I've drank myself into oblivion, pushed those that I love away from me, and tried to kill myself several times. But I was like bad grass that wouldn't ever die. That's because I never found myself worthy of God's love. And just twenty minutes ago I heard a word from God through Reverend Day, but more so as if Jesus, Himself, was sitting

126

right next to me, that I, too, in addition to Joshua, was known before the creation of all creatures, that we were both loved immensely, that there was a plan that our lives would intersect one day, and that through it all His name would somehow be glorified..."

Spence receives a resounding "Praise Jesus!" from the congregation.

He then takes another deep breath and continues...

"I don't know... I feel like I know him so well, but I've never even said more than two words to Joshua... 'Good game' was about as far as we ever got."

He looks down, shakes his head, and smiles...

"But I really feel like we could've been best friends. In fact, in an alternate universe somewhere out there in the cosmos, I feel like we are teammates together in the Major Leagues, as strange as that may sound..."

Spence then slows it back down...

"But the reality of it all is that he's no longer here and I'm a big reason as to why..."

Spence then turns to Reverend Day and goes to speak to him, but then stops himself, and instead turns fully around to look upon the likeness of Jesus Christ being crucified above the choir...

"I no longer question Your intentions, my Lord and Savior. I only ask that You take this burden away from me, somehow, so that I may glorify You moving forward with my life..."

He then begins to cry for about ten seconds, as do most in the congregation who also get teary-eyed, before composing himself once again and pointing towards the casket and photo...

"And tell Joshua that Spence said 'Hi.'"

He walks back to his seat and Reverend Day quickly stands up and shouts "Praise Jesus in the Highest! He's our Redeemer! Come one, come all!"

Mr. and Mrs. Waters embrace Spence when he gets back and once again the praise and worship team begin playing. Dan and Joy are both crying, but it's obvious that these are tears of joy, as they reach over the pew to hug their grown child.

***

The actual burial of Joshua is a private family affair. Being an only child, it's just Mr. and Mrs. Waters that are standing together graveside alongside Reverend Buddy Day as he reads from the Word. There are several hired hands standing off in the distance awaiting approval to lower the casket and fill in the hole once the three of them depart.

Joshua does have a handful of first cousins, but his parents were adamant that they wanted everyone else to remember him in celebration only. They, themselves, recognize that the individual being buried before them was but a shell of what he had once been, especially with regard to his longer-term potential over the last dozen or so years. So, in effect, they'd already "mourned" his loss, albeit slowly as the years passed, considering that he was basically total care, would never realize his Major League Baseball dream, and would never get married or have a family of his own.

They eventually came to accept it and embrace their role as his primary caregivers. But this moment was when and where they were both going to finally say their goodbyes to him, their perfect son, and they wanted it to be more intimate than doing so while hundreds of other people also paid their respects.

Spence understood this and tried his best to stay away. He had spent the evening and the following afternoon after Joshua's death with the Waters getting to know them, listening to stories about their son, and discussing his own future. They even invited Dan and Joy over to get to know them and encourage them not to give up on their own son. He was amazed at how accepting and forgiving they were, especially considering that he thought he was hated by them.

Still, he couldn't help himself, and instead parked his truck in the distance, just outside the back exit of the cemetery, and walked up to a tree about one hundred yards away, attempting to discreetly monitor the service.

Whatever ceremony there is between Joshua and the three of them is a short one. Spence can observe very little emotion during the process, and when it's over the Reverend escorts the Waters back to their car and embraces them before driving off.

The workers waste little time in lowering the casket into the ground and then covering it with dirt. Spence watches them the entire time as the sun begins to fall back over the tree line and the sky turns a beautiful shade of orange. And when they are finally done and gone, Spence slowly and respectfully walks over to the small pile of dirt and looks on for about five minutes, before gently kneeling onto one knee and uttering his thoughts…

"I still don't fully understand it all. But I'm going to live the rest of my life honoring you. I'm so sorry that it's you in there and not me. And I'm so thankful that your parents have chosen to not only forgive me, but to also counsel me. I will always carry your story around with me, because you are now a part of me. Rest in peace, brother… And save a spot up there for me."

Spence then stands up and slowly begins walking to his truck that is parked just outside of the back gate. His steps feel a little bit lighter and the load he is carrying around with him isn't nearly as heavy. And as he nears the exit, Abby pulls up from behind him, turns on the cabin light of her car, and rolls down her window…

"Your speech today was wonderful."

"Thank you."

"I know it was technically a 'celebration,' but I cried a little bit when I saw you."

Spence grimaces with emotion and looks away, before almost forcing himself to look back…

"I have to do better. It's what Joshua would've wanted."

"It's what I want too, Spence. It's what everyone around here wants…"

He tears up and looks away again, before turning back…

"I'm ready."

"Good. I'm praying for you."

"Please don't stop."

Abby then smiles and rolls up the window as she slowly drives away.

Spence eventually makes it back to his truck. It's now dusk, and as he reaches to turn on the headlights and proceeds to put it in gear, he suddenly stops after noticing a brilliant red cardinal swooping down over the hood of his truck and landing on the fence post immediately to his left. The bird, only a few feet away, looks directly at Spence for over 30 seconds, almost as if it knows him, and then proudly flaps its wings several times before flying away.

Spence stays where he is and gazes at the empty fence post for several more minutes with utter fixation. He then takes a deep breath and smiles, before rolling-up the window, putting it in drive, slowly pressing the accelerator, and driving off…

This might just be the first time he's smiled in quite some time. It's nearly dark now as he's traveling home, and he notices that there's no alcohol cravings like he's had beforehand. And unlike what often occurred in the past, he easily drives right past his favorite liquor store.

His mind, now clearer than he can ever remember, begins to drift off once again as he passes the old stomping grounds of his high school…

"Spencer Taylor…"

Standing next to his hallway locker, he smiles a sly smile as he closes it and looks at Christa…

"What?"

"You will most certainly walk me to my car on our last day of class together…"

"Oh, my game doesn't mean anything to you?"

"It's five hours from now…"

"I know… But your car is in the front parking lot and the field is in the back of the campus…"

Christa smiles back and playfully punches him in the arm…

"You take that back."

"Ow." He then sees Coach Gray in the distance… "Coach… Did you see that!? Now I can't pitch tonight…"

Coach Gray interrupts him while laughing, "Christa… There's no 'Plan B' for tonight. Please be gentle with my star pitcher…"

"Oh, whatever," as they all giggle.

Spence continues to walk Christa to her car as banners hanging everywhere display a variety of cheers such as "BEAT BRANDON!" and "TAME THE BULLDOGS!"

It's the last day of school and as usual the baseball team has extended their season beyond the classroom and into the summer with a playoff run. And tonight will determine if they make it to the State Semifinals – or what's often referred to as "The Final Four."

The two of them stop at Christa's car…

"I'll see you tonight," she says smiling. "You're gonna do great."

"I hope so. I'm nervous."

She leans in and kisses him gently on the lips before getting into her car…

"I love you, Spence Taylor…"

He leans down, puts both elbows on the bottom on her car's driver's side window, and whispers… "I'm gonna marry you one day, Christa Johnson."

Christa blushes as she drives off.

He then smiles and waves…

"See you tonight!"

Spence eventually makes it back home from the cemetery. Turning down Myrtle Drive, the gravel road leading to his single-wide trailer, jars him back from his high school playing days and flirtations with Christa into his current circumstance.

He gets out of the truck and notices once again that the screen door hinge is fixed, apparently thanks to his dad. Not only that… But leading up to it there's a mosaic assortment of concrete pavers at the foot of the precast staircase that rises up to the front doorstep. This is of course instead of the rotten wooden pallet landing area that was there beforehand – one which Dan had playfully nicknamed "The Ankle-Breaker."

And as he walks inside it's noticeably cleaner, more picked-up, and more organized than ever before. There's no alcohol or beer cans to be seen and no dishes stacked up in the sink. The breakfast area table and chairs are brand new. Gone is the broken one which had a leg that snapped during his suicide attempt a few fateful nights prior.

Looking towards the living area, the hide-a-bed is tucked away and the sofa that it occupies appears to be slip-covered and now adorned with a decorative blanket. There's also a new rug underneath the coffee table that seems straight out of a Pier 1 Imports catalog.

He walks towards the back to his bedroom, taking great care to undress and hang up all the components of the new suit that his parents bought him the day before. He then places his new dress shoes back inside of the box from which they came and puts them on a shelf in the closet. In doing so, he can't help but notice that his old clothes that were once strewn about the floor and hanging out of drawers are now essentially gone and replaced with seemingly perfectly folded brand-new replacements.

His bed is made and the sheets and pillowcases appear to be not only washed, but also brand new. Again, there's no alcohol or remnants thereof that are noticeable, and come to think of it no ash trays or cigarettes scattered about, either.

A small diffuser blows humidified air nearby on his nightstand, sending the aroma of an essential oil concoction throughout the different sections of his mobile home, although the scent is definitely the strongest in his bedroom, arising from the source. It's a familiar smell to him called "THIEVES" – one that he originally disliked, but it has grown on him over the past several years. Anything is better than the essence of booze and ash trays, I guess.

His mom also diffuses her own entire house and Dan often jokes that she is somehow convinced her favorite essential oils are the cure for alcoholism, chain-smoking, cancer, and AIDS – just to name a few ailments.

The two of them have spent the last several days with their only son sprucing up the place and taking him on shopping sprees for a new wardrobe and furniture. They also stocked his fridge and cabinets with healthy options from the grocery store.

Totally committed to his transformation, they've also gone as far as to make an appointment with a local dentist in hopes of getting his unkempt teeth capped and crowned the following week, having been convinced that this is a life-changing moment for their son, based on his 180° turn in behavior in the aftermath of Joshua's death.

He's even agreed to attend the local Alcoholics Anonymous group meetings, having already been to his first one the night before.

Spence grabs a bite to eat, before sitting down on his couch and having a good look around. And after just a few minutes he lays face down on the floor in front of him and hammers out ten push-ups, albeit struggling to do so and out of breath afterwards. It's enough to make him chuckle at himself. A few minutes later he does ten more… And then ten more.

seventeen – reticent

Spence awakens the next morning after hearing his alarm clock and gets out of bed. His chest and arms are extremely sore, as he attempts to stretch them out. He thinks to himself that he hasn't been this sore since hitting the weight room in high school.

The factory has given him a paid week off thanks to Ralph's insistence on doing so, and he has several more free days before going back to work.

After cooking some ham and eggs, eating, and then letting them settle, he decides to don a brand-new pair of running shoes and set out on a jog down the gravel road towards the main drag. This is a new thing for Spence. Basically reclusive for the better part of the last dozen years or so, electively getting out and about town, much less on foot, isn't something that the townspeople are used to seeing from him.

Other than appearing the part in his new apparel and gear, courtesy of Dan and Joy, he still looks pitifully undernourished and emaciated as he runs through the town and cuts through the parking lot of his old high school. It's there that he runs into Coach Gray, who's out tending to the baseball field...

"Spence!?"

"Yeah, Coach?"

"Come see..."

He stops running at what is probably the best moment, considering that he feels like he's going to die. Coach is a bit older now than how Spence remembers him, and somehow also a bit more overweight. The field, itself, is in decent condition, in large part due to the hours and hours of labor and care that Coach Gray puts into it. The press-box, stands, and outfield wall are another story, altogether. The good news is that everything is structurally stable, aside from the ruins of a nearby batting cage that's resting upon a cracked slab along the outside of the left field fence-line. The bad news is that the whole thing appears to be patchwork repaired. There are brand new pieces of unpainted lumber mixed in with older boards and laid out seemingly in a checkered pattern throughout the ballpark, with many layers and hues of the same color paint chipping off the more timeworn ones. The panels that haven't been replaced yet have all warped and splintered after several decades of wear and neglect, although they remain somewhat functional enough to keep a baseball or player within the confines of the playing field. The scoreboard, while still operative, is rusted, faded, and antiquated, with more than a dozen bulbs that don't light up anymore. However, amidst the disarray, Coach still has the same infectious smile, as he and his former player go find a sturdy bench in a shaded area of the home dugout to sit down and talk.

"How's it been going?"

"Not so good, Coach. I've been struggling, but I think I'm turning the corner and on the right track to bettering my life."

"I see that, son. I never would've pictured you out here running before, but here you are…"

They both share a laugh together…

"I saw your parents a couple of days ago and they told me about Joshua, and how you've been spending time with his parents?"

"Yessir."

"Are you going to be okay, son?"

"Yessir. I think so…"

"Good. Uh… Look, Spence… I don't know how to ask you this, but I could use you around here. You have a lot of baseball knowledge to share with all the kids…"

Spence looks on and says nothing...

"And, most importantly, I think you could use us, too. There's a little over a month left until our first game here, and for the first time in a decade I think I have a team that can compete with the local academies. A few pitchers here and there... We have several players that can really hit... And an overall fast team that can maybe play a little small-ball..."

Spence nods in agreement...

"I want you to help me coach... Specifically the pitchers. Of course I can't pay you anything. But Spence, I'll tell you the truth... And don't you dare tell anyone else, but I love doing this so much that I'd do it for free. And I think you'll feel the same way once..."

Spence starts to respond, but instead pauses to think about it for a second, as coach Gray stops mid-sentence in anticipation of his answer...

"Whaddaya say, son? You can quit at any time, no questions asked. But I think you're gonna love the kids and remember just how much you miss this game. Just come out for one of our practices in the next couple of weeks and then give me your answer. Deal?"

"Sure, coach. It sounds like a lotta fun. Next week is my first week back at work, and I'm also getting my teeth fixed. I have my AA meetings on Tuesday and Thursday nights. I'm sorry, but I can't miss those, and may have to leave early at times. But whenever I'm available, I'd love to help..."

"Sounds good, son. I'll get in touch with you with all the details and you can let me know when you can make it..."

Spence jogs off and Coach gets back to work. He makes it about halfway back home and ultimately has to stop because he's short-winded. It's about two miles from his old high school to his mobile home, and he's beginning to think that he may have been a little overly ambitious on his initial public outing into town by foot. Surprisingly, he's only taken two breaks from exercising since leaving this morning: once to talk to Coach, and just now because he's wheezing and can't quite catch his breath.

He starts to cough, and it gets progressively worse over the course of the next couple of minutes. His hands, that once started above and behind his head after he gradually decelerated into a slow walk, have since found their way to the tops of his knees, as he's now completely stopped, hunched over on the shoulder of the road, and retching – a thick black and nasty substance that tastes like an ashtray eventually making its way up towards the tip of his tongue, before he can spit it out onto the ground. His respirations almost instantly become less labored after expelling the tarry plug, as he thinks to himself how scary it was to not be able to catch his breath for several minutes. But it also crosses his mind about how nice it would've been to have just one cigarette to maybe help with his cravings before that thing began making its way out his body in a fit of protest.

He opts to walk the rest of the way home, making it to the gravel road that is Myrtle Drive over the course of the next fifteen minutes or so. Almost there, he starts to fancy a "smoke" in a really bad way for the first time since Joshua died. And when he finally arrives, he's been lusting after one so badly that he mauls open a pack of Nicorette gum, putting two pieces inside his mouth, both chewing and sucking on them at same time, nearly biting his tongue in the process, and thinking to himself "This sucks." For some reason the alcohol yearnings are much less than that of the cigarettes presently, but now sitting there as the nicotine starts to reach the cells that were starving for it, he remains steadfast and determined to kick both habits.

**

"Hi. My name is Spence… And I'm an alcoholic."

"Hello, Spence."

"I've been sober now for a week or so. I don't really have a sponsor per se, but my friend Dave that I met on my first visit has agreed to counsel me through my journey…"

"That's wonderful. Good job, Dave."

Dressed in khakis and a polo, with a head-full of short grey hair, a full beard, and a slight potbelly, Dave is a local project manager for a design and build construction firm based out of Memphis that offers engineering services, construction, steel fabrication, equipment installation, and mill-right maintenance to automotive, food & beverage, and general manufacturing plants throughout the southeast United States. He moved to the central Mississippi area from Texas twenty years ago when his company, WAYCO Construction, ventured into the sports-market sector and won the bid to construct a new ballpark for Jackson's Double-A affiliate to the New York Mets. Heading up his first big project on a new market expansion into designing and building sports arenas, Dave was stressed and turned to the bottle for relief, almost losing his wife and three kids in the process. Sober now for fifteen years, he's been a local mentor to those also attempting to free themselves from the bond of alcoholism, rarely missing a meeting and now only wanting to help others, like Spence. He acknowledges and smiles back at the group, before deferring back to the newcomer.

"Yes. Thank you, Dave. I didn't really speak much the first time I was here because I wanted to observe from a distance, so to speak. But this time I want to take a moment to explain just how determined I am to get through this journey and onto the other side. I understand that I am powerless against my alcoholism and will always be an addict to some extent. But I also believe in the Almighty Power of Jesus Christ and His healing Grace – and have chosen to take the first step toward Him filled with the faith of a mustard seed – imploring Him to help me move mountains in my life."

There are collective "amens" and "attaboys" scattered amongst the group of about a dozen or so addicts sitting around the circle.

Dave then speaks to the group...

"I spent more than an hour with Spence after the last meeting and was able to hear a firsthand account of his story, one that I vaguely knew since I've followed local high school sports for the past twenty-plus years."

Another member chimes in... "Wait... Are you Spence Tay...?" – and stops himself.

Dave looks his way, as if to say "Really!?" – before continuing… "Spence has graciously agreed to share his story with the group, but I want to remind everyone that what's talked about here in this circle is confidential…"

Spence looks around the group and recognizes one face as someone that was at Forest Hill High School around the same time that he was, but a couple of years older.

"The floor is yours, son…"

Spence places his hands under his thighs and leans forward in his chair, but doesn't know exactly where to start…

Dave gives him a little encouragement… "Just start from the beginning. How you grew up. Were your parents alcoholics? Etcetera."

Spence nods affirmatively and begins his story…

"I had a great childhood. I grew up as an only child. My parents wanted me to have siblings, but could never get pregnant again. Looking back, I think there was a time at about five years of age that my mom had a miscarriage. I remember her being upset, and she was always happy-go-lucky…"

He looks around at the group and gets some head-nods of approval so far.

"My dad played JUCO baseball in Raymond and was always out in the yard with me tossing the ball. I was never a good hitter. But my arm, so I was told since I was about nine years of age, was 'elite'" – adding finger-quotes for emphasis.

Spence stops for a second like he's embarrassed before continuing…

"I'm sorry. I don't want this to be just about me, but it is. I hate sitting in front of a group and saying stuff like my arm was 'elite.' I don't want to sound like I'm bragging, and you'll soon understand that I don't have much to brag about the way my life has since turned out…"

Dave interrupts Spence and the room agrees with him…

"Spence. Nobody here is judging you. We want to hear your story. Although we're all different in how we ended up at this meeting, there are details and minutia in everyone's story that has similarities with that of others – and everybody can come away with either something that personally helps them or perhaps even just some understanding – so that if they ever need to counsel you, themselves, then they have some perspective. You are the newest member of this group and you have us all on the edge of our seats. You don't owe us anything. But we want to encourage you if you'd like to continue…"

Spence looks around, gets multiple acknowledgments, and resumes his story after taking a deep breath.

"Well… Let me back up. My parents weren't alcoholics. I may have seen my dad drink a beer in a social setting a time or two… But my mother? Never. Anyway… By the seventh and eighth grade, I was a pitching 'prospect' for major colleges and universities and was already getting mail and phone calls from them. But I wasn't the only one in the tri-county area who had their eye. Over in Rankin County… Brandon, Specifically… There was also a kid my age that I'd played against since we were young children. His name was Joshua Waters, and he was just an all-around elite athlete. And by the time we were both high-schoolers, not only was he, too, a 5-star D-I college prospect at shortstop, but he was also being projected as a very early first round selection in the 1991 Major League Baseball Draft. He was going to be an instant millionaire, so to speak…"

He stops for a second to gather his thoughts…

"But there was a Friday night in mid-May, our last day of class as graduating Seniors at Forest Hill High School, that we had a home playoff game against Brandon High School, and he hit a towering home run off of me that I couldn't let go of."

The group seems enthralled by his story and the room is so quiet that you can hear a pin drop. Some of them, although not firsthand, begin to recognize what he's saying and can remember the overall story, minus the details. But until tonight they had no idea at all that the person in front of them was a major player in what unfolded.

"So the next time he came up to the plate, later in the contest, we had a commanding lead. The team I played on was just better, all-around. When you played Brandon High School, you simply pitched around Joshua and avoided hitting the ball to the shortstop. What you didn't let happen was him, alone, beat you. And earlier in the game I fell into that trap, and I was pissed off. It didn't help things at all that I could see the MLB scout behind the backstop suddenly showing interest in the game now that he was back up to bat."

He stops for about thirty seconds and seems to be really gathering his thoughts on what to say moving forward. The group remains silent the entire time.

"So… I've never admitted this part out loud, publicly, but I think this is a component of my treatment. What I have to get out of me, especially right here and now. I was upset that he murdered a three-oh pitch that I threw to him in his last at bat and we were so far ahead at that point in the game that I didn't want to just walk him, like I was told to do by my dugout. So I decided to hit him. More specifically, to throw the ball at his ribs as hard as I could. Now, this wasn't a controversial thing. I'd been instructed numerous times in the past to bean people in high school by my coaches, whether in retaliation for one of my teammates getting hit or just to keep them from crowding the plate. It also goes on in both the collegiate game and in the Majors…"

Again, he pauses and starts to get a little emotional…

"It's just that this time I was doing it out of my own frustrations and from my own will. And so I threw it as hard as I could right at his ribcage, only to let it get away high and with a bit more arm-side run than usual. It hit him in the head at 95 miles per hour and sent his helmet flying high in the air, landing far from where he was…"

There's a collective gasp from the group. Again, about one-third of them are hearing it for the first time, one-third is only slightly familiar with what happened, sans the details that they are now receiving, and the last-third is very familiar, one or two of them perhaps even having been at the standing-room only playoff baseball game.

"I remember him twitching on the ground for several minutes after it occurred with seizure-like movements. I don't know about anything medically-speaking today, but even as a high school senior, I knew that wasn't a good sign. So I just stood there in disbelief with my hands behind my head, as my teammates attempted to console me out on the mound. Joshua was eventually carted off to an awaiting ambulance and showed no movement in the process of that. I was so afraid. Coach Gray could see it in my eyes. And even though nobody had warmed up, he took the ball from the home plate umpire, patted me on the butt, and said 'Good game,' all while inside of me I was in the beginning process of dying a slow, torturous death. I walked over to my dugout. And I'm still not sure if my teammates and the other coaches just thought I just needed my space or what, but nobody said a word to me. So instead of walking inside, I simply continued past the crowd and into the parking lot. Eventually I made it home – walking, just lost in my thoughts. And that's where my parents ultimately found me after desperately looking for my whereabouts after the game was over."

Spence notices a few of the attendees wiping their eyes…

"That pitch that I threw at Joshua was the last time I held a baseball in my hands. I lost all interest and only heard about Joshua's prognosis over the following weeks through hearsay. But I couldn't for the life of me go see him or face his parents. Instead, I turned to the bottle and fell deep inside of a depression, losing my confidence, my promising career, and…"

Spence's emotions start building up as he says this, so much so that he cannot even get the last thing he lost out of his mouth.

Dave gets up, walks over, gently puts a hand on his shoulder, and whispers… "It's okay, son… Take all the time that you need. But I do think you need to verbalize it…"

Spence then breaks down to the point of a cold sweat as nearly everyone in the room is either wiping away tears or blatantly sobbing along with him, now invested in both his story and his well-being.

He then gathers himself enough after taking a deep breath to finish his thoughts…

"... And the girl I was gonna marry."

And at that point he bends his head over his knees and wails uncontrollably, as several more attendees get up to console him. After a few minutes he looks up, and despite looking malnourished beforehand, after throwing crying and sobbing into the mix, appearance-wise, he almost looks like death... But then he somehow musters up the ability to continue...

"I have to see..." He stops involuntarily to gather his breath... "I see her all the time and have to pretend that I don't still love her..."

Spence stops once again as his emotions continue getting in the way of what he wants to say... "I wrecked Joshua's life, those who loved him's life, my own life, Christa's life, and my parents' life... Who've still never given up on me..."

He then stops and takes a tissue that is offered, trying to clean himself up as everyone goes back to their seats. Dave asks him if he'd like to say more...

Spence looks around the room before continuing...

"And so here I am after beating myself up over the better part of the last twelve years... Tryna grasp the concept that I deserve to feel better, turn my life around, and live it to the fullest after paying a penance which, in my opinion up until a few days ago at Joshua's funeral, that I honestly thought I deserved worse."

He then stops himself, realizing that he left out a significant part...

"Joshua lived the last twelve years – not as a professional baseball player, where he belonged, but as a total care invalid that would've basically been bed-ridden, if not for the care of his devoted parents, who gave him the best life he could've possibly had, considering what I took away from him. He recently died after a bout with pneumonia."

Dave speaks up, helping him by guiding the conversation...

"Spence... and how was it that you ultimately atoned for what happened to Joshua, decided to make a change, and now we find you here in front of us?"

"Oh, I didn't 'atone' for anything at all. Of course I've always had remorse, thereby ruining my own life and future. But the process that brought me here is complicated. For one, I was drinking so much that I started hallucinating and found myself reliving parts of my life that I wish I could both have back and take back. And that ultimately led me to the doorstep of Joshua Waters' parents' home the night after he passed away. Something made me knock on the door, and when Mr. Waters answered it, I fell into his arms and asked for forgiveness for what I'd done."

There's at least one person in the group that says "Amen" aloud.

"Mr. and Mrs. Waters were so merciful towards me. They stayed up with me, tucked me in on their living room couch after I passed out from exhaustion, and spent the following days with both me and my parents reliving the days of old when their only sons were fierce competitors out on the baseball field, and both still had bright futures."

Spence then realizes there's one last thing to tell that would explain him being there in front of the group...

"And so a few days after that we had a 'Celebration of Life' for Joshua. And let me tell you... It was most certainly a 'celebration.' Anyway, still in a funk and processing all that surrounded me – considering we were there, on that day, and for that cause, solely because of me, alone – after listening to the Reverend give a five to ten minute 'sermon,' I came to the full conclusion that my grief, my self-destruction and sabotage of my own life, and my insistence that I didn't deserve a better life was no match for the Grace that Jesus Christ offers..."

Spence is then interrupted by a resounding "Amen!" from all attendees.

He then looks up and says...

"I want my life back."

"Hear, hear! Son."

Dave speaks with excitement for the group as a collective applause rings out amongst it.

"That's one helluva story. But the better one is gonna be the one about your total redemption!"

The group claps again, before one, and then all of them say "Thank you for sharing, Spence."

Dave then redirects the attendees, some of them still with tears in their eyes and others now offering handkerchiefs out of their own pockets, and begins to close out the night's meeting, as they all stand up and hold hands...

"Dear God, grant me the serenity to accept the things that I cannot change, the courage to change the things I can, and the wisdom to know the difference... Amen."

eighteen – clean

The next few days are quite different for Spence in relation to how his life has played out over the last dozen or so years. For one, he wakes up spontaneously without an alarm clock and spends most of his mornings, afternoons, and nights sprucing up both the interior and exterior of his mobile home, instead of drowning his thoughts with liquor.

His mom and dad come over to help-out with whatever home improvement project is on the docket for the day and the three of them often go out to eat, seem to enjoy each other's company, and openly converse now, instead of how it had previously transpired when he was reluctant, distant, silent, and didn't eat much at all.

They say that moms know best and are the first to recognize things about their children. That noted, Joy has even noticed a change in the facial structure of her son since the previous week, when he was at his worst. His eyes aren't as jaundiced as they were before and his sockets no longer appear to be cavernous, sunken-in, or plagued with dark circles. Hydration and a more normal diet have changed the appearance of his skin and he's also already showing signs of filling out his new wardrobe that they recently purchased for him. His lips, once dry, chapped, and cracked in several places, now appear to be moist and lubricated. He even reaches into his pocket from time to time to re-apply more Chapstick.

His teeth, though, are still horrible. It's obvious that he's taking better care of them, but the damage has already been done. That was one thing that she spoke to Dan about. If their son was going to have a complete restoration in his life and undergo a total transformation of his body, his teeth would have to be addressed, too. They agreed that investing in his smile would also help out his prospects of meeting someone romantically in the future – although both secretly held out hope of him and Christa one day reconciling.

Speaking of his old high school girlfriend, Spence had also been secretly showing interest in, at the very least, her well-being. He knew that she was a single mom now, which apartment complex she lived in, and had more recently been going slightly out of his way attempting to discreetly drive by it – perhaps maybe to just get a glimpse of her face, even if it was from a distance.

Despite his turnaround though and his consuming desire to see it all the way through, one thing he couldn't shake was his insistence that she deserved better than what he had to offer – the baggage, the recovery, and the lifestyle void of discretionary money to spend.

Everything wasn't all hunky-dory either when he was alone. Despite staying busy, he still had debilitating cravings for alcohol and was now basically "addicted" to Nicorette gum. He could handle the tremors in his hands, but the stomach cramps he would experience at various times were both taxing and exhausting – as if every cell in his digestive tract was in violent protest against his new lifestyle change.

His parents had witnessed one such unfortunate episode that brought him to his knees and called an ambulance on his behalf. Spence, knowing what he was up against, having been warned at his meetings and committed to the process, refused to go with them.

His Alcoholics Anonymous sponsor, Dave, was on speed-dial and had proven to be patient with him and his many inquiries, knowing that the first weeks and months were the most difficult to navigate in regards to maintaining one's sobriety. This had been one instance in which Spence called him and he showed up right away to talk down both the paramedics and his parents, while educating them about the body's resistance to change.

It did seem as if every day it got maybe a little bit better though. A gradual increase in feeling better ultimately leads to a complete healing – so Dave ended up counseling his parents during this time, too – who weren't naive enough to think that this would all just go away immediately; however, they were generally unsuspecting of the entire drawn-out process.

Spence also periodically visited the parents of Joshua Waters. He'd already mowed their lawn without being asked and would often show up just to see if they needed anything at all. Mostly all they wanted to do was talk about him and how he was doing.

It was no longer about himself, and he was coming to the realization of just how selfish he had been to make it that way. Instead, his desire was increasingly becoming that of helping others, wishing he'd have done it that way all along. And, interestingly enough, he found that in doing so, it went a long way in helping to temper all the urges he personally had instead of having to just fight through it all with nothing else to do.

And on Sundays, he attended church. The beginning of every week was now given totally to God – the Reverend Buddy Day also agreeing to counsel and be available to the recovering addict.

***

Spence clocks in and heads to his post. It's Monday and it's his first day back at work. From a distance, Ralph looks up and does a double take, hardly recognizing him, before moseying over…

"Well, well, well…"

Spence grins.

"I have to say that you look pretty good, Spence. Cleanly shaven? What's up?"

"Oh nothing. Just a different mindset. Going to meetings at night and fighting cravings during the day. All the fun stuff."

"I'm proud of you, son. Your dad is, too. I just spoke with him last night."

"Oh yeah?"

"That's right. And he's never sounded happier when discussing his son with me."

Spence smirks as Ralph grabs him by the shoulder and gently squeezes it a couple of times, before walking back to resume what he was doing.

148

"Uh… Wait… Ah… Ralph. Did my dad tell you that I'll need the afternoon off tomorrow so that I can get my teeth worked on?"

Ralph nods yes and says that it won't be a problem.

Spence is way more productive than ever before. In fact, it's now the others in the assembly line that cannot keep up with him. He playfully looks around and jokes with everyone around him that was once frustrated that he was always lagging behind…

"Let's go… Still waiting… Guess I'll use all this extra time and do some lunges or sumthin…"

He's much more likable in sobriety. His coworkers also can't help but notice his changing appearance for the better, during what's basically only the beginning stages of his transformation. It's as if he's a totally different person, altogether… And they slowly come to the understanding that beneath the surface of what had been a hurting individual, there is yet another one that's quite a presence, commands attention, and is full of life.

Spence continues through his day, clocks out, and drives straight home – after detouring down the road towards Christa's apartment, of course. And while passing by it his mind begins to drift…

"But Spence, I love you."

Spence stares straight ahead and won't look her in the eyes. She's come over to his childhood home and his parents have brought her back to his bedroom. He won't leave it and that has them worried. He also claims he's not traveling with the team, nor is he playing in the Mississippi High School State Championship Semifinals that are in just a few days.

"I'm sorry."

"You're sorry? You're sorry!? Spence… I've planned my whole entire life moving forward with you. Going to Mississippi State with you. And all you can say to me is 'I'm sorry?'"

Spence says nothing at all, as Christa begins to cry. He doesn't even attempt to console her. He simply looks forward towards the Nolan Ryan poster hanging on the wall of his bedroom, as if he's staring one hundred feet past the wall, itself.

The two of them sit in awkward silence for several minutes. The person in the room with her is not the same one she's been dating over the past three years. His eyes are distant, and his affect is strange. She lets him know as much, and he's unaffected by what she says.

"Just say that you don't love me, and I'll leave, and you'll never have to see me again."

At this point he very purposefully looks up and makes eye contact...

"I don't love you..."

A horn blowing stuns him awake. He's at a stop sign, with two cars behind him, and he hasn't yet proceeded forward. One driver has his hand out of the window and is imploring him to go. Embarrassed, he makes a right turn and continues home.

***

"Oh wow!"

"Let me see, son!"

"Wait a minute, mom."

There was a mold made of Spence's teeth at sixteen years old, shortly after his braces came off, so that a removable retainer could be made for when he slept. They had never been so perfectly straight as they were, then, and the only concern that Joy had expressed to the dentist now reconstructing her son's mouth at thirty years of age was the possibility of an unnatural look, with no similarity, whatsoever, to what nature had once bestowed upon him.

Spence turns the hand-held mirror over and looks more closely at himself. The other side is magnified. His mother, insistent upon seeing it herself, finally just slaps the mirror down upon his lap and then puts her face directly in front of his, before immediately bursting into tears.

Sensing her concerns before agreeing to help, Dr. Genard, his parents' dentist, had contacted Dr. Cope, Spence's childhood dentist, to obtain the imprint – which he still had in a storage closet where he kept old dental records and files – and then reconstructed each tooth identically to what he once previously had.

Thankfully Spence's teeth had enough of a solid root foundation, despite his neglect over the years, and the dentist was able to dedicate four solid hours of his day to file down and build onto his existing teeth. Not only that, but he had an actual scaled to size guide and was able to reconstruct each individual tooth precisely identical to the way that God had once made them.

They weren't too white… Or too big… And, perhaps most importantly, they didn't feel like unknown rocks inside of his mouth that closed awkwardly or that he had to spend a lot of time getting used to.

It was a remarkable transformation that had every dental hygienist and even the office workers moseying back to personally witness what all the "oohing and ahhing" was about.

Once again, thought Joy, Spence was looking more and more like his previously handsome self…

And this made her happy.

nineteen – despondent

Dave is unavailable and Spence isn't doing too well on this particular night. That's the thing about addiction. It's taking just one day at a time and some days are simply better or worse than others. The truth is you're always an addict and each sunrise is just another fight for sobriety, complete with its own unique temptations and empty promises to avoid.

The good news is that his smoking habit is pretty much non-existent; the cravings having resolved over time and the black tarry sputum that ultimately made its way out of his lungs, little by little, in fits of protest against him exercising, no longer find him hunched over and retching in order to clear them out of his system.

Spence only wishes it was as simple as a piece of gum that he could chew to help satisfy his yearnings for alcohol, as they have recently surpassed the intensity of his urges to light up. And tonight the tremors aren't just limited to the hands, themselves. Instead, it's full-body involuntary convulsion-like episodes that have him scared and perhaps justifying a relapse.

He's diaphoretic and exhausted, having burned who knows how many calories. And in between one of these episodes, he tries to reach Dave by phone one more time – but remains unsuccessful. Complicating matters, many of his peripheral muscles have started cramping up, rendering him nearly totally immobile, and therefore incapable of leaving home to get himself an alcohol fix.

Both helpless and hopeless, he calls out for help, only to look out the window to find the windchimes hanging from his front porch now blowing and ringing out vigorously, in what might otherwise appear to be little to no breeze outside…

"Spencer... Spence."

He startles and opens his eyes to find the stranger inside his mobile home. What's bizarre is that he's experiencing this hallucination once again, but for the first time not only is he completely sober while doing so, but he's also in so much pain and discomfort that it isn't necessarily worrisome.

"Spence. I'm here to help you get through the night. Here... Drink some of this electrolyte solution and let's get you lying down..."

And as the stranger lays him down, Spence starts with the full-body convulsions once again and screams in agony, while sweating profusely, stopping only because he hears a subtle voice that sounds a lot like Christa's calling out his name, resonating from what appears to be an adjacent room – or perhaps even closer. Confused, he cries out "Christa?!" several times, but gets no answer. The stranger now seems to be preoccupied for the moment, whispering and motioning towards someone in the distance behind him that Spence cannot see. But he soon turns back around to hold him down and comfort him until the tremors and aches subside. Eventually he falls asleep from exhaustion.

twenty – hopeful

It's a new day. It's also the weekend and the sun is shining brightly. The night before was a tough one, for sure. But, as mentioned with addiction, some days are just better – and this was sure to be one of those days.

Spence calls Dave and tells him about his night and how the stranger had appeared to him while sober. Dave apologized for not being available, claiming that his grandchildren had spent the night and his granddaughter had unknowingly used their landline to talk to her junior high boyfriend until the wee hours of the morning, all while never informing her grandfather that someone was trying to beep in.

He has plans for the day to go visit with the Waters and mow their lawn, before leaving around lunchtime and heading out to the high school to meet the baseball team.

Coach Gray has told them about the former All-State pitcher that was stepping in to help coach, and many have already searched him on the internet. Although there isn't much on it relating to Spence's back story, there are articles talking about the kid who threw in the low-to-mid 90s that gave up baseball and fell hard into alcoholism. That noted, there are no major national publications available online that implicate Spence in the tragedy that befell upon Joshua Waters. There are some local ones that speak of the duo as the talented tri-county area athletes that played high school baseball back in the early 1990s. But with the recent news of Joshua's death and the ability to ask questions in a closely connected community, at least one of the kids has made the connection and has already started talking to the others.

Spence walks up to Coach Gray as the kids are almost finished warming their arms up, and he calls them all together near the center of the diamond…

By now Spence has filled out a little. He's still thin. But the change he's made has already added some impressive muscle tone. And to be totally honest his teeth having been restored gives a lot more credence to his general appearance than what it would have been had he shown up unshaven, disheveled, and still with discolored and rotten teeth.

His clothes are also more in-line with today's standards. And although he's anywhere from 12 to 15 years older than most of the players, he doesn't necessarily appear to be ancient or on par with the general vibe that Coach Gray puts forth, who's both overweight and pushing sixty years of age.

"Boys… This is Spencer Taylor – and I've asked him to stop by to meet you."

Spence nods at the group and they acknowledge him back…

"He will be coming around when his schedule allows and will specifically be coaching the pitchers. I have personally seen Spence hit the high 90s with his fastball…"

A senior named Rex chimes in from the back of the group… "Yeah. At someone's head…"

Most of the group chuckles in disbelief that he said it, and Coach Gray's immediate reaction is to lunge after the kid; but Spence puts his arm out and stops him…

"That's okay, coach."

Spence looks directly at the kid who said it and then glances at the rest of group before continuing…

"You're right. I hit someone in the head and it changed both of our lives. Congratulations on having the internet and coming up with your own conclusions, based on what your grandpa told you. And trust me. You can't say something bad enough about me or call me any type of name that I haven't already said about or done to myself. And I've totally beaten myself up over the last twelve years because of it."

He now looks straight at Rex…

"But before that fateful night, I was most definitely legit and headed places. Coach Gray can attest to that, and that's why I'm here. And it's something you never lose until age says that you can no longer do it. As a matter of fact, at thirty-years-old I can still strike out the best hitter on this team, and I haven't even touched a baseball since I walked off this field for the last time, more than a decade ago…"

The team lets out a generalized snicker, indicative of being unimpressed…

[Spence with a serious face] "Let's do it, then… You pick out who I'll face."

The kids start talking and begin to get a little bit rowdy as they chant… "Rex! Rex! Rex…"

Coach Gray moves in to stop all the commotion and Spence holds him back once again…

"I've got this, Coach."

Rex already has a bat in his hand and is strutting towards the plate. He then steps back into the dugout and, both loudly and sarcastically, says "Oops… I'd better get my 'helmet,'" adding volume and finger quotes for emphasis.

Spence isn't mad. Instead, he's actually amused at his cockiness.

Rex is a senior who's had an impressive run at Forest Hill High School. He's started at shortstop since he was a freshman and has already committed to play for Ole Miss next year. Athletically, he stands out from the rest of his teammates.

Spence borrows a glove and toes the rubber, before looking at Rex…

"You won't even touch it. I guarantee it."

"Bring it," responds Rex.

A catcher in full gear sets up behind the dish, before Spence, who's apparently itching to go, motions for Rex to hurry it up and stop clowning around. It isn't lost on anyone, including the two that are squaring off, that Rex is also the individual who smarted off earlier. And looking at his overall demeanor, there isn't anybody that would ever accuse him of lacking confidence, as he steps into the batter's box and assumes his stance.

Spence, without throwing a warm-up pitch, takes a full wind-up and delivers a fastball over the heart of the plate for a strike.

There's now a collective silence from all the kids who were previously cheering Rex on.

Coach Gray giggles and says, "Strike one."

Rex, who was only in the beginning stages of starting his swing, looks up and smiles...

Coach Gray, estimating the pitch at nearly 90 miles per hour, quips "You're gonna have to be quicker than that, Rex."

Rex gives him a head nod and steps back in...

He again takes a full wind-up and throws another heater, center cut, and Rex takes a full swing, only after the ball hits the mitt.

The kids go wild with excitement and laugh at Rex's feeble attempt at being on time. They'd never personally seen a pitch over 90 miles per hour outside of a big stadium, and hitting it is a whole'nother thing. Spence even musters up a smile, as Coach Gray adds a subtle "Strike two," soft enough to not embarrass the kid, since all his teammates were now making jokes at his expense, but loud enough for Rex to still hear.

Rex chimes in... "Alright. I've got this now," and throws in a little swagger, as if he's trying to psyche himself up.

Spence then looks over at Coach Gray, and without saying anything, he says everything about the next pitch.

Rex is still grandstanding in the box when Spence puts both feet on top of the rubber, slowly takes one step back with his left foot while bringing both arms over his head, plants his right foot in front of the rubber, and pushes off while striding toward the plate in a powerful motion, his arm soon following…

Everything about his intentions and actions screams "fastball" as Rex, having started extremely early this time, sees the ball out of his hand coming straight for his head, and instinctively drops the bat, before falling backwards to the ground. The pitch then breaks over the middle of the plate for strike three…

The kids go wild and storm the mound towards Spence, jumping up and down at what they'd seen. Rex looks at the coach and smiles, before dusting himself off and walking out to the mound to congratulate him.

"Okay… Okay… Maybe I can learn a thing or two from you."

Spence shakes his hand and brings him in for a hug…

Coach Gray comes out to the mound to say, "It ain't fair to be able to throw that hard AND have a curve ball that breaks like that. I've always thought it was your best pitch and that you should throw it more."

***

The evenings that follow are better than the one that had Spence jonesing for fix and risking a backslide into dependence upon the bottle. There are still headaches, tremors, and stomach cramps to deal with, but nothing remotely close to what he was experiencing on that particular night.

He's still curious about the stranger appearing when he did though. Being an unabashed drunk that abused alcohol on a daily basis kinda explained it beforehand. But him showing up nearly two weeks after sobering up had him questioning everything – especially considering that all he did was console him instead of taking him to some distant point in his life that led to where he is now. There was no lesson to learn and no task to complete. It was as if he actually cared about him.

Hearing Christa's voice in the middle of it all was also confusing. Spence is acutely aware that just the thought of overhearing her voice had him crying out in despair, apparently touching a spot in his heart that he thought he'd suppressed long ago.

When he's not attending an AA meeting, coaching the kids, or helping-out the Waters during his free time, he can usually be found shoring-up a shortcoming in or around his mobile home. Dan and Joy are there nearly every day, while Spence is at work, cleaning up, replacing subfloors, addressing roof leaks, and adding furniture that his mom finds "on sale" at the local hip furniture stores.

And tonight Spence, himself, is busy working on a task at home as he indulges in the luxury of watching cable programming on his brand new television set. As it turns out, when you're not spending hundreds of dollars a week on booze and cigarettes, there's usually money left over to purchase the things you've never been able to before.

The project that he's undertaking isn't sprucing up the house though. Instead, he's busy with pen and paper, writing a letter to Christa. It's no coincidence that in doing so, his attention is diverted back and forth between the words he's putting down and a rerun of her favorite TV show from back in the day - The X Files.

Feeling nostalgic, he's drafted several copies over the last hour and then ripped them all to pieces, not exactly knowing how to put his thoughts into free-flowing words. But eventually he hits his stride and pens a note that's both from the heart and has no visible errors. He signs and folds it neatly, before placing it in an envelope, setting it on the coffee table in front of him, leaning back on the couch, extending both arms, and taking a deep breath.

For the first time in a long time, he's enjoying life and planning a future, instead of feeling despondent and disheartened.

***

The note sits on top of Spence's coffee table for a couple of months as he goes about his daily life. His parents have noticed it sitting there adorned with Christa's name on the envelope and have even considered trying to steam it open in an attempt to pry into his life, but have instead chosen to give it all to God and His perfect timing.

They're optimistic though that Spence's turnaround might ultimately lead to a reconciliation between the two of them. But they also understand that pushing it might have the opposite effect. It's something they've come to appreciate over the years – that well intentioned attempts to help with their son's decision-making often made him choose the opposite of what they had intended for him – which is why they choose instead to say nothing at all about her, even though they want it so badly for him.

Baseball season has since started for the boys and he has the pitching staff hitting on all cylinders, having only allowed an average of 1.5 earned runs over the first dozen or so games. The hitting hasn't yet caught up to the pitching, and Coach Gray gives all the credit in local interviews to Spence. Interestingly enough, and in a strange turn of events, Spence has already been approached about a paid assistant coaching position at Brandon High School next year, which is ironically Joshua's Alma Mater.

But Spence is focused on the here and now, using the Alcoholics Anonymous mantra of "one day at a time" in every aspect of his daily life and decision making.

Speaking of AA, he's still attending the meetings twice a week and his longings for respite in the form of whiskey, beer, or cigarettes are more controlled than ever. Dave has also counseled Spence through another process that he must complete regarding the program. Part of the twelve steps of recovery promoted by Alcoholics Anonymous is identifying those you've wronged in the past because of alcoholism and, where appropriate and safe to do so, making amends with them.

That noted, Joy eventually notices that the letter is gone while sprucing-up his mobile home one day and calls Dan over to let him know. She's giddy with excitement and, with her fingers crossed, her husband has to remind her that their son must make his own choices on his own timeline.

"Oh... You're no fun," she giggles.

As for the note, itself, Spence has taken it and placed it underneath the visor of his truck, all while making the road that Christa lives on a permanent part of the route both to and from pretty much anywhere he goes.

Eventually on one Friday morning, and he's not sure exactly why, he decides to pull into her apartment complex and considers wedging the envelope inside her door. It's still dark outside because Spence has now made it a habit of getting up and exercising in the early mornings, eating a good breakfast, and being the first one into work. He gets out of his truck and walks up with the intention of doing so, but holds it in his hand for a few more minutes, pondering the contents...

"Christa... I hope you and the children are doing well. I've been thinking a lot lately and taking a good look within. What I've found isn't pretty. It's ugly. I've asked God for forgiveness and found His Grace to be overwhelming. I wanted to reach out to say that I'm sorry for all that I've put you through and humbly ask for your forgiveness. For what it's worth, you deserved better than me and what I put you through. I also wanted you to know that I've never stopped loving you. I just stopped loving myself. [signed] Spence."

He then places the letter in the door and walks away.

twenty-one – reformed

It's later that same Friday evening and Spence is sitting on a bucket in front of the entrance to the dugout along the first base line. He's wearing a full baseball uniform with a short sleeve "batting jacket" embroidered with the Forest Hill High School emblem around his upper chest. In only a couple of months' time, he's personally transformed himself from a rather timid looking wannabe assistant that couldn't quite fill out his baseball pants into a bold signal caller that appears as if he's only slightly older than the players he coaches, and in much better physical shape.

His team has had a surprising season so far that nobody really saw coming, aside from perhaps Coach Gray. And even then, one might say they've surpassed what he ever thought they would do thus far into the season.

Tonight's opponent is Gulfport High School. They are and have a history of being a baseball powerhouse. They're ranked number one in the state, top ten in the nation, and have yet to lose a game this year. They're in the tri-city area for the weekend to play two games: One tonight against Forest Hill and another tomorrow in Clinton.

Spence has saved his ace, Tyler O'Dowd, for this game, and it's paid off so far. Gulfport has tagged a couple of balls pretty hard to the warning track, but by pitching around their two best hitters, he's managed to leave them frustrated and stranded on base, only mustering one run across the plate.

And to contrast this Coach Gray has made the opposing pitcher, no slouch himself, work himself high into the pitch count by instructing the kids to not swing until they have two strikes. This strategy has also worked out. After getting a few leadoff walks and then stealing second base, he's content with bunting them over to third and, when the time is right, squeezing them home.

Six full innings into the game and with the score now 2-1 in favor of Forest Hill, the two teams are heading into the top of the last inning.

The first batter of the inning again flies out to the warning track – his second time doing so this game – and the second one rolls one over to the shortstop, who throws it to first base in time to get him.

There's now two outs and the three-hole hitter is up to bat. Spence calls for an off-speed pitch and he swings at the first offering, lining it over the first baseman's head and into the corner for a stand-up triple – the tying run now on third base and the four-hole hitter stepping up to the dish.

Spence stands up and calls timeout, before walking out to the mound. His pitcher has thrown more than one hundred pitches now and he has someone else warming up that he doesn't trust in this situation. He brings the infield into the conference with the pitcher and catcher…

"You've pitched a great game. Don't worry, I'm not taking you out. This has nothing to do with your abilities or what I think you can do. It's me sticking to our gameplan and not letting their best hitters beat us. One of them just hit a triple. We're not going to give the other two the chance…"

He then looks at the catcher…

"We're going to intentionally walk the next two batters…"

The kids interrupt him by groaning…

"Listen to me. This is their fourth time around in the batting order facing Tyler. Statistically they are due for a big hit. This is our best chance to win this game. Our BEST chance…"

The kids come around to his logic and say, "Let's do this!"

Spence walks back to the dugout, sits down on the bucket, and turns his head and smiles at Coach Gray, before winking and sarcastically saying… "This is what you pay me the big bucks for."

And as he says it with a smirk, the catcher, still standing tall behind the plate as the clean-up hitter steps into the box looking like he wants to hit, extends his right arm…

Everyone boos as Spence smiles. Even some in the home-team stands jeer, but most are just asking each other the obvious question of "Why are we putting the winning run on base!?"

Coach Gray even says as much, and Spence just smiles.

After walking the clean-up hitter, the next one steps up and the catcher, after looking over at Spence to confirm, again stands tall and extends his right arm…

The crowd then goes nuts with the booing and jeering. Now everyone on both sides is disagreeing with the strategy. Coach Gray stands up, obviously frustrated and in agreement with them, and steps into the dugout, essentially leaving Spence on an island by himself out in front of the home team's stands.

After intentionally walking his second batter in a row, loading the bases, and hearing the crowd, the pitcher then looks over at his pitching coach, who now feels compelled to walk out to the first base line, but not across it, and briefly reassure the kid – while offering more encouragement…

"You've got this…"

Tyler watches the batter step into the box as he toes the rubber, comes set, looks the runner back at third, and strides toward the plate…

Off-speed, the sixth batter in the line-up swings early as the umpire makes a "Strike" gesture with his hand.

Spence yells out "Good!" – knowing that he was sitting on a fastball.

The next pitch, a fastball, comes in about waist high and a bit inside. "Ball."

Spence throws his hands up in the air, really wanting that call.

"Where was that, Blue!? Up?"

Spence is totally into the game and lobbying for his player on the mound, who's thrown way more pitches than his coach's liking.

The next pitch, again off-speed, is maybe a bit off the outside corner of the plate – but it's called "Strike two." Spence smiles, while understanding that he probably prompted that call with his previous actions to the pitch beforehand, as the opposing coach standing next to third base now throws his own arms up in the air in disbelief.

The next pitch is obviously low, bouncing into the catcher's mitt for ball two, the count now two balls and two strikes. The kid in the box digs in and Tyler delivers off-speed again for a "ball" heading for the dirt, but the batter check swings. An appeal to first base is unsuccessful and the count is now full…

Spence doesn't want to throw him a fastball, but he doesn't have much of a choice in the matter. He knows that with two outs and the bases loaded, the runners will be going on the next pitch, needing either a strike or a ball actually batted into play somewhere to either win or have a chance at winning.

Predictably, it's a fastball down the middle to inner half of the plate and the batter turns on it, hitting a towering shot to left field as the opposing fans start going wild, but then hooking about twenty feet left of the foul pole and landing nearly 75 to 100 feet on the other side of the fence…

The batter, rounding first base, jumps into the air and falls to the ground in disbelief, as Spence looks over at Coach Gray with a smile, before turning to the stands and seeing many of the parents giving him "what-for" regarding his controversial decision making.

He knows that he got away with one as the batter steps back into the box…

"Time."

The third base coach gestures for time to be called and the umpire grants it. And as the opposing coach is talking to the batter and his runners that are on base, Spence walks out to the first base line and brings his catcher and pitcher in. He looks at all the infielders and motions for them to stay where they are, telling them to get the easiest out on a ball that's put into play, while also reminding them that the runners will be going on the pitch – thereby making first base the likely best option. He then looks at the pitcher…

"Tyler… Are you having fun yet?"

"I was until he smoked that 'nuke' that went foul…"

"Tyler… Remember when I showed you how to throw the deuce?"

The kid nods his head. He'd spent several of the early practices showing the kids how he used to throw the curve ball. This particular one, although his best pitcher, hadn't quite mastered the technique, so it wasn't in his current repertoire of pitches.

"Well… We need it for a strike right here. Look at me, Tyler… Just throw it hard so that it will break for a strike and fool him. If you throw it too softly it will dive into the dirt and potentially walk him. Overhanded and as hard as you can yank it. I think you can do it. I believe in you. Just one more strike and it's over. He won't even swing at it if you throw it just like I described. Trust me."

Spence then sits back down on the bucket and doesn't even send in a sign to the catcher. The pitch soon comes in high out of the hand, making the hitter buckle, bend backwards, and give up on it. It's the most beautiful curve ball that drops in for what surely must be a called strike three, and Spence bounces off his bucket and heads over, jumping clear across the chalk-line towards his pitcher with a fist-pump, before it's even called by the umpire… "Attaboy!!!"

The batter doesn't even turn to look at the umpire and the third base coach immediately spins back toward the dugout. The music soon starts playing really loud, as he high fives the pitcher and all of the infielders, before turning to his own hometown crowd and motioning for them to get up and be louder for the kids, who just knocked off the number one team in the state of Mississippi. The players then gather at the first base bag and walk across the infield to shake hands with the opposing team, before coming back around and stopping just in front of the dugout, where Coach Gray is waiting. He tells them just how proud he is and then defers to his pitching coach. Spence takes a bit of time before speaking and uses it to quickly scan and look at every single player's face.

"This was indeed a team win. Coach Gray had a strategy for offense and scratching a run or two across the plate and I had one for pitching. But our plans don't work unless you execute them for us. And tonight you did so to perfection."

He then points over to the Gulfport team that's having their own post-game conference around the third base area…

"If we try to go toe to toe with that team over there, not only do they beat us every single time, but we likely get 'run-ruled.' But… Don't miss this… Whether it's with baseball or in life… When you have a plan and you stick to it, even when the circumstances around you begin changing and those surrounding you say 'You should do this or that…' When you take a deep breath and stick to what you know, without falling into the trap of temptation… Well, then it will be much rarer that you are sitting over here with the regret that you didn't see it all the way through. The plan, that is… Thank you for trusting us as coaches. And well done. Let's close it out…"

The team then comes together in a circle of hands to chant "One. Two. Three… Rebels!" one last time, before they all start grabbing rakes and packs of synthetic dirt and begin patching up the parts of field that had wear and tear from the game. A news reporter finds Spence around the entrance to the dugout and asks him for a short interview. He obliges…

"Coach Tay…"

[interrupting] "Please, call me Spence."

"Okay. Spence… You just handed Gulfport High School its first loss of the season. What can you most attribute your win to tonight?"

"It's just the kids, Jerry. We can coach until we're blue in the face, but if the kids don't perform to their capabilities, it's all for nothing. And tonight they did exactly what we asked them to do…"

"Speaking of that... There was a point in tonight's game that you, as a coach, were being booed by the fans of both teams for putting the winning run on base..."

"That's right, Jerry. But we had a plan going into the game to not let their better hitters beat us, and we stuck to it until the very end..."

"I must admit it was fun to watch. I've never quite seen it play out like it did..."

"Yeah... [smiling] For a split-second there, when he tagged that ball foul down the left field line, I thought for just a moment... But fate was on our side tonight."

"So how do you come up with these game 'plans' against teams like this?"

"Well, for me it's easy. Ever since I was young, I hated to lose more than I enjoyed winning ballgames. It might sound strange, but winning just felt normal. Losing though... It just stung really bad and stayed with me. And Coach Gray and I make a great team. He thinks from the perspective of 'How can we win this game?' and I counter with 'How can we avoid losing it?' And tonight that's what happened. We got two hits and had a total of five base runners. On the scoreboard you'll see that we were victorious. But when you look closely at the box score tomorrow, you'll understand that somehow we didn't lose it. And again, that was our plan all along going into it."

"Well, congratulations. That was some of the best coaching that I've ever personally witnessed..."

"Thank you, Jerry. God bless..."

The teams and parents soon disperse, as the parking lot slowly empties. Coach Gray walks over to Spence, who by now is always the last one to leave, and reminds his assistant to turn off the lights, before congratulating him once again on being an outstanding coach.

Spence sits there in the dugout looking over the scorebook, wondering to himself how they actually won that game, and he smiles at the thought of it. He then walks over to the light switch that's on one of the poles and pulls it down, watching the field go completely dark.

There're only one or two dimly lit lights on in the parking lot now and the visibility is marginal, at best, as he takes a couple of equipment bags, throws them upon his shoulder, and makes his way towards his truck that's parked in the back corner.

And as he approaches it, he can make out that there are actually two vehicles together and a person standing in front of his truck, awaiting his arrival. It's so dark that he can't tell that it's Christa until he's about twenty feet away. He then smiles as he walks up to her…

"Oh my God… Your teeth!"

He keeps smiling big, as he sets his bags down…

"Yeah… They were a gift from mom and dad."

"They're amazing!"

"Thanks."

She looks so beautiful. She's got on a pair of shorts and a matching top, while her hair appears as if she's just stepped out of a luxury salon. And to be honest, she doesn't look like she's aged a minute since their high school days. But by now he's right up on her and it's a bit awkward because they're close enough to be touching, kissing even, but instead the two of them just keep smiling and conversing…

"Where are the kids?"

"My mom and dad took them…"

"And they knew that you were coming to see me!?"

She giggles and says, "Heck no!"

Spence laughs too and replies, "Well, I can't blame them…"

"Great game, 'Coach.'"

"How long have you been here?"

"I saw the whole thing. I'd forgotten how much I loved baseball. But my favorite part was always seeing you out there on the field, and tonight sure brought back a whole lot of memories."

"Yeah. It's bringing me back, too. I'll tell ya… I can still pitch, Christa. I went twelve years without touching a baseball and struck out our best hitter on three pitches…"

"Oh, I believe it. You were always so amazing."

"Do you want to go grab a bite to eat with me?"

"No. I just want to stay here with you and talk…"

Spence smiles at her and nods… "You got the letter?"

"I did."

Spence smiles even bigger…

"I've been crying all day long…"

He now stops smiling and shows concern… "I'm so sorry, Christa. I never meant to…"

And at that point she strikes him in the chest as hard as she can, surprising him and pushing him backwards a bit…

"Christa!?"

She then hits him again, and again, and again, over and over and over five to six times, each time a little more forcefully and with him backing up a bit more, until he finally grabs her by the shoulders and pulls her in close for an embrace, at which point she breaks down crying, and so does he…

"You hurt me…" – as she continues to wail.

"I know I did, baby. I'm so sorry. Can you please forgive me?"

She continues to cry into his chest for the better part of the next three to four minutes, as he caresses her hair and rubs her back, begging her for forgiveness…

And then she finally looks up at him, her eyes now swollen and with her mascara running…

"Spencer Taylor… I have always loved you… And I've always dreamed of a life together with you. It didn't matter to me if we grew old here in our hometown or in some major city somewhere with you playing baseball. I just wanted to be with you…"

Three…

Two…

One…

Pause…

[there's several seconds of inaudible mumbling in the background]

And suddenly there's a blinding flash of light that pierces through the twilight of introspective thought. It's both irritating and disconcerting. It's also unsettling insofar as being abruptly awakened from an intense dream, caught somewhere between what's real and what isn't, with rational thoughts initially supporting both worlds as reality.

Spence can overhear the windchimes at his front door, but it's strange because he's not at home… And soon he's there, alone, standing in that same dimly lit parking lot where he was just holding onto Christa. But now it's just he and his pickup truck…

He begins to yell…

"Christa!"

"Christa!"

For a moment it all felt so good, but then…

"Spence."

Spence is jump-scared by the stranger, as he quickly turns around to find him standing there…

"Wait… Where's Christa!?"

"Spencer. Christa is fine. Don't worry…"

Spence, still in the parking lot and now standing alongside the stranger, again looks all around and calls out for Christa…

"Spence… Calm down. I'm going to redirect you here. You can see and hear me right now and think that you're totally awake, but you're actually in a very deep trance-like state of being. A hypnotic state, if you will. Listen, the windchimes you've been hearing were for when I had to personally show up and assist you at refocusing. And at one point I also had to help you work through a tough night of alcohol withdrawals and delirium tremens. Spence. You've been on a long journey and I'm the one that's guided you there. You've had both highs and lows, wins and losses, and come through on the other side a significantly changed man. I've walked you through a life that you've never known, but one that's been very real to you somewhere deep inside. So in a few seconds, when I count to 3, and ring these chimes, you will then be totally awake and aware. You may or may not remember much about what we've talked about. But hopefully your subconscious mind is forever changed. Are you ready?"

Spence is listening, but he is also still looking around the parking lot for Christa…

"Spence… I said you've been under a deep hypnotic state… Take a good look around if you want… But you won't find Christa here any longer because this, son… This is not your reality."

Spence is confused and he continues to look around, almost frantically.

"You're not real."

"Oh, I'm very real. And when I count to three you are going to wake up a changed man…"

"One…"

"Two…"

(windchimes) "Three…"

Once again there's a blinding light, as if someone flipped on a switch too quickly and then began dimming everything into focus.

"Welcome back, Spence. You've been in a deep hypnotic state for the past four-plus hours."

The person speaking to him is the same stranger, black, long beard and everything, that's been appearing out of nowhere. He's dressed in the same outfit and sitting in a chair directly in front of him.

"How do you feel?"

Spence thinks about it for a second, much like when a dream feels so authentic that you wake up and for a split second think it was real, and he begins to slowly understand, once again, that his reality is much different.

His wife, Christa, is sitting in the same room…

His wife! Christa! She's sitting in the corner with a very concerned look, just over the shoulder of the would-be stranger.

The stranger looks back behind him, nods to Christa, and she gets out of her chair and walks over with tears in her eyes, before kissing him on the lips.

"Welcome back, baby."

Christa then looks at Dr. Olgivy…

"I'm assuming the same rules as the last time?"

Dr. Olgivy nods affirmatively.

Spence looks on in a confused state.

"We can perhaps be a little more direct with him this time, Christa…"

Dr. Olgivy then pauses for about ten seconds as if he's pondering whether or not to ask the next question…

"Spencer. Do you know who I am?"

Spences nods affirmatively towards Dr. Olgivy and then turns and squeezes Christa's hand.

"And do you remember why you're here?"

Again, he nods yes...

"I figured so. There's often a bit more clarity after the second hypnosis session. But that still doesn't clear him to drive. I will go over my notes tonight and submit my report with my recommendations by tomorrow afternoon."

"Wait... Is there a chance that he still might not be cleared to play?"

"I don't like to give yes or no answers so quickly, Christa. There's no such thing in what I do. It's not just black and white. There're gray areas that are up to interpretation. I like to go through both sessions thoroughly, compare my notes, and then write my report. And while I like both of you, I'm not bound by my emotional response to Spence's story. I'm only bound by my professional opinion of the treatment that I provided and his reaction to it. Of course we've made lots of headway here. But to give you a yes or no answer right here and now? I'm sorry, but I just can't do that."

"Wait just a minute. So you're telling me that I just watched my husband relive a childhood trauma, try to kill himself, convince himself that he no longer loves me, mourn a friend that he never even lost, go through alcohol withdrawals while calling out my name when he isn't even an alcoholic, and then fall in love with me all over again when he never even lost me in the first place – and then you're going to sit there and tell me that what he did over the last few hours, not to even mention the entire first session nightmare that he endured, might not be good enough for you!?"

"Mrs. Taylor... Don't do th..."

"Mrs. Taylor!? Mrs. Tay!?"

Christa abruptly grabs her purse and Spence's hand and storms out the treatment room door toward the side exit. Dr. Olgivy doesn't even attempt to follow. By now it's dark outside, and as she opens the door, the two of them are immediately swarmed by paparazzi and cameras going off in their faces to the point that they're completely still and unable to move forward or backwards.

"Spence: Is it true that you hit Joshua Waters in the head during a high school game and that it required a hospitalization?"

"Spence: Did you hit Joshua Waters on purpose back then? How about Yuli?"

And just then Christa feels a huge tug on her arm that's coming from the other side of the wall of people, sending both her and Spence tumbling into them so hard that a few of them actually fall to the ground. It's Abby, who's come back to pick them up, and she's having none of it, while yelling at all the people to get a life.

"You two okay?"

"Yep."

"Good. Let's go." She then looks toward the paparazzi and other reporters and tells them they should be ashamed of themselves.

They get into Sergei's SUV and drive back to the house…

"Y'all done made me lose my religion on these people and now I'mma be on Entertainment Tonight showing my ass. We've got to get home though. The game's almost halfway over by now…"

twenty-two – optimistic

It's still a mess getting into the neighborhood as they drive by all the news trucks and reporters.

"You know… I've at least got to give these people a little more credit than the idiots back there because they are just looking for some info, and maybe a pic, and not just rammed all up your ass and invading your medical privacy."

Christa nods in agreement as they drive through the gate and pull into the neighbor's garage…

"Spence. You still planning on jumping the fence to get back home?"

"Abby?!"

The two of them burst out laughing, just thinking about the goings-on earlier in the day.

Spence and Christa thank Sergei and the three of them maneuver through the two backyard gates, before entering the house and saying hello to Dan, Joy, and the children. The game is on in the background and the Red Sox have the lead 5 runs to 4 in the top of the 7th inning.

Spence doesn't even stop to watch or ask, and instead goes straight back into the master bedroom and lays down on the bed.

"So… How was it!?"

"It was nearly as awful as before."

"And is he cleared to play yet?"

"We won't know anything until tomorrow afternoon. I'm going to go make sure that my husband is okay."

Christa hugs Abby and thanks her for being there like a true friend, before kissing her children and saying goodnight to both them and the in-laws. She then walks into the bedroom and he's sound asleep. Sawing logs. However you want to say it. He's exhausted and spent, so she just snuggles up closely, wraps her arms around him, and cries.

***

"Post-traumatic stress and sports. Tell me Dr. Phil… How does it occur? And what can be done about it?"

"Well, Oprah… As you know, this isn't necessarily my field of expertise, but I believe…"

Christa turns off the television, rolls her eyes in disgust, and looks at the clock. It's nearly 4pm on Thursday afternoon and Spence is still sleeping from the night before. It's no wonder though, considering that she saw him physically manifesting the symptoms of delirium tremens and severe muscle cramping while under hypnosis. It was so scary to watch that at one point she went against the rules and spoke up, while trying to make sure he was going to be okay, which only made things worse after Spence heard her, became confused, and began calling out her name. Dr. Olgivy was not a happy camper. But to his credit, he cared for Spence during the whole ordeal, giving him fluid to drink, and massaging his cramped muscles. She could only imagine what he was experiencing while under hypnosis because the scenes he'd describe to the psychiatrist were both vivid and detailed, like you were almost right there alongside of him as he traversed a different reality than what he knows. One thing she did appreciate, however, was the sweet note that she got to hear him read about her when he was under. She blushed from her side of reality and appreciated the fact that in both universes he's now experienced, the two of them end up together in the end as soulmates, thinking to herself that it has to say something about his self-worth to his subconscious brain.

And just then the phone rings with the caller ID registering from the Tau Center. Knowing it's Dr. Olgivy, she takes a deep breath and answers the phone...

"Hello."

"Christa..."

"I prefer Mrs. Taylor..."

She can hear a long, genuine belly laugh from Dr. Olgivy on the other line, before clearing his throat and continuing...

"Mrs. Taylor... First and foremost, I must inform you that the two of you left so quickly last night that I forgot to give Spence back his firearm. Being a legal carry, I've turned it into the local police district, and they have told me that they will run it through their system, before returning it to you at your residence. That noted, I've also made and submitted my final report on Spence's treatment while under my care to the Boston Red Sox organization, to Major League Baseball, and to the MLB Player's Association, and recommended that he be allowed to resume playing starting tomorrow – with no restrictions. Please tell Spence that I'm rooting for him and to make me proud."

Christa begins to cry, thinking to herself that she's cried more in the last week than she has in her entire life.

"And while I've got you on the phone, let me address some of your concerns from last night, when you left in such a hurry. As I see it, during my direct care – and looking at the very core of his being – your husband found acceptance and forgiveness in the name of Jesus Christ, conquered an addiction that had a stronghold in front of an entire community, and recommitted and reconnected with his soulmate after fighting seemingly insurmountable odds that he had made up in his own head. I mean think about it. Was there anything that you saw about his reaction to hitting Yuli that was rational at all? No. That's because it came from deep within, an unease at the bare root of his subconscious mind, and we went in there, pulled back some curtains, and attacked it where it thought it was safe. But do you want to know what really matters to me? All of that was great. But do you want to know what my main job was while on retainer? It was simply to get Spence to somehow remember what it was like to throw a pitch with confidence and without fear. That's it. Unfortunately, all the rest of what you witnessed was standing in the way."

"Thank you, Dr. Olgivy."

"Spence faced it all like the true warrior that he is. I know that I pushed him to the limit, but I did it knowing what a tough son-of-a-bitch he is. What you saw, though… I have to tell you… I wouldn't do that to just anyone. I believe Spence is ready. And I must say that 'I've got a good feeling about all of this…'"

"Praise Jesus…"

"Oh… And Chris… Uh… Mrs. Taylor… I just want to also say that every man deserves to have a wife like you in his corner. Well done."

Christa hangs up the phone and looks at both Abby and Joshua, who just walked through the door…

"Well?"

"YES!!!"

"Wait, he can play!?"

"Yes!"

The three of them all hug it out in the kitchen, as Christa and Abby continue dancing around for a few seconds thereafter…

"No restrictions…"

"Well, where is he? Meat!?"

"Joshua! He's still aslee…"

And just then Spence walks into the room from the master bedroom and Joshua picks him up and gives him a huge bear hug.

"Holy crap, Meat! I've missed you so much!"

Spence smiles, as Joshua puts him back down.

"Let me see your eye, fool!?"

"Oh, it's fine. You should've seen what my eye did to his fist."

"Who was it?"

"That doesn't matter. What matters most is that the team misses you and, most importantly, we need you."

"Who won game five?"

Joshua looks over at Abby and Christa…

"He's been asleep since we got home last night, before the game was over, and I didn't want to wake him up."

"Damn, Meat! What in the heck did that head-doctor dude do to you!?"

Abby chimes in, trying to calm her husband down… "It was pretty involved, Joshua. He's been put through the wringer trying to get back out on the field with you."

"And now you're cleared to play again, right!?"

[looking at Christa] "I don't know… Am I?"

"You are!" – declares Christa, while giving Abby a playful high five. "Dr. Olgivy just called to let us know."

"So, what happened last night in San Fran, Joshua?"

"Same as before, Meat. We couldn't hold a late lead, and now we've got to win two at Fenway to take the series."

Spence looks on with concern. Another late loss by the team has surely added to the media firestorm that's just a few hundred yards up the street and beyond the gate.

***

It's now late in the afternoon on Thursday and it's been another "travel" day for the two teams. More than 3,000 miles away from each other, the Red Sox left San Francisco early this morning and Skip has given them the rest of the day off to regroup, thinking at this point that an additional practice will likely only fatigue them.

The series is now back in Boston for game six on Friday and, if necessary, game seven the following evening. The Red Sox are hoping to force a deciding game seven, while the Giants are simply content with closing it out tomorrow night and perhaps flying back for a parade in San Francisco on Saturday.

One thing is for sure though, if it does go to a final game seven, there will be starting pitchers on just three and four days rest available for both teams, each manager having already confirmed as much.

And although Spence has indeed been cleared to pitch, which is huge for Boston, the Red Sox nor Major League Baseball has officially released that information out to the media just yet.

twenty-three – clarity

The Waters have invited the entire clan over to their house for the evening, including Dan and Joy, so that they can also visit with Joshua's parents, who just flew into town. The pair don't seem to notice Spence hugging them both just a little more tightly than usual and are oblivious to his most recent closer connection to them while he was under hypnosis.

There isn't really anything special planned, other than Joshua grilling up some burgers and all of them just sitting around enjoying the company of one another, while the kids frolic around in the pool.

Joshua's parents, again unaware of their deep connection with Spence in his alternate reality, start telling stories from back in the day about Joshua and everyone begins laughing out loud, as the tales of his practical jokes and shenanigans grow.

Mrs. Waters then decides to share one particular story that happened in the aftermath of her son being hit by Spence's errant pitch…

"Now, we were very worried during the ambulance ride because he'd been knocked out cold, and when he regained consciousness, he was still confused about where he was."

Christa glances over at Spence, who's been laughing along at all these tales, while listening intently, and she initially considers butting-in and stopping the story right there. But she also loves Mr. and Mrs. Waters a lot and doesn't want to appear rude – especially considering that they only have a basic grasp on the subject of Spence's recent struggles. She then looks over at Abby, who's sitting across the room, but on the same wavelength as her and ready to step in. However, they both decide to just see where Joshua's mom is going with this…

"And when we got to the Emergency Room, they immediately scanned his head, before coming back to us about fifteen minutes later to say they couldn't find any bleeding. That was surprising because the hospital had already arranged for him to be transferred out via helicopter and informed both of us that he had a neurosurgery team on standby in Memphis, just waiting for his arrival, before rushing him back for emergent surgery. They acted as if the CT Scan they were doing prior to transferring him out was just a formality that would save precious minutes and seconds once he got to Memphis."

Mr. Waters then steps in to help move the story along…

"So instead, they called off the Life-Flight and diagnosed him with a bad concussion. Now, at this point, even though he had a headache, he was awake, lucid, and starting to ask relevant questions, but they still wouldn't let us take him home. Rather, the doctors wanted to keep him overnight because they couldn't believe that he didn't have a brain bleed after taking a fastball to the head…"

Abby winces at how casually he just said that and considers interrupting, but doesn't.

"… I tried to tell them that the Waters family males all had hard heads… But they wanted to make sure they weren't missing anything, so they woke him up every hour, on the hour, throughout the night to do neuro-checks, and then decided to scan him again the next morning, for good measure…"

Christa remains worried about where this story is headed…

"Well, the next thing you know we were there in the hospital for the next five to six nights because the neurologist on his case was claiming that he now had to fly in 'this' and 'that' specialist from all over the country to be certain that every precaution was taken. We were starting to get upset. We really wanted to trust the doctors. But Joshua, who was on some type of protocol that had him in a dark room with limited interaction and absolutely no visitors outside of his family, was beginning to get restless and was ready to go home. Another thing that we weren't being told at the time was that the Red Sox, who were already planning on taking our son in the upcoming draft, were scheming behind the scenes, using the local neurologist to consult with, and eventually sending in their own doctors to come personally evaluate their potential prized prospect – word having reached them from the scout at the game that things didn't initially look so good. Which is fine. But we must've seen like five or six different doctors from all over the country, and nobody would tell us anything definitive. We were just getting the runaround."

Mrs. Waters then takes back over describing the story once again…

"So, all the while the Boston Red Sox organization had been pulling the strings of the attending neurologist until they were ultimately satisfied that Joshua was going to be okay. And finally, nearly six days into his hospital stay, we got discharge orders for the next morning. So, on that last night at the hospital, we were both standing outside with Abby late in the evening, hugging and seeing her off, and lo and behold who walks straight up to us but Spencer Taylor, himself…"

"Oh, I think I remember that…" – says Spence.

Dan and Joy both verbalize about never having heard this story.

Mr. Waters then chimes in…

"Yeah… Ole Spence didn't look all that well. You could tell that he was still distraught about what had happened. He apologized and then asked if he could see Joshua. Well, his mom and I knew that Joshua was just fine, but we still wanted to go in and ask him if it was okay for Spence to come inside for a short visit, just in case he wasn't up for it. I remember telling him that the boy looked like he was worried sick. So, anyway, Joshua says with a straight face and concerned look, 'Yes, absolutely let him in,' so I went back outside and told Spence what his room number was… And that he was expecting him. I mentioned nothing at all about his condition because I didn't think that I needed to, since he was getting discharged the next morning…"

Joshua then interrupts and starts laughing…

"Now this is where I've gotta pick up the story. I knew I had about five minutes before he showed up, and there was a hospital supply room directly across from mine. So, I ran over and grabbed everything that I could out of it… Tubes, bandages, tape, oxygen masks… You name it, I took it. I then frantically took the long cushiony bandages and wrapped my head up like I was wearing a turban. I taped three or four IVs to my arms, put some fluids up on the poles at my bedside, and ran an oxygen nasal cannula into my nose. Then, at the very last minute, when I heard the double doors to the unit opening up and then his voice at the nurses station, I took one of those plastic suction sticks like they have at the dentist and stuck one end in my mouth and hooked the other end up to a suction line, which resulted in this horrible wet sucking sound from steadily vacuuming up all the spit in my mouth. And so finally I laid back in my bed, closed my eyes, and tried my darndest to keep the straightest face that I could when I heard him walk into the room…"

"Oh, I definitely remember this part…" – Spence says while smiling.

"So anyway… Meat walks in and the first thing that I hear him say is 'Oh no…' as he starts to breathe heavily. Then he pulls up a chair and sits next to me, and I can hear him sniffling, I think… But to be honest, the suction thingy in my mouth is so loud now that I can't hardly hear a thing AND, get this… It's starting to actually hurt, like it's ulcerating the underside of my tongue or sumthin…"

The group all starts to laugh…

"And then he starts crying and saying that he's sorry for this and that. As for myself, it's all that I can do to not burst out laughing. But I'm also thinking 'Come on, Meat. You can't be this gullible to not realize that I'm faking here!?' I was wanting him to hurry up and figure it out for selfish reasons because my mouth was hurting from the suction and my nose was starting to burn from all the oxygen blowing in it, which I had turned up really high for more of a sound effect, I guess… I know it sounds mean, but I was a kid just trying to have a little fun after being couped up for five or six days…."

And then Spence speaks up…

"Alright… So let me finish this story from my vantage point. I sat there for about ten solid minutes, pouring my heart out to this guy, and praying out loud for his well-being, all while thinking that he's on death's door, when his mom and dad both walk into the room with a confused look, wondering what the heck is going on…"

By this time everyone has busted out laughing, but Spence continues with the story…

"So Mr. Waters sees me sitting there with tears falling from my eyes and then he looks over at his son laying in the hospital bed with all of these bandages, IVs, and tubes coming out of his nose and mouth, and he immediately yells 'Joshua!?!?!?'"

This is the first time that Christa, Abby, Dan, or Joy have ever heard of this story, and they are all bent over in hysterics that Joshua would go so far as to put all these tubes inside himself in an attempt to appear really sick…

"And so Joshua startles and starts shaking like he's having a seizure or something. Then, when he can't hold it anymore because his dad is on to what he's doing and is now reaching across the bed attempting to pull out all his bogus lines, he immediately starts cracking up and spitting out all the tubes and stuff. Well… Me, foolish and having apparently taken the bait, hook, line, and sinker… What do I do!? I'll tell you what I do… I start freaking out and calling for all the nurses to hurry-up and get in there to help him because now his own father is tryna kill'em… So the nurses all spring-up from their chairs and hurry-in to check on what's going on, at which point he finally just sits up in the bed, as pretty as you please, turns to look at me, and in the calmest voice says, 'Wassup, Meat?'"

Mr. Waters interrupts, "Yeah. Those nurses were so upset with 'you' that they tabulated all the stuff 'you' grabbed off the shelf that night and added it onto the hospital bill that they sent 'me.'"

Spence chuckles and then looks at Joshua to ask…

"Joshua. Didn't you even grab a urine bag and pour Mountain Dew or something in it and then hang it from your bedside?"

Joshua responds, almost embarrassingly, but also proud that he was so clever…

"I did. There was other stuff, too that I can't quite remember. I was just thinking that I had about five minutes to try to make myself look really sick and… Well, I guess it worked," as he bursts out laughing…

"Oh. My. God. Just when I thought you couldn't have possibly been even more immature than what I remember…"

"Yep. And then you married me," as he makes a goofy face toward Abby.

Joshua then gets serious for a moment… "But… What came of that silly and awkward encounter though is what you see right here today." He then points to his best friend… "I had to convince Meat over there to go pitch in the State Championship tournament for his high school. Abby and I both made the trip to go see him play. And it was there that she got to meet Christa and the two of them hit it off. As a matter of fact, the four of us [pointing to the two wives] had an instant bond, doing lots of stuff together both before and after I was drafted by the Red Sox…"

He then looks over at his friend to say…

"Spencer… It may be a strange way to meet your best friend. But I'm here to tell you there are no accidents in this life. It was all meant to be. I want you to know that I love you. You're the brother that I never had, and I'll always have your back."

Abby and Christa tear up as the two of them bro-hug it out in front of everyone. It's also not lost on anyone that it was probably the first and last time they'd ever hear Joshua addressing his friend by his actual given name.

"Meat" had become a term of endearment that Joshua always used for Spence. He picked it up while watching the classic baseball movie "Bull Durham." Normally it is reserved for rookie players that have more physical talent than they do intellectual smarts. But it is also utilized for pitchers that tend to throw easy balls to hit right down the middle of the plate – often referred to as "meatballs." And while Spence was far from the literal definition of the slang word, he had become an easy target for its use, considering that Joshua had taken him yard at a distance of 400 feet in their last game facing one another.

A full twelve years together as best friends and never having once used his name…

Despite their wives and parents getting emotional at its use, the two of them hardly even notice as they pat each other on the back and disengage.

***

Spence and Christa decide it's time to leave and go about giving everyone a hug before doing so.

It's about 11:00pm and Dan and Joy have chosen to stay a bit longer to continue catching up with Joshua's parents. The kids are already tucked into bed, both sets having convinced their respective parents to agree to a sleepover at the Waters' house.

Notwen Avenue has sidewalks on both sides of the street; however, only one side is lighted. The Taylors strategically decide to walk on the unlit side. And after passing a few houses, they crest a small hill and can readily see all of lights from the news vehicles that are still busy staking out the gate.

"You ready?" – Christa asks with a playful giggle…

"Race ya!" – Replies Spence…

The two of them then dart across the street and through their front door…

"I won!"

"I opened the door for you."

"I entered the house first!"

"Whatever…"

They soon embrace in the foyer and Christa goes from playful to serious for a moment…

"Spence…" [now looking straight into his eyes] "How come you never told me the story about seeing Joshua at the hospital?"

"I don't know, really. It's like I'd forgotten it entirely, but when Mrs. Waters started telling it, I suddenly remembered."

"Do you think that your brain did something to compensate? Attempting to protect you? Like what Dr. Olgivy described to us?"

"Hmmm… Maybe so… Like Mr. Waters said, I was in a pretty bad place at that point. It was six days after I'd hit him and he was still in the hospital, so I was expecting the worst…"

"Did you go by yourself?"

"I did. Coach Gray had come over to the house a couple of nights before, wanting me to come back so I could pitch in the State Championship, and when I was reluctant, he said that he could arrange a visitation through Brandon High School's head coach, who was his [and my dad's] good friend…"

"But you still said no?"

"I did. And then a couple of nights later I decided to go up there on my own…"

"Not knowing anything about his condition, whatsoever?"

"When I walked into that hospital room, I had no idea of what to expect."

"Joshua can be so goofy sometimes."

"I know, right!?"

"Well, you weren't talking to me. I know that much. I came to see you and you were very withdrawn and mean. And as far as I knew you weren't even going to play, until your mom called me the night before to say that you had decided to play, and then asked if I wanted to ride along with them…"

"Yeah. When I told him that I wasn't going to play, in true Joshua form, he busted out with 'The hell you aren't!?'"

"And that was it?"

"Well, he spent several minutes telling me that if I wasn't going to do it for myself, then I at least had to do it for him. And then he just blurted out that he was getting discharged the next day and was coming to make sure that I actually made the trip and pitched..."

"And the rest, as they say, is history?"

"I guess so."

"I love my life, Spence Taylor, and that we've lived across the street from our best friends for nearly a decade."

"Yep. I've never even really thought about it, but if I hadn't gone up to the hospital on that night, then my life likely ends up eerily similar to the one I lived under hypnosis..."

"You're absolutely correct. The last thing you ever told me was that you didn't love me. That night definitely righted your ship..."

"Pinch me..."

"Why?"

"Because you're so beautiful that I have to be dreaming..."

"Oh my... That's straight cheese. But I love it..."

She then grabs his hand and leads him towards their bedroom...

"Let's get some sleep because you have TWO big games coming up...."

twenty-four – encouraging

It's Friday morning and it's game day. Christa is silently optimistic that Spence is closer to his normal self, seeing his reaction to both the stories told the night before and his playfulness with her on their stroll back home. The sheer nature of the one told by Joshua's mom – considering her casually mentioning Spence beaning her son in the head and their uncertainty during the ambulance ride to the hospital – had been enough to mentally trigger and derail the husband she's had over the past two to three weeks. But with him laughing and playing along with it, not to mention actually contributing his point of view that had everyone else bent over in stitches from laughing so hard, she suspects his subconscious mind has perhaps turned the corner. She also enjoys seeing him smile once again.

His never having shared that particular memory with her and apparently going as far as to block it from his own mind is both disturbing and fascinating at the same time. She's now even more impressed with Dr. Olgivy for hitting the nail on the head regarding Spence not having the successful career he's had based on talent, alone, and that his brain had likely been protecting him all along, up until the fallout from last batter he faced. That noted, she's now more hopeful than before that the treatment he endured will be worth it in the end.

The players are having lunch catered in the clubhouse under the stands at Fenway Park and are being asked to be there by noon. The game, itself, isn't until 7:30 pm tonight, but Skip wants to use the extra time to go over the gameplan with the players and provide all the necessary treatments for the nagging injuries that have added up, it having been a long season. He also wants to evaluate everyone, considering he's now in desperation mode and needing another win before even having a shot at being a world champion and hoisting the Commissioner's Trophy for the third time over the last decade.

Ledbetter has been a gamer so far, especially when taking his age into account, and is on tap to pitch in a deciding game seven, should they make it there. But in the meantime, he wants to know exactly what arms he has, and who appears to have the hot hand.

Spence, wearing dress pants and a sport coat, is waiting for Joshua to pick him up and take him to the ballpark. Christa and Abby will be riding together later on, after picking up their own respective parents at the airport, and plan on arriving closer to the scheduled game time – while all four sets of grandparents are content with watching tonight's game from the comforts of home and spoiling the grandchildren in the process.

Spence gives Abby, the kids, and his parents a kiss as Joshua is pulling into his driveway, and walks out the front door. He gets into the car with his friend and hears "Are you ready?"

Spence looks at him and nods affirmatively before saying, "Let's go finish what we started..."

"Right on!"

Joshua makes his way towards the neighborhood gate, prompting his friend to start laying his seat back.

"What are you doing?"

"I don't want the attention, Joshua. You get enough of it, as it is, without me."

"Meat... You're 'fixed' now! It's time to 'own' the attention you've been getting and maybe go looking for some endorsement deals or something."

Spence only laughs as he keeps reclining his seat back, now essentially all the way flat.

And just as the two of them are pulling out of the gate and beginning to make the turn onto the main road, Joshua suddenly stops the car and rolls down the windows…

[now pointing at the supposedly empty passenger side] "He's right here!"

"Joshua! What are you doing!?"

And of course, the media and the paparazzi start running over to where they are, screaming over one another, and asking questions…

"Taylor, is it true that you've been cleared to play!?"

"How's that make you feel, Spence!?"

"Joshua, does your head still hurt from getting hit in high school?"

He allows them to get a little bit closer and then speeds off, chuckling to himself…

"Sorry, Meat… I'm just having a little fun."

Spence just rolls his eyes and smirks, as he brings his seat back up and Joshua turns on the radio. It's a pregame ritual for him to play 80s hard rock and sing aloud at the top of his lungs. He's been doing it for years on his way to ballgames.

Spence takes out his wallet and opens it. Inside there's a compartment that is separate from the credit cards and cash, where he pulls out a tiny bag of dirt. He looks at it closely, while feeling the graininess from the outside of the thin plastic packaging, rolling it around between his thumb, index, and middle fingers. His mind then begins to drift…

"Taylor… Come see…"

Spence walks over while half dressed in baseball pants and an undershirt in preparation for his upcoming Saturday afternoon game in Pawtucket, Rhode Island. He plays for the Paw Sox, the Triple-A affiliate of the Boston Red Sox.

It's early September, 1993, and Spence has been phenomenal since being drafted. As a dominant sophomore pitcher that played in the most premier conference in college baseball against the best competition outside of the high professional leagues, and more recently a Golden Spikes Award winner – handed out annually to the best amateur baseball player in the United States – the Red Sox front office personnel, in desperate need of a shut-down closer to anchor all of the recent talent they'd acquired and justify the money spent, had implemented a plan to fast-track Taylor's ascension to "The Show," provided that he met or exceeded all the expectations that were placed on him.

Spence was unaware that this wasn't normal, even though Joshua stressed to him that it wasn't. Historically, all drafted rookies, especially out of high school, but also those taken from collegiate teams, go straight into developmental rookie ball for the remainder of the season in which they were taken. But Spence, having pitched very well in the Southeastern Conference against quality competition that were using very hot aluminum bats, also known as "Gorilla Ball," was assigned straight into Double-A ball with the New Britain Red Sox, where he quickly surpassed all expectations.

It was such a whirlwind of "move here and go there" after being drafted that he and Christa decided to ditch their plans for a big wedding and drive to Bristol on a midweek off-day, where Joshua and Abby met them, to get married by a Justice of the Peace – with plans of having a big reception the following off-season back in Jackson.

And after only a few weeks in New Britain, he was soon promoted to the Paw Sox, where again he outpaced any and all predictions of his ability.

"Step into my office, son."

Skip Jenkins is the current manager of Boston's Triple-A affiliate. He had once played twelve seasons for the Red Sox, making two All Star games, before age started to catch up to his body. Citing his love for the game and his loyalty to the organization that once took a chance on him, he transitioned into coaching within the lower developmental leagues, where promotion after promotion has now landed him in Triple-A Pawtucket.

Not only this, but he's also currently on the short list of candidates that Michael Thompson, the General Manager of the Red Sox, is considering to be the steward of all the recent talent that has been acquired by Boston – not at all happy with the present manager and hoping for a return on investment of all the trades made and money spent over the last several years trying to build a team to contend with the Yankees.

He's also been an unsuspecting beneficiary of the talent surrounding him lately. He's won the International League Championship four times over the last five years, with several future Hall of Famers helping out his cause. And all the players simply love him.

"Please, Spence. Sit down…"

"Yeah, Skip…"

"Taylor… I wish I had a better way to tell you this, but I'm just going to cut to the chase because of time constraints. It's September now and Major League rosters are expanding in preparation for the playoffs that will be starting soon. The Red Sox have been mathematically eliminated, but feel like you could be the missing link next year and beyond that could help them keep leads and take their unbelievably talented roster to the next level…"

"Wait… Skip?"

"Son… They want you to get some big-league experience, without all the pressure of a playoff push, so that hopefully next year you can step-in and be the shut-down closer that they're currently in need of. They believe in you that much. So, I want you to pack your bags as quickly as you can because Michael Thompson's private plane is waiting on the tarmac in Providence to take you to New York City. And if the Red Sox have the lead tonight late in the game, you need to be mentally prepared to come in and pitch to help ruin those bastard's season…"

"Wait… I'm pitching tonight!? For Boston!? In Yankee Stadium!?"

"If everything falls into place, son, then… Yes, you'll be closing the game. And they're playing so well right now that it's more than just a possibility."

"Wait… Can Christa come with…?"

"As long as you can both be there within an hour…"

"Can I use your phone, Skip?"

"Absolutely. Let me give you some privacy. Congratulations, kid. You're gonna be something special. I just know it. Strike every one of those bastard Yankees out tonight."

Skip shakes his hand and walks out of the office, before closing the door behind him. Spence is a softy, and he starts crying before Christa even picks up the phone…

"Hello…"

Composing himself… "Hey baby."

"Happy Birthday you big stud… Does anybody even know?"

"Nope. And nobody cares."

"Well, I do…"

Christa then starts to sing her husband the Happy Birthday song, when he suddenly interrupts her…

"I need to know something… Are you ready for the game tonight?"

"Spence… I'm trying to sing you Happy Birthday, and you're being rude. Are you okay? What's wrong?"

"I just want to know if you're ready for the game tonight? If you're excited about it?"

"Uhhh… Yeah? I'm ready. I just got off the phone with Abby and she's in New York City with her parents right now for Joshua's game, so I'm a little late getting out the door. I think it's supposed to be hot this afternoon, so I'm trying to figure out what I'm going to wear because it gets cold when the sun starts to…"

"Christa… Listen to me. I want you to pack a suitcase with some rather cool weather clothes. Maybe a windbreaker…"

"Okay…"

"And meet me in an hour at the airport in Providence…"

Christa lets out an audible gasp. She knows exactly what this means, and her voice increases with excitement…

"Spencer Taylor!?"

"I'm pitching in Yankee Stadium tonight. In just a few hours from now… And Michael Thompson's private plane is waiting for us at the airport…"

She starts to cry… "I knew you could do it, baby. I just knew it."

"Can you meet me there in an hour!?"

"Yes. I'll be there. I love you so much and I'm so proud of you!"

Spence then hangs up the phone and calls home…

"Dad."

"Hey, son. Happy Birthday! Your mom and I are just sitting here listening to the pre-game on the radio and waiting for it to start."

"Dad… I don't know how to tell you this… But I'm getting called up…"

"You're what!?"

"There's a plane here in Providence that's waiting to fly me and Christa to New York City…"

Dan starts to get emotional, thinking about all the times he's thrown the baseball outside with his son since he was a little boy…

His mother sees her husband and quickly grabs the phone…

"Spencer!? Is everything okay!?"

"It's perfect, mom. I'm pitching in Yankee Stadium tonight, but I must leave soon so that I can catch my plane."

"Oh, son. I'm so proud of you."

"Thanks, mom. I'll try to call y'all tomorrow. I love you. Can you tell dad that I love him?"

"Yes, honey. I will. He's sitting right here next to me and blubbering like a baby right now…"

"Okay… Just tell him for me. I've gotta go."

Spence hangs up the phone, walks outside of Skip's office, and into the locker room, where his teammates start cheering for him and singing Happy Birthday…

Skip walks over and hands him a tiny empty plastic bag, about the size of a half-dollar, with a Ziplock seal. He then pulls the same kind of bag out of his own pocket to show Spence…

"Taylor… You see this little bag of dirt? I took this sample the first time I stepped out onto a big-league field. In my case, it was from around the third base area in Kansas City – Royals Stadium – they just changed the name to Kaufman Stadium this year. Anyway, I keep this thing in my wallet till this very day to help remind me to never take the talent I was given for granted. I encourage you to do the same thing tonight at Yankee Stadium and soak it all in before throwing your first pitch…"

"Meat… Meat!?"

Joshua is now reaching over and tapping him on the shoulder as they are turning into the players' parking garage… "We're here."

Spence takes the small bag of dirt and places it back into his wallet, before they exit the vehicle and walk up to the first checkpoint. Security is fired up about seeing Spence again…

"Go get'em, Dawg!"

Many of his teammates and the crew refer to him as "Dawg," in reference to him being a Mississippi State Bulldog Alumni who likes to wear maroon and white every chance he gets. In fact, he still visits Starkville on a regular basis in the offseason, where he has a suite in Davis Wade Stadium overlooking Scott Field. It also fits considering his all-business demeanor when out on the mound.

Spence smiles as he walks into the clubhouse and starts shaking hands with his teammates.

"Look who's back!" Pointing at his friend, Joshua brings way more attention to his returning than what he wanted…

The others soon chime in…

"Spencer… You're a celebrity now! Can I have your autograph!?"

But most of them come over to bro-hug and welcome him back.

And then the rookie outfield sensation Cameron Moon walks over. Spence has no idea that he's the one who was badmouthing him and fighting with Joshua on the plane. His best friend looks on with concern, closely monitoring the situation from nearby.

Speaking in a thick accent he tells Spence, "I'm glad you're back, Dawg. Let's get this thing done," before high-fiving and bringing him in for an embrace.

The team moseys through the buffet line and eventually finds their seats among the scattered tables, before Skip walks up to the front of the room and addresses them.

"Boys, we need all arms on deck tonight to get this win…."

He then looks around and finds his closer…

"Taylor… That includes you."

Spence nods in agreement, as the team looks back at him and shows support…

"The only one who 100% won't be pitching tonight is Adam [Ledbetter]. I pushed the old man to the limit in game three out in San Francisco, where he threw 126 pitches and gave us a good chance to win. And of course we blew it, of course with a little help from the umpires. Anyway, I've spoken to him personally and told him my plan. So, he's gonna pitch one helluva game seven for us tomorrow night on a full five days' rest. But we must get there first. And in the meantime, if I need to pitch a different person every inning of this game, I most certainly will…"

Adam nods in agreement and interjects, "I'm confident that we'll get it done and tomorrow night we'll be walking off of the field as World Champs…"

The team explodes with excitement!

"Damn right!"

"We're the best team in baseball history! Let's do this!"

Skip continues… "I've been talking to the coaches and we're also going to pitch around the three-hole hitter – Encarnacion. We aren't going to let him beat us. He's been hot at the plate and has hit three home runs so far in this series, alone. We are going to avoid him if we can. We may even consider putting him on base as the tying run rather than trying to get him out. But we'll make that decision if and when we get there… Now, let's all eat and then go get some good swings and throws in… And then let's go out and win this game!"

The team then cheers Skip on as he goes around high-fiving everyone.

***

For an older stadium, Fenway Park is still a very modern ballpark insofar as the amenities that it offers to both players and fans. There have been multiple attempts over the years to approve the construction of a newer and bigger baseball stadium for the Red Sox nearby, but they all ultimately failed for various reasons, not the least of which was the majority of the public opinion wanting to keep the charm and mystique of the historic venue in the face of nearby rival cities that were choosing to do the opposite with their own aging ballparks. But that didn't mean they couldn't upgrade what was already there, so over years the city has approved numerous improvements and enhancements.

Originally built in 1912 and then essentially rebuilt in 1934, it has since undergone various modifications and renovations. Bound by its location in Boston's densely populated Fenway-Kenmore neighborhood, it is bordered by Yawkey Way and the streets of Van Ness, Ipswich, Lansdowne, and Brooklyn Avenue. After ensuring enough room for the fans to sit, these constraints seemingly necessitated some of the park's most peculiar features including, but certainly not limited to "The Triangle," "Pesky's Pole," and "The Green Monster."

Despite all the technological advances that occurred over the years and decades since it was built, where upgrades like video boards and luxury boxes were added to further increase its allure and bring it roaring into the twenty-first century with some degree of relevance, those in charge of Fenway Park have also chosen to preserve many traditional nuances – such as a narrow foul ground territory, a hand-operated scoreboard spanning the facade of "The Green Monster," and keeping a short wall in extreme right field that still remains only 302 feet away from home plate – allowing fans to feel up close and personal to the players.

Further adding to its appeal, it is limited by its capacity to hold a crowd of no more than 38,000 spectators – thereby leaving baseball enthusiasts and purists a beacon of yesteryear – or perhaps just a small glimpse into the past that might be indicative of what it was like to sit and watch such iconic Red Sox players as Babe Ruth and Ted Williams out on the diamond.

The first time Spence ever pitched in the famous stadium, he was awestruck and kept turning around in circles, taking in a visual 360° panoramic mental photo after every single strikeout. And as far as he is concerned, there is still nothing more strikingly beautiful in sports today than a packed-house at Fenway Park and the stadium abuzz with excitement.

By midafternoon, everyone is lounging around in the state-of-the-art locker room that's adorned with televisions, leather recliners, and a custom sound system, while allowing their food to settle. There are some jokes that are being passed around by the guys, but the mood is considerably more serious than that of the previous playoff and World Series games played this season, especially when considering the finality of a possible loss tonight. Those that had needed to go get their ailments addressed by the trainers were now beginning to file back in, one by one, and starting the process of getting dressed for the upcoming game. Spence does the same.

There are several batting cages that populate the underbelly of Fenway Park. Connected to the locker rooms on both the home and visitor's side, they soon start filling up with players from both teams looking to get-in some pre-game hacks. Meanwhile, Spence and the other available pitchers go in the opposite direction, following the hallways that parallel the fence line beneath the right field stands, hanging a sharp left, and then continuing on until ultimately reaching the door that opens up into the right-center field bullpen.

Alas, there's nowhere for Spence to hide now as the whole area is open to all cameras and sets of eyes within the ballpark. Skip is already standing out there, too, alongside the pitching coach, ready for someone to step up and show something that he can work with later tonight.

"Well, first thing's first. Let's get warmed up."

A few of them choose to step over the short wall and onto the field by the warning track to get their throws in, while others stay inside the pen. And once they're all warmed up, Skip again speaks up…

"Taylor, you're up. Let's see what'cha got."

Spence toes one of the rubbers as the other mound next to him remains completely unmanned. He's keenly aware that all eyes are now on him. Some of the Giant pitchers in the opposing bullpen even stop to watch out of curiosity. The last time this occurred was two weeks prior when he failed his bullpen session miserably.

He motions towards the catcher that a fastball is coming, does a half wind-up followed by a high leg kick, strides forward, and then throws…

It's strike one, center cut, at 99 miles per hour.

Skip glances over and smiles at the pitching coach…

He delivers another one, again a perfect strike, with no change in velocity.

He then proceeds to throw a total of ten pitches, all in the zone, three of them 100 miles per hour or more, and all located where he was told to throw it…

"Alright, Taylor, I've seen enough…"

"Just one more, Skip? I feel good."

Skip humors him and turns to address another player…

Spence then motions that a curve ball is coming, while Skip is half paying attention, and proceeds to throw the most beautiful breaking ball for a strike, prompting the catcher to immediately pull his mask off and tell'em that he's never seen a pitch break that hard…

"Where in the hell did that come from, Taylor?"

"It's something I've been working on lately. I used to throw it a lot back in high school…"

"Good to know…"

The catcher then heads over to the other bullpen catcher to tell him about the pitch that Spence just threw to him. He's very animated and using his arm in a sweeping motion while trying to describe it.

twenty-five – fortuitous

"Well, here we are, about to start the top of the 9th inning in game six of the 2003 World Series at Fenway Park, and I'm not sure if anyone saw this story coming…"

"You're right, Ted. Skip had made no secrets about it being a 'committee' approach to Boston's pitching line-up tonight…"

"But, to his credit, he also said that he would evaluate everyone who's available and go with the apparent 'hot hand' based on pre-game performances, having not yet named a starter for up to two hours before tonight's first pitch…"

"And here that surprise starter is… Jason Burns is once again taking the mound, and tonight he's vying for a complete game shutout in what would be one of the most clutch performances that I've ever seen from a young pitcher."

"Well, talking to Skip right before the game started, he said the young lefty came to him this afternoon claiming to still have a bitter taste in his mouth about how game three ended with him out there on the mound, begging for the ball again tonight, and asking him to place the team on his shoulders…"

"Yep. And he said he also looked phenomenal in pregame warmups, so he had a good feeling about it and went with his gut."

"And boy has that decision paid off. Taylor is now warming up in the bullpen just in case, but Skip is staying with the hot hand of Burns, who's thrown 110 pitches so far and simply pounded the strike zone, pitching mostly to weak contact, with four strikeouts, and only surrendering a total of three hits…"

"You know, Ted. Assuming this 4-0 lead holds up for the Red Sox, this might be one of the gutsiest head coaching calls, in addition to player performances, that I've ever seen. It's like he came out of nowhere to shut down a very tough San Francisco Giants team in a must-win game on a big stage."

"That's right. It's also worth noting that even though this isn't technically a 'save' situation, being up by more than three runs, you know that Skip would have Taylor out there pitching the 9th inning and shutting things down if the last three weeks hadn't played out as they have..."

"Oh yeah... I agree with you one thousand percent on that. There isn't any question that he'd pat the young lefty on the butt and say, 'Good job,' while handing the ball over to the veteran closer, Taylor."

"That noted, Skip appears to be going with his gut once again..."

"For sure, but I guarantee you that if anyone makes it on base, we will see Taylor..."

"Here we go... And it's a first pitch swinging, weak ground ball to Waters, who charges in and makes the throw to first on the run!"

"That was a big league play right there. Waters has been quiet tonight at the plate, but his glove has been solid, Ted. And it's the little things that he does like that, even when he's 'Oh-for' at the dish, that make him the best shortstop in baseball."

"Ted... Waters is wincing after making that play and looks pretty uncomfortable... Like he strained an oblique or something..."

"You're right, Tom. That's not something that any Red Sox fan wants to see, considering they have one more game to win..."

"And would you look at that? It's another first pitch swinging, and it's popped up to the infield... Who wants it? Anyone? And it's Waters, once again, calling off the third baseman for the 2nd out..."

"He called everyone off, caught it, and looked like he was in pain once again after raising his arms to catch it and quickly lowering them. He then handed the ball off to the third baseman rather than throwing it around the horn, himself..."

"I saw that, too. And right now he looks to be favoring that right side pretty significantly..."

"You know, the Giants haven't exactly done themselves any favors here tonight against Burns. Yes, he's throwing strikes and pitching a great game. But their pitch selection – or more specifically what they've chosen to swing at, considering how much he's been around the strike zone, has been interesting. It's like they can't pick it up well out of his hand..."

"Mitchell now steps into the box and takes ball 1."

"The one-oh... It's ball 2."

"Ball 3..."

"Waters is now jogging in to have a quick conversation with the youngster..."

"He's smiling as he runs back to short, but looks to still be guarding that right side..."

"I agree. It's bothering him, for sure..."

Spence has stopped throwing pitches in the bullpen and is simply looking on now...

"If he puts Mitchell on base right here, I'd bet my house that we'll see Spence Taylor pitching to the top of the line-up..."

"No doubt..."

"And there's strike one. He was taking all the way there, Tom."

"Yes, indeed. And the three-one? It's strike two!"

"Needing baserunners, Tonglet probably had him taking there, too..."

The count is now full as the Red Sox faithful are on their feet cheering and anticipating a game seven here at Fenway Park tomorrow night...

And it's a ground ball straight back to Burns, who fields it cleanly and turns and runs to first base, before giving an underhand toss…

"And we'll see you tomorrow night for game seven!"

The Boston players don't want to appear too excited because there's still another game yet to win; however, they all take turns congratulating and hugging Jason Burns on his complete game shutout, as a reporter soon grabs and pulls him aside for a postgame interview…

"Jason. Game six of the World Series on a stage like Fenway Park, and you decided to show up with ice water in your veins? How'd this happen?"

"Well, Erin, I just felt really good all day long. We lost game three back in San Francisco largely because of me, and I wanted to make amends to my teammates. So, I asked Skip for the ball."

"You most certainly did, and you've set the stage for a classic showdown tomorrow night, their ace verses yours…"

"Yeah. It has all the makings for an exciting game. I know that Adam will be pitching on a full five days' rest tomorrow and that he'll keep us close – hopefully with a chance to win at the end… And now with Spence back, we're feeling pretty confident. The ninth was definitely a lot easier to pitch, knowing that he had my back, should I have needed him…"

"Well, there you have it. Game seven is tomorrow night at 7:30pm eastern time and the weather is forecast to be perfect. Let's take it back to Ted and Tom…"

"Thank you, Erin. Well, Tom…"

[laughing] "Ted… Did you expect anything less than a deciding game seven between these two great teams?"

And as the two of them are wrapping up the broadcast, Joshua Waters can be seen chasing Burns around the infield with a plate of shaving cream, while holding the area around his rib cage with his right arm…

***

One of the things that Skip hates the most about being the manager of the Boston Red Sox is having to talk to reporters. One could hardly blame him in this case. As the rest of his coaches and the team get to shower and revel a bit in their game six victory, he's bound by his contract with both the owners of the team and Major League Baseball, itself, to stand behind the team's podium and in front of a backdrop emblazoned with the team logo, not to mention its corporate sponsors, within fifteen minutes of the game ending in order to address the press. And lately the questions have simply worn him out. Tonight, however, everyone seems to be singing his praises and not second-guessing him, so he's a bit more forthcoming with his answers.

"Skip… Do you have a crystal ball or something?"

[laughing] "Look. Based upon our talk beforehand and his warm-ups, I truly expected Burns to have a good game. But let's be honest. I think he gave up the first of their three hits tonight with two outs in the top of the first inning and, I'm not sure if you noticed or not, but I'd already called down there and asked for another arm to be up, stretching and getting warm…"

The reporters laugh as Skip continues to chuckle…

"I wasn't going to take any chances tonight. I'd have brought in Taylor before the fifth inning, if I thought it would help the team…"

"Speaking of Taylor… Is there a reason that you didn't put him in to pitch the ninth?"

"Absolutely. We had a four-run lead and… Well, considering what Spence has been through, I thought him just being out there in front of the crowd throwing the ball in the bullpen was something that he needed, and all the pitching coaches said he looked great. I'd have put him in if anyone would've made it on base."

"So tomorrow night with a lead and the World Series on the line, it's Taylor?"

"For sure. We do not have the record-setting season that we had, with the most wins in baseball history, without Spence Taylor. If it's a save situation, you're damn-right I'm putting him in."

"Skip. We saw Joshua Waters favoring is right side…"

"Yeah… I think he might've strained his oblique on that slow roller to short to start the 9th inning…"

"And his status for tomorrow?"

"Well, unless Joshua is missing a leg out there tomorrow, I don't think I could keep him off the field. Hopefully we can treat whatever it is and get him as close to 100% as we possibly can…"

"And Ledbetter?"

"Yeah… Adam is ready to go and looking forward to the opportunity to carry us tomorrow night out on the mound…"

Skip then realizes that he's surpassed his contractually obligated ten minutes of press time and abruptly ends the session by saying "Thank you," getting out of his seat, and walking off the stage – as the reporters all sound off numerous additional questions, while trying to speak over one another.

twenty-six – "strategery"

The Boston Red Sox players each have two assigned parking spots in the player's garage: one for them and another for their spouse and/or family. It sits both underground and adjacent to the first base side of Fenway Park, with an entranceway that's a full block away from the stadium and flanked by security.

There's a tunnel that connects it to the clubhouse and locker room, with an elevator that leads up to a suite that is dedicated to the wives and/or girlfriends. If children, parents, or extended family will also be attending the game, there is a dedicated section just in front of and outside of it that comes with many of the same amenities, including a wait-staff, unlimited drinks, and meals. It is specifically reserved for the extended families of coaches and players for no extra charge, up until twenty-four hours prior to the scheduled game-time – at which point those seats then become available to the public for a premium price.

Christa and Abby watched game six from the wives/girlfriend's suite, but chose not to stay and meet-up with their husbands afterward. Instead, they hurried home together, attempting to beat any media that might be lurking nearby, and to also relieve the grandparents from the responsibility of caring for their children.

"Meat, I may need you to drive..."

The two of them walked out into the player's parking garage together, just as they had also arrived, and Joshua is now struggling to get comfortable in driver's seat. Spence notices that he can't even reach up to grab the seatbelt without significant discomfort.

"Yep… You're gonna have to drive us. But first you've gotta to come over here and help me out of the car."

Spence gets out of the passenger side, walks over to the driver's side, and grabs Joshua's left hand. Joshua then takes his left leg and gingerly places it outside of the vehicle with the toe of his shoe touching the ground…

"Okay… On the count of three… One… Two… Three!!!!"

And with that Joshua let's out a loud moan, as Spence pulls him from his own car…

"What in the hell did you do?"

"I don't know, Meat. But I can hardly move my right side."

"We need to go back inside and get you some treatment…"

"No, we can't. Someone might see us and realize that I'm hurt."

"Newsflash… You are hurt, Joshua."

"I know that – and you know that… And tomorrow Skip and the whole team will soon know it. But we can't let the other team know the extent…"

Spence goes about helping Joshua into the passenger side before coming back over, starting the vehicle, and then proceeding home.

Joshua soon reaches over with his left hand and presses a button on the steering wheel, which makes a "ding" sound. He then says, "Call Skip…"

The car responds back to him in a computerized, but soothing voice, "Calling Skip…"

"Fancy," Spence quips.

[after a couple of rings] "Hey Joshua… What's up, son?"

"It's not good, Skip."

"Your rib area?"

"Yes."

"You don't think you'll be able to play tomorrow night?"

"Skip… I've got an idea, but I need you to hear me out. The Giants don't know the extent of my injury, and they always try to pitch around me anyway. That's part of the reason I've been stinking it up lately at the plate because I haven't been getting anything good to hit and I was being selfish. But now I'm good with just going up there and taking every pitch. I think I can get at least two walks on the night as a designated hitter. You can still put me in the three-hole and as long as I don't swing, they'll be none the wiser…"

"I don't know, Joshua. That's quite a bluff. Can you even run, much less slide if you needed to?"

"Skip… I prolly can't slide. But there's nobody else that can get on base like I can. They don't want to pitch to me in a game seven, just like we don't want to pitch to Encarnacion…"

"'Don't let their best player beat you, especially in a game seven,' right? I think it's a helluvan idea, son. We can move Cameron from center field into his true position of shortstop, put you at DH in the three-hole, and they'd just think that you're well enough to bat, but limited with movement when making plays out in the field…"

"Those are my thoughts, too, Skip."

"And what about BP before the game?"

"We just don't say anything to anyone. The last time the Giants saw me I was chasing Burns around the infield with a shaving cream pie. So, I'll just stay underground, and they can assume that I'm taking my hacks in the cage while I'm getting treatment…"

"We probably need to keep it from your teammates, too… At least the extent of it. Is Taylor in the car with you?"

"I am, Skip."

"Spence… Don't utter a word to anyone about the magnitude of his injury, and we'll just have him in the treatment room for the whole pre-game, before listing him as a late scratch in the field, but still batting in the three-hole as the DH…"

"Skip… I know everyone was singing your praises tonight, and rightly so. But if this works out and we somehow win tomorrow's game with what we've been through this postseason, it's gonna be the stuff of legend…"

[laughing] "Let's see what tomorrow brings…"

"Bye, Coach…"

"Get some rest…"

***

Joshua is using rapid and shallow breaths, while employing a slightly forced hollow sounding whistling technique, in an attempt to temper the pain around his right rib cage as he gets into Spence's vehicle…

"Wassup, Meat?"

"Let me guess… You're still planning on playing, aren't you?"

"No doubt."

"How will you even run if you happen to get on base?"

"I'm gonna make sure that I'm doped up, Meat," he says while smiling.

The roles are reversed this morning thanks to Joshua's injury. Spence, having long since been cleared to drive by Dr. Olgivy following his second hypnosis session, is now the one tasked with getting the two of them to the ballpark both safely and on time. There are also only a few news trucks and reporters left outside the Notwen Avenue gate, most of them now gone after having seen Spence warming up last night in the bullpen and assuming that it is no longer a story. Some still remain, though, unconvinced until they see him out on the bump performing in front of 38,000 fans and a live television audience in a high-pressure situation.

It is now well known, having been reported in the media, that he's undergone at least two intensive psychotherapy treatments under the care of a South African psychiatrist. And many of Dr. Olgivy's former patients, who are also professional athletes, are beginning to speak out in favor of sports psychology for the first time, without any shame. It's only taken two weeks of the subject being front and center in every mainstream news cycle, once the World Series started and Boston's future Hall of Fame closer was essentially "missing in action," to finally give these people a voice. Spence, himself, though, remains uninterested in speaking to reporters. And even if he wanted to, he is still bound by a gag-order issued by Skip until the season is completely over later in the evening.

As for Christa and Abby, they, along with the children and all four sets of grandparents, will be attending tonight's game, making good use of the other three assigned parking spaces in the player's garage and the reserved seating in front of and below the suite for the wives and girlfriends.

Tonight's contest is projected to be the most watched game in the history of baseball. There is a newer, faster internet connection that is starting to gain legs, and people are using it all over the world to "stream" the live video of sporting events from the website of the broadcasting network. In short, you don't necessarily need a cable TV subscription anymore. You only need what's referred to as an "Ethernet" connection.

This has Christa very worried. She still isn't quite sure of what to make so far regarding her husband's complete recovery, and she's secretly praying that the Red Sox can somehow win tonight's game without Spence even making an appearance. It's not that she doesn't believe in him. It's just that she personally sat-in and witnessed everything he endured with Dr. Olgivy and the depths into which both his mind and body were taken. And somehow if he were to get out there on the biggest stage she could possibly even think of – such as the latter innings of a World Series game seven at Fenway Park – and struggle once again… Or, even worse, have a complete nervous breakdown in front of an international audience…

Well, she doesn't even want to let her mind go there. That may be the reason why she's been on her knees at her bedside lately, selfishly imploring Jesus to guide her husband and make him whole again, while at the same time asking for His will to be done – and then opening her eyes to embarrassingly glance around at their wonderful life, thereby reminding herself that if Spence never steps onto a baseball field ever again, they're still very blessed.

Spence pulls into an unmarked, but heavily secured garage entrance off Boylston Street and weaves his way down into what is basically the belly of Boston's Children's Hospital, some area hotels, and shops. After parking, he gets out of the driver's side and, with his head on a swivel looking for anyone that might see them, walks around his sport utility vehicle towards Joshua, grabs his left arm, and on the count of three he heavily assists him in exiting the car, as he moans in agony once again.

The two of them walk past a couple of checkpoints and through the tunnel leading towards the locker room, as one attendant fist-bumps them both and tells Spence "Give'em Hell, Dawg."

They are the first players to walk into the clubhouse. The only people there are the caterers, coaches, and trainers – who are asked to show up an hour or more before the players start arriving.

Skip walks up to Joshua…

"Still the same?"

"Yes… Maybe even worse."

"Let's get you in the treatment room before anyone sees you."

He then looks at Spence…

"Taylor, fix him a plate so that he can eat while he's in there."

Skip then turns to all the coaches and calls them into the treatment room with Joshua…

"We all know what's going on here… This is a bluff, and I own it. But like I've already said, we don't want any of our players even knowing the full extent of his injury. Cameron will do just fine at shortstop. I have no issues with that, whatsoever, since it's his true position. But by listing

Joshua to bat in the three-hole as the DH though, like we would normally do, it will hopefully obscure any doubt about his ability to perform… Because even with him hurt, he's still our best chance at getting a baserunner or two against their ace, because they're sure to try to pitch around him, just like we are with Encarnacion. And with Adam pitching for us, that may be all that we need."

Spence then walks in and hands Joshua a plate of food, complete with everything he likes and nothing that he doesn't.

"Taylor… I'm going to need you tonight. You've got your head straight, yeah?"

"Skip, I've never felt better."

Skip then turns to the team doctor and nurse…

[pointing at Joshua] "Can he have Toradol?"

"Yes. Both now and another dose just before game time…"

[interrupting] "What else can he have?"

"Well, we have these large numbing pads that are coated with both menthol and lidocaine. Those should help him if we put them on closer to game time…"

"And what else?"

"Other than treatments and calculated massaging, I'm not sure what else can be done, Skip… I'm pretty sure he has a torn oblique, and I'm conflicted between my medical opinion of what's best for him and your coaching opinion of wanting him out there…"

"It's his choice! And he's one tough son-of-a-bitch! Don't you dare put that on me! It's game seven of the World Series, dammit!"

Joshua then intervenes…

"I wanna play, Doc. I'm not going to go out there and do anything to further damage it."

The team doctor and Skip walk outside the treatment room. Both Joshua and Spence can see them having a heated discussion just beyond the door, before they begrudgingly part ways. Skip then walks back into the room...

"Don't make me regret this, Waters..."

He then closes the door behind him as a nurse nearby draws up medication using a hypodermic needle and syringe.

twenty-seven – approachable

Part of the pregame ritual for pitchers is standing deep along the warning track in the outfield and "shagging" the balls that their teammates hit during batting practice.

Spence, a veteran now of nearly ten years for the Red Sox, could most certainly claim the seniority card and simply let the other pitchers get the job done. But he loves being out there on the field in any capacity, whatsoever, having dreamed of being a Major Leaguer since he was a child. And the thought of chasing balls around to keep him loose, while perhaps being able to see a kid's face light-up when he gets to personally hand them one that his future Hall of Famer best friend hit... Well, there's just not many feelings in life that are better.

Spence walks through the tunnel connecting the locker room to the dugout and climbs up the three short steps that lead out onto the field. And as he begins to run out there to his station in the outfield, he hears a familiar voice behind him...

"Spencer! Spence Taylor..."

He turns around to find his old high school baseball coach standing there at the fence-line, right at the front corner of the home dugout...

"Coach Gray!!!"

He shakes his hand quite vigorously and continues... "Why didn't you tell me you were coming!?"

"Well, son, you have a lot going on... But I didn't want to miss this for anything."

"Where are your seats?"

"They're right here, son. Next to the dugout. I had to pull some money out of my 401k to get them," he says while laughing.

"I'm gonna pay for them. Game seven of the World Series!? How much were they? I'm going to pay for them…"

"No, you're not. And it's just me here. I wouldn't miss it for the world…"

"No doubt…"

"Is your dad here? I'll be in town for a few more days and would love to meet up with him…"

"Yessir… He'll be here…"

Spence then points up towards the suites that are just under the press box on the Boston side…

"He'll be up there… And we can definitely make that happen…"

"Alright, son. I'm proud of you. Go out there and have some fun…"

"I will, coach. Great to see you!"

And with that Spence runs out onto the field and stands on the warning track out in right-center, as his teammates take batting practice.

Noticeably absent, to him at least, is Joshua's commanding presence out there hitting bombs over The Green Monster and putting on a show for the incoming crowd. But none of his teammates seem to even notice it, much less the other team.

And just then a ball comes his way. He fields it off the ground using his bare hand and hears "Mr. Spence! Mr. Spence!" coming from over closer to right field, along the fence-line. He walks over to a young boy, about 9-10 years of age, who's wearing a Spence Taylor jersey, standing there with his own father. Spence then has the dad pick the boy up and place him on the other side of the short fence, before posing for a picture with him and pulling a sharpie out of his back pocket. He takes the ball and signs it…

"Throw with conviction! Spence Taylor #58."

He goes on to hand it to the boy, before having his dad pick him up and back over into the stands. And as he walks away, he overhears the boy's voice saying "Wow!!!" – turning around to see him examining the ball thoroughly. It makes him smile as he settles back in at his station...

twenty-eight – improvisation

"Well, Ted. We've got a classic brewing here late in game seven of the World Series at Fenway Park. Both Waters and Encarnacion have been non-factors tonight, each having drawn two walks, Waters with one strikeout looking, and Encarnacion with a hit-by-pitch."

"Yeah… The two sides have simply pitched around them, Tom. But something's definitely 'off' with Waters. He hasn't swung the bat even once tonight… And he looked at three straight perfect pitches in his last at bat…"

"You're absolutely right. I think he might be more injured than the Red Sox have let on, and perhaps now the Giants have finally figured it out, too? He didn't take BP…"

"That's right! He didn't even take batting practice on the field before the game. And I hardly even noticed…"

"If he's truly injured that badly and Skip put him in the lineup-up as the DH in the three-hole as a bluff… Perhaps suspecting that they'd pitch around him?"

"Wow. You don't think?"

"I wouldn't put anything past Skip… That's why he's where he is and I'm where I am… He's a master at game-planning…"

"In any case, Ledbetter has pitched a gem here… A three hitter… And has not allowed a single run to cross the plate tonight…"

"The old man's still got it… Only to be matched by the Giants' ace though, Kevin Powell, who's also pitched seven strong innings of shutout ball, himself."

"And as we head into the last half of the eighth inning, Taylor is now warming up out in the bullpen, and we've got the bottom of the order due up for the Red Sox."

"Well, depending on how this inning goes, we'll definitely see Cameron Moon stepping up the plate and, if he somehow gets on, a likely stolen base attempt…"

"But for now it looks like San Francisco is sticking with Powell out on the mound… And why not?"

"Yeah… But they've got their-own big closer in Moorhead out there just dying to come in and wreak some havoc, should the Red Sox get anything going."

Spence is all warmed-up now out in the bullpen and spends most of his time perched on the mound and watching the game closely from beyond the outfield fence.

"Powell has been great tonight, but Moon will be up to see him for the fourth time in the last two and a half hours, and that might be enough for Tonglet to go ahead and bring in Moorhead to help keep the Red Sox bats at bay, trying to negate any chance of late-inning heroics…"

"Speaking of… Is it now time to pinch hit for Waters? Or do you keep him in there?"

"I hate to say it, but I'd probably pinch hit for him…"

"And here's Powell… Strike one."

"He's been all over the zone tonight, Tom."

"He has… But his velocity has decreased a little. He can get away with that as long as he locates…"

[interrupting] "Strike two…"

"You were saying?"

"Oh, I'm a big fan. Don't get me wrong. But you've got the rookie sensation Moon, as the lead-off hitter, coming up after the first two

222

batters, for the 4th time tonight… And I'm not sure that I'd let Powell face him again. I'd go ahead and bring Moorhead in to get one extra out, try to maybe scratch a run across in the top of the ninth, and then bring him back out to slam the door…"

"And there's strike three, swinging…"

"It's hard to lay off of that pitch down and away in the dirt when you've got two strikes on ya…"

"For sure…"

"Powell still looks confident and composed out there in his eighth inning pitching…"

"And it's a weak roller back to Powell… He fields it… And it's in time at first for the second out…"

"Strikeouts and weak contact…"

"Just what the Giants ordered…"

"And in steps the rookie, Cameron Moon."

"It looks like they might be keeping Powell in to face him…"

"Moon is oh-for-three tonight, with three strikeouts. That may be why Powell is being allowed to pitch to him for the fourth time…"

"Powell delivers to the plate…"

And it's a hard ground ball through the right side, just beyond the first baseman's glove…

"That was my concern, Ted. He knew that Powell wanted to get ahead in the count, and just sat on a fastball and hit it hard for his first hit of the night, a single to right field…"

"And that might be all for Powell here tonight, as Tonglet goes out and Kevin hands him the ball…"

"Well, the San Francisco faithful that made the over 3,000 mile trip to Boston are surely standing up now and showing their appreciation for him, as he walks off the field…"

"And even some Red Sox fans are clapping out of respect, too…"

"Knowledgeable fans know baseball, Ted. And he showed up today and gave his team a good chance to win it…"

Chad Moorhead opens the gate in the San Francisco bullpen that leads out onto the field and sprints out to the mound in the center of the diamond, his own classic way of entering every game that he pitches. At the Giants' home stadium, he does the same thing, except with "Welcome to The Jungle" playing from the loudspeakers. Spence looks on with a smile and thinks to himself about how he'd probably be so out of breath once he got there that he might need an oxygen mask.

Moorhead has been pivotal for the Giants this season. He's come in and closed games, without giving up a blown save all year. He's had a few close calls, though, largely due to a lack of control to start innings. The Red Sox have scouted him well and know this. Like Taylor, his MO is to overpower you with a fastball, another fastball, and then change things up with an even harder fastball…

"At twenty-three years of age, this is the second full season for Moorhead, who's come in with two outs in the bottom of the eighth to try to shut down Boston – who now has just a little bit of life with Moon over on first base and Sanders coming up to the plate…"

"Do you even try to send Moon, here?"

"Not for the potential third out."

The first pitch Moorhead throws to Sanders is off the plate for ball one at 100 miles per hour…

"Ted, I know that there's a batter and a pitcher facing off right now, but I can't help but watch Joshua Waters warming up in the on-deck circle. He's holding the bat up for about a second in his stance, but then quickly setting it back down… There are no practice swings at all, whatsoever…"

"Yeah, Tom. He's hurt. If Sanders gets on and he bats…"

"Surely not… Huh? You've got to go with someone else in that situation…"

"I don't know. If Joshua tells Skip that he wants to bat, then…"

Moorhead delivers the second pitch and it's ball two…

"He's amped up, Tom."

"Too amped up, Ted"

Ball three from Moorhead is high at 102 miles per hour…

"And there's ball four in the dirt and it's all the way to the backstop…"

"Now this is interesting because it is gonna be Waters who's coming up to the dish…"

"Just listen to this crowd, Ted. They obviously don't see what we see, right?"

"I don't think they do. All they see is the speedster Cameron Moon on second base, 180 feet away from home plate as the go-ahead run, Sanders on first, and their MVP future Hall of Famer stepping into the box…"

"Moorhead steps off and looks at Moon on second base…"

"Big situation right here…"

Moorhead then delivers and it's ball one.

"If you look closely at Waters, Ted, you can see him wincing when he holds the bat up in his stance…"

"Ooh… Nice observation there. Yeah, he's hurting pretty bad…"

"I think all that Moorhead needs to do is settle down a bit and throw a strike here…"

"And it's ball two in the dirt…"

"Moorhead looks at Moon again and delivers…"

"Ball three high in the zone at 101 miles per hour…"

"He's struggling, Ted. He has an easy out right here, and he can't even sniff the strike zone…"

"And here comes Tonglet out to try to settle him down, and I'm sure to tell him exactly what you just said."

"It looks like Skip is also using this opportunity to speak with Waters and the two baserunners…"

Moorhead gives all his infielders a fist-bump, as Tonglet walks off the mound and back towards the visiting dugout.

"There is nobody warming up in the Giants' bullpen… This is Moorhead's game to win or lose…"

"And there's strike one over the heart of the plate. The count is three balls and one strike…"

"Moorhead looks Moon back to second base and then comes home…"

"Strike two!"

"All it took was a mound visit, Ted?"

"I guess so. But now the count is full and there's two outs, so the runners will be getting a head start on this next pitch…"

"Moorhead again steps off. He knows the runners are forced and will be moving on the next pitch…"

"Once again, you have to ask yourself 'Do the Giants not notice what we both see about Joshua Waters?' He will not swing. In fact, he cannot swing…"

The television cameras quickly turn to Abby, who's looking on with concern while Christa, with her eyes closed, appears to be praying out loud behind her…

Moorhead comes set and then strides forward towards the plate as both runners are now moving. And right before the ball comes out of his hand

Waters inexplicably drops his bat, chokes up high towards the barrel with both hands, and lays down a beautiful bunt in the grass along the third base line. The third baseman, who was playing mid-range and caught off-guard, charges and bare-hands the ball, before his forward movement demands that he throws it almost underhanded towards first base.

Waters races down the line giving it all that he has. It is painfully obvious that he's hurting now, and everyone knows it when, at the last second, he extends his arms and slides headfirst into the bag.

"And the throw pulls him high and off the bag! Waters is safe! He was safe, anyway… But Waters is safe at first on a headfirst slide!"

The first baseman comes off the bag when he must jump for the ball and, after catching it, his momentum forces him to turn his back ever so slightly to home plate. Meanwhile, Moon, who started on second base, has long since rounded third and is now being emphatically waved home by the third base coach…

"And here comes Moon!"

"We're gonna have a play at the plate!"

"He's safe! He's safe! Joshua Waters laid down a perfect bunt that the Giants never saw coming and, with the runners going on the pitch, Moon was able to make it all the way home and dive in safe!"

"Let's look at it again, Ted, 'cuz it was pretty close…"

"He's safe! Wow! What a play by the Red Sox!"

"They knew all along that, if the count got to full, Waters was going to bunt with two strikes and the runners going!?"

"Yes, they did. And that's undoubtedly what Skip was telling them in the huddle when Tonglet made the mound visit after the count got to 'three-oh…'"

"Oh my… I've never quite seen anything like it in all my life, Tom."

"An unbelievable call from the Boston manager Skip Jenkins to take a one run lead in the bottom of the 8th inning of the World Series, and perhaps set the stage for Taylor to come in and redeem himself..."

"Well, it appears that they're now gonna send out a pinch runner for Waters... And listen to this crowd get up on their feet and go nuts for this man..."

"Wow... I'm getting chill bumps. That's the face of the franchise right there... Obviously hurt... And playing through it... All heart... What an unbelievable ball player. And it's been a true joy to watch him compete over the years."

"And now he's not trying to hide the pain anymore, Ted, as several of his teammates come out to help him off the field..."

"They're basically carrying him, Tom."

"Again... Just wow."

A camera quickly pans over to show Abby and Christa, who are both crying while they listen to and watch the capacity crowd giving Joshua a standing ovation, as he gingerly walks with assistance off the field.

The following batter goes on to hit a "can of corn" to the center fielder for the third out, and the inning is now over...

"Hold on to your hats, people. We're gonna see Taylor facing the top of the order and Encarnacion in the top of the 9th inning, who'd like nothing better than to spoil his return to the mound here at Fenway."

twenty-nine – immaKulate

Spence walks in slowly from the bullpen that sits beyond the outfield fence, as his teammate passes by to assume his own position in center field…

"I've gotcha, Dawg."

He smiles back, as he methodically continues towards the mound. It's speculated that Spence loses one or two warm-up pitches every time he makes an appearance because of his slow, deliberate approach. After all, baseball has long since become a commodity, and when the commercial break is over, the people making the television deals behind the scenes want the audience to see nothing but action in a game where, quite frankly, there isn't a lot of it – their reasoning being that nobody is interested in watching someone warm-up from a barstool or their couch at home.

As such, there has been a lot of talk lately about perhaps adding a pitch clock and other rules to increase the pace of play. Spence, as a baseball purist, wants nothing to do with that. Instead, he wants to keep the game, warts and all, as it is now, staying as close as possible to the way it was when players like Mickey Mantle, Ted Williams, and Babe Ruth once played. That noted, he realizes it's a losing battle, and is therefore unsure about pitching too much longer, having been long since annoyed with the trend of rushing what he feels is a beautiful game-flow.

The capacity crowd filled with mostly Red Sox faithfuls is still going nuts from the disbelief of what occurred in the last half-inning, so much so that it's difficult to determine if any of it is related to the fact that the most dominant closer of last decade is coming in to perhaps close the door on a game seven win in the World Series for Boston.

It's an unbelievably loud atmosphere that has Christa on edge, considering that her worst fears for her husband are now in play. She looks on with concern, while dissecting every warm-up pitch that he throws.

"So far, so good," she thinks to herself.

Out on the mound, Spence is all business as usual, showing little to no emotion. There's a throw down to second after his last offering and his teammates toss the ball around the horn, before congregating out on the mound, patting him on the butt, and taking their positions behind him.

Moon winks at him and says, "Bring us home, Dawg."

"We're back here at Fenway Park and, boy, has it been a treat to watch so far…"

"I'm still in shock, Ted. I guess I should've seen it coming, but…"

"I never saw it, Tom. I mean I've seen a lot of baseball in my lifetime, and it never even crossed my mind… I guess because we're so used to seeing Waters out on the field hitting bombs…"

"Well, in hindsight it totally makes sense, with him being hurt… But in that moment? I think you're right… And that we're not alone in our reaction…"

"And now we have Taylor back in his original role out there on the mound after a long absence in the postseason…"

"I'll be interested to see what we've got here. It's one thing to throw strikes to just a catcher and a mitt, and a whole'nother one to pitch to a live batter…"

"Taylor, going with the full wind-up as usual, as he faces the top of the order, starting with Ramirez…"

And as Spence delivers the ball to the plate, it comes out higher than he wants, up in the zone at first, before tailing hard towards the batter with quite a bit of arm-side run.

Ramirez, initially committing to the offering that starts up and in, but still in the zone, ends up abandoning his swing while his hips rotate and his arms continue to move forward, instead quickly leaning his torso way back in an involuntary attempt to avoid being hit by the ball…

Christa immediately stands to her feet and shouts "Oh no!"

"Ooh… That almost got'em…"

"Yeah… But it looks like he swung, Ted."

"I think he did, Tom."

The Red Sox then appeal to the first base umpire, who confirms that he did indeed swing with a hand gesture strike call…

"And here comes Tonglet out of the dugout, and he's not a happy camper…"

Ramirez looks on and is not thrilled, himself, with a pitch that almost hit his back shoulder, but is now technically a strike.

"Let's look at the replay from the side…"

"I mean… He offered at it. That's the right call, Ted. I don't think anyone could argue that it's not a swing. Of course it wasn't pretty. In fact, it was kinda scary. But a strike is a strike, I guess…"

By this time the manager of the Giants is all up in the face of the first base umpire, who's just standing there taking it, surely being spit on with every word that Tonglet yells from three inches away.

Spence, out on the mound after having received the ball back from the catcher, looks on and can hardly blame Tonglet for his reaction. The pitch was eerily similar to the last one he threw to Yuli Rodriguez. Ramirez wasn't as close to the plate, though. Still, he's a bit shaken up as Moon jogs up to the mound and gives him some encouragement.

"I know that no umpire wants to eject a coach in the top of the ninth inning, game seven of the World Series, and that's why first base umpire James Williams is showing a little more restraint than usual here… But

Tonglet has to be treading on thin ice at this point, especially considering that it's the right call and it is being confirmed to both the crowd and all of the other umpires on the large video screen out in center field as he's still arguing."

"Yeah. The crowd is now booing him, pointing to the video board, and telling him to sit down…"

"Back to Taylor, though. That's some first pitch to throw after what he's been through…"

"Yeah… But right now it doesn't appear that he's bothered…"

From her vantage point, and without the luxury of having a camera to zoom in on his face like the television audience and announcers have, Christa sees it differently, having known Spence intimately now for about fifteen years. There's a demeanor about him that he gets when he's nervous. She can't quantify it, nor does she expect anyone other than herself to notice it. But she can surely recognize that things aren't starting off well with his mindset.

And after about two to three minutes of Tonglet reaming out the first base umpire, he finally makes his way back to the San Francisco dugout, as the Red Sox fans egg him on and berate him for delaying the game.

Ramirez then steps back into the box, as Spence confirms the sign from the catcher. But before starting his wind-up, he steps off the rubber, first with his right foot and then the left, and takes his hat off to wipe his brow. He then turns around, walks back towards the base of the mound, and picks up the rosin bag, throwing it up and catching it a few times with his right hand, the powder spewing into the air all around him.

Christa can see it and now the crowd is apparently catching on, too… Things aren't looking good.

"Skip asks the umpire for time, as he walks out from the dugout… Wait a minute. That's not Skip!"

"Nope. Not unless he's about thirty-five years younger now and five inches taller, Ted…"

Joshua, having been pinch-run for in the last half-inning and no longer eligible to re-enter the game as a player, is now on his way out to the mound. He's wearing a navy blue and red lightweight windbreaker and carefully considering his steps along the way.

Spence, still with his back turned, realizes that his coach is coming out to talk to him when the infield starts to walk in towards the mound. Joshua sees this and waves them off using his left hand – the only one he can still move at this point. The crowd begins to increase in volume as soon as they start realizing that it's actually Waters, and not the Red Sox manager, coming out to talk to him. Spence finds this to be strange and turns around, only to discover his best friend standing right there in front of him, smacking on a wad of bubble gum.

"You hav'n fun yet, Meat!?"

Spence, now surprised, cracks a smile and raises his glove, while attempting to cover his mouth when he answers, "I don't know if I can do this, Joshua."

He gives a concerned look back at him, before replying, "Well, I think I see the problem. It looks like you've 'got a million-dollar arm, but a five-cent head' out here. I know your old man is in the stands with his camera and all, but if you concentrate on breathing through your eyelids like a lava lizard, then I'll work hard on finding a live rooster so that we can take the curse off Cameron's glove over there. And I'm not sure if you ever got Abby and I a wedding present, but candlesticks always make a nice gift. I can see if we're still registered somewhere ten years later, so that maybe you can get us a place-setting, or perhaps a silverware pattern."

Spence, unable to continue with the straight face and concerned look, immediately bursts out into laughter with his best friend. Here they both are, out on the mound in the biggest moment of his professional career, and Joshua, true to form, stays in character by referencing the wacky dialogue from the famous mound visit scene in the movie "Bull Durham." The cameras catch the laughs and giggles between the two of them.

"This is fun to watch, as they seem to be candidly having a conversation and telling jokes during a big moment."

Joshua then quickly gets serious for a second, knowing that his time out there is limited. "Meat, listen to me… You were made for exactly this…"

Christa and Abby look on, as Spence suddenly starts to look more fidgety, now that Joshua has sobered it back down a bit between the two of them. His body language is very concerning.

"Spencer, look at me, Dawg…"

Once again, for the second time in the last 48 hours, he hears Joshua using his given name, prompting him to look up and make eye contact…

He then holds up eight fingers and says, "You only need eight more pitches. That's it. Now show me the little leaguer, the eighteen-year-old, and the most dominant closer in the history of baseball that I once knew…"

And with that, Joshua turns around and walks back to the dugout to another standing ovation…

"How is he?" – asks Skip.

"Terrible. But I think I may have found something…"

Christa is now covering her eyes with her hands and peeking through her fingers, as the television camera once again finds her for a close-up. Encouragingly enough, Spence appears to have a slightly different disposition than before, when he stepped off the rubber and tried to gather his thoughts.

The count is zero balls and one contentious strike, as Spence steps back onto the rubber, goes into his wind-up, and delivers…

"Strike two, swinging!"

"He simply beat him with that one, Ted."

"Yep. 101 miles per hour… Here's my best fastball… Try to catch up to it."

The capacity crowd at Fenway wants more and starts cheering loudly again, as he stretches towards the plate with the "oh-two" pitch…

"Strike three, swinging, high in the zone…"

"Another Taylor special, Ted. 'Here's my heater high in the zone and I dare you to try to hit it.'"

"Yeah… You can definitely say that Taylor is back after that sequence of pitches…"

Christa has taken her hands down from her face as she and Abby smile and high-five each other in the stands. His mother and father, more reserved and tending to the children further down in the aisle, also begin to recognize the Spence of old, as he circles around the back of the mound and receives the incoming ball from the third baseman. He's not being cocky at all. But it's the business-as-usual approach that they've both come to know and love.

"Three pitches, three strikes, Ted."

"Yeah. A little unconventional, Tom… But a start to an inning like we've grown accustomed to seeing from Taylor in the past."

"And now it's the left fielder Hanson standing in the way of the Red Sox winning their third World Series in the past ten years…"

"Don't forget Encarnacion, who's on deck, Ted…"

"Oh, I'm not. But Hanson is no slouch, himself, batting above the .300 mark, and he has one of the few hits for the Giants here tonight…"

"Yep. And he's a four-time All-Star…"

Spence, looking as confident as ever, acknowledges the sign from the catcher and stretches toward home plate…

"Strike one, looking…"

"That one came in at one-oh-two, Tom…"

"It's not even fair, Ted."

"No, it isn't."

"There's another one at 102 miles per hour and Hanson was so late that he might as well hadn't even swung the bat…"

The Boston crowd is louder than ever before now, having recognized that Spence is not only back, but better than ever before.

"And it's strike three, again swinging."

"Once again, high in the zone… And it's just so hard to catch up with it."

Spence circles around the back of the mound again and receives the ball via the third baseman for a second time in the inning…

"Just one more out, Dawg!"

Joshua is smiling big from the steps of the dugout and using his one good arm to slap the padded railing in front of him, as Encarnacion steps up to the plate.

The Giants, as a part of the National League, will rarely get to play the Red Sox during the regular season, barring any rule changes in the future that allows inter-league play between both it and the American League. As such, Spence has never faced Encarnacion outside of spring training, where he's encountered him only once, giving up a double off the left-center field wall.

"And here's the game, Ted, with the Red Sox clinging to a 1-0 lead."

"This should be interesting. Mateo loves hitting fastballs – and Taylor loves throwing them…"

"The first pitch… And it's fouled off!"

"Encarnacion almost came out of his shoes swinging at that one, Tom. And this Boston crowd has definitely quieted down since he took that big cut."

"Yeah… It looked like he was on time for that one and just missed it."

"Well, don't look now, but Taylor is technically only two pitches away from pitching that elusive immaculate inning. Can you imagine him finally getting it right here, tonight, on this stage, after what he's been through the last couple of weeks!?"

"I can't. But let's see strike two first, before we start to speculate. Taylor has teased us both in the past…"

And just then Spence delivers his second pitch, and out of his hand he almost immediately regrets it. It's about mid-thigh, upper 90s in velocity, and headed towards the inside corner of the plate, where Encarnacion is known to like it. His eyes get really big, and he hammers it down the left field line, headed for the foul pole on top of The Green Monster.

"And there's a long drive! If it's fair, it's gone!"

"It's looks like it's hooking, Ted…"

"And it's just foul by about ten to fifteen feet…"

"That would've tied-up the game."

"Wow. Like this game needs any more suspense at all…"

"I think we may have made some baseball fans somewhere out there watching this one play out tonight."

"It's been a true classic. And I'm honored to have called it."

Encarnacion, having rounded first base, stares Spence down as he slowly walks by him, cutting through the middle of the infield while on his way back to home plate. Spence has no response, acting as if he doesn't care.

"That was 'strike two,' Ted. And once again Taylor finds himself one pitch away from an immaculate inning…"

"That he does."

Spence then steps both feet onto the rubber and looks at Encarnacion, who's now assumed his batting stance and is awaiting the pitch. But instead, he just stands there with both feet perched on the rubber, ball in glove, appearing ready to start his wind-up at any moment, but not doing so. An awkward seven to ten seconds passes, before Encarnacion asks for time and the umpire grants it. The batter steps out of the box and glares at the pitcher, who has now stepped off and back onto the rubber. He then steps back into the box and takes a few loose practice swings...

Spence glances over to Joshua, who's impatiently standing at the top of the dugout steps, just waiting for his turn to run out onto the field, not caring at all, whatsoever, about further injuring himself in the ensuing celebration.

He also looks over to Coach Gray, standing on his feet near the corner of the dugout and cheering loudly, along with the rest of the crowd.

His mind then starts to drift back to some of his memories, while both real and under hypnosis, and he quickly begins to recall several snippets that are now bouncing around in the back in his head...

Joshua's dad speaking to him when he was at rock bottom: "Joshua used to talk all the time about wishing that he was your teammate, instead of having to always play against you. He said there was something special in you... And that your curve ball was the best strikeout pitch he'd ever seen..."

Coach Gray walking up to the mound after he struck out Rex: "I always thought it was your best pitch and that you should throw it more..."

His conversation with his ace, Tyler: "Remember when I showed you how to throw the deuce? Just throw it hard. I believe in you. Just one more strike and it's over..."

He then pictures Joshua in his hospital bed, starting to crack-up laughing with all the tubes coming out of his mouth, up his nose, and IVs hanging from his arms...

And finally there's Christa, crying as he holds her tightly in the dimly lit parking lot: "Spencer Taylor... I've always loved you... And I've always dreamed of a life together with you. It didn't matter to me if we grew old here in our hometown or in some major city somewhere with you playing baseball. I just wanted to be with you..."

"'Time' is called by the umpire."

"Actually, Tom, I think it was Palmer who called it, and he's now asking the home plate umpire for a new ball to take out to Taylor, before he goes out to make sure that he's alright."

The catcher trots out to Spence and hands him the new ball, while taking the old one and rolling it towards the dugout.

"You okay?"

"Yeah…"

"Let's blow this one by him, high in the zone, and celebrate…"

[interrupting] "I'm throwing the deuce."

"Spence… I've never even seen you throw a curve ball. Skip wants a fastball up…"

"I don't care what Skip wants. This is my strikeout pitch."

The home plate umpire walks out to break-up the meeting. Spence immediately looks over at his old high school baseball coach and, without saying anything at all, he says everything in that moment about the next pitch. Coach Gray, anticipating precisely what's coming, nods in agreement.

He then looks up to find Christa in the stands, covering her face with her hands yet again, and then over to his parents, both smiling while each holding one of his children in their arms.

He's steps back onto the rubber after delaying this pitch for a good two to three minutes now, slowly takes one step back with his left foot while bringing both arms over his head, plants his right foot in front of the rubber, and pushes off while striding toward the plate in a powerful motion, his arm soon following…

"And this for an immaculate inning and another World Series title for the Red Sox…"

Everything about his intentions and actions screams "fastball" as Encarnacion sees the pitch out of his hand coming in high, gives up on it, and then buckles helplessly after realizing that it's going to be a strike just before it breaks over the middle of the plate...

"It's strike three! Oh my God it's strike three, looking! On a curve ball of all things! It's pandemonium here at Fenway as the Red Sox players rush the field! And it's an immaculate inning finally for Taylor!"

Spence, never one to celebrate too much or gloat, tosses his glove high into the air and then turns his back to home plate. Now facing towards center field, he raises both hands in the air as if he's worshipping, if only for a moment, before being tackled by his best friend, the catcher, and the rest of the infield, and ultimately being further piled upon while still on the ground by his other teammates coming in from both the outfield and the bullpen.

Christa is now sitting back down and cannot contain her emotions, as everyone around her celebrates. Abby, jumping up and down with the grandparents and children, soon notices and bends over to get face to face with her. She says nothing at all. She knows... And simply chooses to just allow her to let it all come out right there in front of her, before hugging her tightly.

Joshua is at the bottom of the dogpile, along with Spence, out in the middle of the infield, and in intense discomfort. But he couldn't care any less because he asked for it and has the whole offseason to recover. And as it disperses and the players are pulled-off one by one to the roar of the crowd, the two best friends at long last emerge to find one another for one final embrace...

"Not so damn hard, Meat! I'm hurting!"

Spence realizes that he's forgotten about Joshua's injury... "My bad..."

"Nah... Bring it in! I'm proud of you, Meat..."

thirty – lucidity

Author's note: The last chapter of "immaKulate" immediately follows this short message. I want to thank you for purchasing my first novel. It is my hope that you were able to visualize the characters within and vividly see the scenes playing out in your own mind while reading it.

I priced this book on the lowest end of the "novel" spectrum with hopes that I might be able to offer it at a bargain price and make you feel as if you got a lot of value out of reading it. Afterall, most of the eBooks with this much content are priced in the $6.99-$9.99 range.

As such, I would greatly appreciate you doing me two favors, either now or once you finish the book. 1) Please take the time to leave a short review on whatever platform you purchased it from so that it can bump-up in the eBook algorithm and 2) tell at least one friend who you think might also enjoy reading it. Thank you.

FOUR PLUS MONTHS LATER

The Taylors have decided to use Spence's World Series Championship bonus winnings to help them pay cash for a house on the water, just northeast of Jackson, where a dollar goes a lot further than what it does in Massachusetts. The Ross Barnett Reservoir is a man-made body of water that is 33,000 acres in size and was formed in the 1960s after the Pearl River was dammed. It's a drinking water resource that also serves as a recreational area for boating, fishing, water-skiing, and camping. There are dozens of restaurants and bars on its surrounding shores and a large destination waterpark just off the southwest corner. Sixteen miles long and seven miles wide at its maximum width, it separates the counties of

Madison and Rankin, while a spillway controls the potential floodwaters that might otherwise cause havoc downstream.

Spence and Christa spent lots of time out there on the water with friends and family while growing up, and would often marvel at some of the neighborhoods being developed and the homes being built around it. But there has always been one street and a series of waterfront lots that Christa has had her eye on for many years. So, during the last off-season, when her husband had a business meeting scheduled in Southwest Jackson, she flew down with him, at which time they purchased all three pieces of land and began the process of building a home and swimming pool that they could only dream of back in high school. A little over a year later, the Taylors had just completed putting the finishing touches on it and arranging all the new furniture, when they had to abruptly leave to be on time for the dedication, which is about a thirty-minute drive.

And once they arrive at Spence's old high school, he steps out of his SUV with his family, including his mom and dad, and they all walk up to the new entrance gate, complete with bricked-in pillars and an iron archway. Dan walks through and eventually runs into someone he knows, soon calling for Spence to come over.

"Spence. I want you to see someone. Do you remember my good friend, Ralph?"

Spence looks up and shakes his hand. Ralph is exactly the way that Spence remembered him under hypnosis, down to his mustache and mannerisms.

"Yessir. Ralph? I remember you well. Are you still supervising down at the factory?"

Ralph looks over to Dan, who shrugs his shoulders, indicative of not knowing how or why his son would know or remember that. He would come over from time to time to have a beer with his father, but as Spence got older, Dan's weekends ended up revolving around his son's baseball schedule. He may have even seen a few of his games in high school. But, other than perhaps in passing, he didn't ever remember mentioning to Spence that he worked at the factory, much less what his actual job title would've been. He then turns back to answer Spence's question...

"Uh… Yeah. I'm still a supervisor there for maybe another year or two. But I plan on retiring soon."

"Spence… Ralph brought his grandson up here to hopefully meet you…"

A young boy then emerges from behind him. He's about eight years old and is wearing an "old-school" Forest Hill High School 'Spence Taylor' baseball jersey, obviously custom made, complete with the name "Taylor" and the number 58 on the back.

"Wow… Would you look at that!? I don't think I've ever seen anyone wearing my Forest Hill jersey before."

"Yeah. His grandmother is a pretty good seamstress and she put that together for him as a Christmas present this past year. His parents can barely get it off him to wash it anymore…"

Spence then gets down on one knee… "What's your name, buddy?"

"Connor."

"Connor? That's a great name. Do you want me to sign your shirt?"

Connor nods yes to Spence, who turns him around, pulls a Sharpie out of his pocket, and signs it.

Spence then points around… "Are you planning on staying to see all of this?"

Connor looks down shyly, but then picks his head up and answers, "Yessir."

"Good."

Spence then turns to his dad and Ralph… "Maybe he can be my bat-boy this year?"

Ralph looks a little bit confused, as Spence once again shakes his hand. Dan starts explaining to him what his son was talking about, as the crowd continues to grow around them. The school's principal then grabs Spence's arm, quickly ushering he and his family to their seats.

The press conference is scheduled to be outside on a beautiful Monday afternoon in early March. The table and backdrop are adorned with the emblem of Forest Hill High School. There is a large grandstand and press box towering over them with a sign that reads "Spencer Taylor Stadium" across the facade, near the top. Flanking out to both the left and right, the grandstand continues down towards the baselines and dugouts. It's a sprawling state-of-the-art baseball stadium with a brand-new turf field, dugouts that are cut-out underground, locker-rooms beneath the stands, a weightroom, and a rather cool outfield fence-line that isn't all that different from that of Fenway Park. There's also a huge scoreboard and video screen just beyond the left-center field wall, and a dedicated "Student Section" that is labelled "The Right Field Lounge," an obvious ode to "The Left Field Lounge" at "Dudy Noble Field – Polk-DeMent Stadium" in Starkville, where Spence played collegiate ball; it having its own elevated entrance gate, concession stand, and pricing.

Joshua and Abby Waters are both in attendance. Now about to start his twelfth year of baseball at the highest professional level, he has been given permission by the Boston Red Sox organization to show up to spring training in Florida a little bit later than the rookies and veterans with less experience – the ownership and front office personnel also wanting to make sure that they've given his right side enough time to recover.

The final touches are being confirmed before the ceremony starts. A soundperson does a quick mic check, before making sure that all the cords are covered with a rubber tented bridge apparatus and taped down accordingly. Spence happens to glance over to the other side of the podium and notices another familiar face. Dave, his mentor and sponsor from his Alcoholic Anonymous meetings while under hypnosis, is also sitting at the ceremonial table. After making eye contact, he gets out of his chair and walks over to Spence and the family, offering his right hand as they both greet one another.

"Spence."

"Dave?"

"It's good to see you again. I hope you are pleased with the job that WAYCO Construction did on the new stadium and field. I also wanted to thank you again for coming to find me a year ago when my new navigation system got me lost and took me down some obscure gravel road a couple of miles away…"

Spence looks at him with confusion…

"You don't remember? It steered me down 'Myrtle Drive,' where I tried to turn around and eventually got stuck in a ditch in front of a dilapidated mobile home."

Spence starts to remember and chuckles aloud as it all begins to make sense…

He had flown down from Boston with his wife, and while she was tending to the matter concerning their new house being built, he was on the southwestern side of town and waiting to meet Dave at Forest Hill High School. The plan was for the two of them to have dinner and discuss pricing and options regarding the construction of a brand-new stadium and field for the baseball program. But after getting lost, stuck, and having spotty cellphone service, he reluctantly called Spence from the landline of the run-down trailer.

"That's not exactly how I envision meeting potential new clients. But I have to say that you were a good sport about it."

With one tire hanging over a culvert and another one barely touching the ground, they had to enlist the help of a wrecker service to come pull Dave's vehicle out. Meanwhile, the mobile home's occupant, who was thin, bearded, foul-mouthed, and disheveled in appearance, knew exactly who Spence was and offered them both a beer as they waited. Spence politely declined, while Dave mentioned that he was a recovering alcoholic. It took a while for the towing service to show up, and in the meantime Spence had to use the bathroom, so the man allowed him to use the only one he had in the back of his trailer. It was then and there that he got a really good look at the entirety of the mobile home, surprised that anyone could live in such filth.

Dave's truck was eventually freed, and the two of them ultimately ended up having dinner together and coming to a handshake agreement, before finalizing the plans a few weeks later, which basically became a strategy that would leave the 2003 version of the high school baseball team having to play their entire schedule away from their home field to accommodate the project – a complete teardown and rebuild – an idea that Coach Gray ran by the kids and got a unanimous approval, even from the seniors who would never get to play a game on it.

"It wasn't a big deal at all, Dave. And of course, I'm extremely happy with the job that your company did, bringing the plans we made that night at dinner to life. Thanks so much."

And just then the sound of feedback rings out from the podium, as Coach Gray steps up to the microphone in front of a now rather large media crowd that also includes students, parents, alumni, and former baseball players…

"I've been coaching baseball for a very long time here at Forest Hill High School and this amazing stadium behind us is a dream come true. It has been gifted by a former Forest Hill alum, State Champion, SEC Champion, Golden Spikes Award Winner, three-time World Series winner, nine-time All-Star, and a future Hall of Famer that once walked the halls of the very school that's sitting behind all of you. It's been a work in progress over the last fourteen months, after being torn down, ripped up, and stripped bare – essentially starting out from scratch. And from what I understand it was initially drawn-out on a paper napkin at a business dinner between Spence and Dave Hardy over there, with WAYCO Construction. Isn't that correct, fellas?"

Dave and Spence both acknowledge the story with a head nod and a smile.

"And not much has changed from what was initially conceptualized on that crumpled-up napkin, that is when compared to what you see behind us right now… At least that's what the two of them told me. But just look at it. It's more beautiful than most college stadiums. Spence spared no expense in building it and we will get to enjoy it here at Forest Hill High School for many more years to come…"

The press continues to snap pictures as the large crowd around them cheers.

"And before we cut this ribbon here in front of us, I think Spence has a few words that he wants to say…"

Spence, who's sitting next to his wife and two kids, gets up from the table and walks up to the podium…

"Thank you, Coach. I also want to thank my beautiful wife, my two amazing children, and my parents who are here with me today. Nearly thirteen years ago I stood out on that mound that's just beyond this grandstand behind us and the last pitch I ever threw from it nearly killed somebody. It's the most scared that I've ever been in my entire life watching him seizing out on the field and then lying motionless as they carted him off. As far as I was concerned, that was the last time I was ever going to touch a baseball. But life has a funny way of turning something very bad into something good. And God's Grace abounds all around me. That noted, I can almost guarantee you that I have one of the most unique ways of meeting my best friend, and he's standing right over there…"

The crowd cheers again as Spence and the cameras point over to Joshua, dressed nicely and standing there with his own family.

"I can also tell you that I even wanted to name this field 'Joshua Waters Field,' but neither he nor Coach Gray would ever agree to that. However, Joshua did donate a cool $1 million to our efforts here, which is another reason you now have the monstrosity that is currently sitting behind us bearing my name."

Again, everyone claps as Joshua points back to Spence and says, "Love ya, Meat!"

"And so, it is with that in mind that I would like to ask both Coach Gray and Joshua Waters to step up here with me. I've arranged for three pairs of ceremonial scissors and each of us gets one…"

The three of them then go on to cut the ribbon and pose for the cameras.

"And there's just one more thing…"

But before he says anything else, Spence hugs Joshua and asks him to come up to stand beside him, as they make their way back to the podium. Once there, he clears his throat…

"I have been in touch with the Boston Red Sox organization and Major League Baseball and…" Hesitating for just a moment… "And I'd like to use this time, the place where it all started, and who I'm standing here alongside, to announce my official retirement from professional baseball…"

There is a collective gasp that comes from the crowd as the camera shutters start closing more quickly than before. This is seemingly out of nowhere because Spence is technically in the prime of his career, with at least four to five good years left in the tank. It had also been announced earlier in the month that the Red Sox were trying to entice him to stay beyond his current contract, with an even larger contract extension. But after talking it over with Christa, they decided that it was best to keep their house in Newton, Massachusetts, but to also build one down here and leave professional baseball, altogether, essentially going out on top as a World Champion.

Christa sits there with the kids, smiling and wiping back tears.

Joshua, who also has tears in his eyes, then reaches for the mic…

"I'd just like to say that five years from now, I will get to repay all of his compliments when I'm giving his Hall of Fame induction speech."

The crowd goes wild again.

Coach Gray then gets up and Joshua hands him the microphone…

"That's right, Joshua. But that's not all. I have one more announcement. I'd also like to introduce you to the newest assistant baseball coach here at Forest Hill High School, Spencer Taylor."

Baseball players, both former and current, are all in attendance and there's a deafening roar of excitement that vibrates through the crowd. Spence slowly walks up to the mic again…

"Thank you. I'm very excited about this opportunity and look forward to getting to know all the players, former players, and parents. Thank you all for coming."

***

The Taylor family hangs around for a little while longer after the press conference ends, while the news of Spence's recently announced retirement from baseball has already reached a national level. Christa hugs Joshua and Abby, before kissing the kids, who are headed out to board a flight bound for Orlando, where he will start his spring training for the upcoming 2004 baseball season in Fort Myers, Florida.

"We'll look after the house. You aren't planning on selling it, are you?"

Christa smiles… "Not anytime soon… And I'm planning on visiting you often."

Abby starts to cry as the two of them embrace one more time for about thirty full seconds. Spence and Joshua go to shake hands once again, but eventually they just hug it out, too. Joshua appears to wipe another tear from his eye as they disengage. That, too, should be national news.

Dan and Joy then pile into the large SUV with them and the whole family heads out for the new home they just built on "The Rez." But shortly after leaving, Spence happens upon a familiar road in the distance with a makeshift hand-painted sign that reads "Myrtle Drive." Intrigued, he slows down and turns left onto the gravel road…

Christa looks up, "What are you doing!?"

"Oh nothing… It's just a shortcut…"

"A shortcut to where!? You're gonna get us all killed!"

And just then he starts slowing down as he comes upon a rundown mobile home with an old beaten-up pickup truck sitting out front. He stops the vehicle, puts it in park, rolls down his window, and just stares at it…

"What is it, baby?"

Spence doesn't answer. Instead, he simply looks on, deep in thought, for some reason preoccupied with the trailer now in front of him.

Christa suddenly startles in the passenger seat and yells "What was that!?"

A brilliant red cardinal has just swooped down, from out of nowhere, in front of her windshield, and landed on the mailbox, just to the left of the driver's side window. Maybe two feet from the car's door, Spence says nothing at all. He just watches the bird, who then turns to look at him, seemingly unafraid, for the next twenty to thirty seconds, before proudly flapping its wings a few times and flying away.

Christa is starting to get a little bit antsy while sitting there as Spence is seemingly fixated on the mailbox. It's now been a couple of minutes and they still haven't moved for some reason. He then looks up once again and focuses his attention beyond it. There's a precast staircase leading up to a wobbly screen door and some old beaten-up windchimes dangling beneath a worn-out awning that are starting to ring-out ever so faintly in the growing breeze...

"Look... Spence, I'm not sure what's going on with you. But the kids are hungry, I don't feel too well, and I'm starting to get a little nauseated. I'm gonna have to pee very soon, too. So, here's a deal that I'll make with you right now: If you want it that badly, then let's please just go buy it. I've always told you that I'd follow you anywhere. I meant it, then, and I still mean it now. And if that means we'd have to live in that thing right there, then so be it."

She then reaches over and gently strokes the back of his right hand that's resting on the gearshift... "Otherwise, let's just drive over to our beautiful new lake-house, and you can enjoy a drink or two while we relax on the dock and watch the sunset together."

Spence looks over, smiles at his wife, rubs her tummy, and winks. He then glances back at his children and parents, before rolling-up the window, putting it in drive, slowly pressing the accelerator, and driving off...

About the Author

John Marble lives in Southeast Louisiana with his wife and three boys, where he works as a nurse-anesthetist. Originally from Jackson, Mississippi, he's a big Mississippi State fan and a long-time baseball enthusiast. He spends most of his weekends traveling to different cities and watching his kids play the sport that he absolutely loves.

Made in the USA
Columbia, SC
04 August 2024

39543872R00139